Aidan Carr was born and brought up on the Fylde coast in Lancashire, where he was educated by Jesuit nuns and the Irish Christian Brothers before reading law at Manchester University.

After qualifying as a solicitor, he provided representation in The Shipman Inquiry and, more recently, was retained by British Cycling to represent their lead physiotherapist in both the UKAD and House of Commons Select Committee investigations into alleged wrongdoing in cycling and the subsequent General Medical Council's prosecution of the Team Sky doctor.

He is an ardent sports fan and Vice President of Broughton Park RUFC, where he coached youth rugby. He is a lifelong supporter of Manchester United and was previously the Honorary Solicitor to the Association of Former Manchester United Players.

Aidan lives in England and Italy, where he continues to coach youth rugby at Viareggio RFC.

To my family – especially my wife, Shirley.

To my professional colleagues, in which I include 'the opposition' – and the Tribunals - they know who they are!

To my best friends, Phil and Gayle, for their generous hospitality in New Mexico, when I was first getting to grips with the incipient 'Wonderbra Manoeuvre'.

The publication team at AM – again, they know who they are.

Aidan Francis Carr

The Wonderbra Manoeuvre

Austin Macauley Publishers™
LONDON * CAMBRIDGE * NEW YORK * SHARJAH

Copyright © Aidan Francis Carr 2024

The right of Aidan Francis Carr to be identified as author of this work has been asserted by the author in accordance with sections 77 and 78 of the Copyright, Designs and Patents Act 1988.

All rights reserved. No part of this publication may be reproduced, stored in a retrieval system, or transmitted in any form or by any means, electronic, mechanical, photocopying, recording, or otherwise, without the prior permission of the publishers.

Any person who commits any unauthorised act in relation to this publication may be liable to criminal prosecution and civil claims for damages.

This is a work of fiction. Names, characters, businesses, places, events, locales, and incidents are either the products of the author's imagination or used in a fictitious manner. Any resemblance to actual persons, living or dead, or actual events is purely coincidental.

A CIP catalogue record for this title is available from the British Library.

ISBN 9781398446878 (Paperback)
ISBN 9781398492820 (Hardback)
ISBN 9781398492844 (ePub e-book)
ISBN 9781398492837 (Audiobook)

www.austinmacauley.com

First Published 2024
Austin Macauley Publishers Ltd®
1 Canada Square
Canary Wharf
London
E14 5AA

The Medieval Christian Hippocratic Oath

Blessed be God the Father of our Lord Jesus Christ who is blessed for ever and ever; I lie not. I will bring no stain upon the learning of the medical art. Neither will I give poison to anybody though asked to do so, nor will I suggest such a plan. Similarly, I will not give treatment to women to cause abortion neither from above nor below. But I will teach this art to those who require to learn it, without grudging and without an indenture. I will use treatment to help the sick according to my ability and judgment. And in purity and in holiness I will guard my art. Into whatsoever houses I enter, I will do so to help the sick, keeping myself free from all wrongdoing, intentional or unintentional, tending to death or to injury and from fornication with bond or free, man or woman. Whatsoever in the course of practice I see or hear (or outside my practice in social intercourse) that ought not to be published abroad, I will not divulge, but consider such things to be holy secrets. Now if I keep this oath and break it not, may God be my helper in my life and art, and may I be honoured among all men for all time. If I keep faith, well; but if I forswear myself may the opposite befall me.

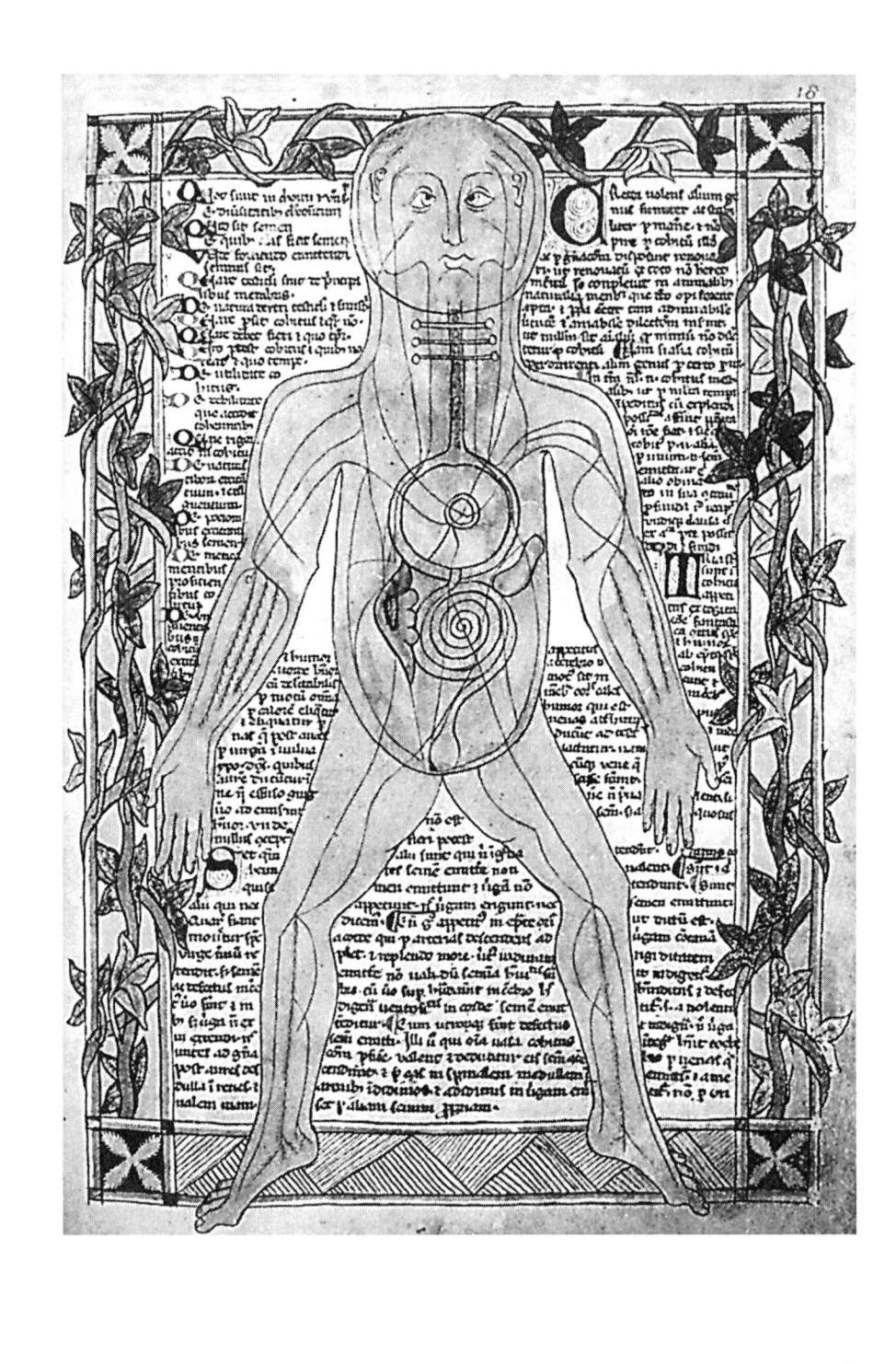

Foreword

The General Medical Council (GMC) is the body responsible for keeping the register of all doctors practising in the UK. Only the GMC has the power to erase a doctor's name from the medical register. It exercises these powers through its fitness to practise procedures.

With these procedures, the GMC should protect patients from dysfunctional doctors, who, because of their misconduct put patients at risk of harm. It has been suggested that the GMC does not have the protection of patients as its priority; its priority is the interests of the medical profession.

Dame Janet Smith
Fifth Report of The Shipman Inquiry

Although Dame Janet severely criticised the GMC for failing to have the protection of patients, upholding standards in the medical profession and properly discipline doctors who were found guilty of misconduct, as its priority she decided not to recommend that the GMC should be deprived of its fitness to practise function.

Instead, The Shipman Inquiry recommended wholesale reform of both the culture of the GMC and its fitness to practise procedures—so radical and far-reaching were these reforms that the criticisms summarised above could not be levelled at the GMC now—woe betide any doctor who departs from the high standards set out in *Good Medical Practice* and its predecessor, the Hippocratic Oath, for their reputation, livelihood, career and very possibly their liberty will be at risk.

GENERAL MEDICAL COUNCIL
SANCTIONS GUIDANCE
SEXUAL MISCONDUCT

This encompasses a wide range of conduct from criminal convictions for sexual assault to sexual misconduct with patients, colleagues or others. Sexual misconduct seriously undermines public trust in the profession and is particularly serious where there is an abuse of the special position of trust a doctor occupies. Erasure from the medical register is likely to be appropriate in such cases.

Sexually motivated conduct is, to put it simply, conduct motivated by sex.

Book One

Chapter One

**APARTMENT 26
MERRION RD
BALLSBRIDGE
DUBLIN 4**

3:00pm
Wednesday 6th of January 2016

Saoirse

Saoirse Fitzgerald was reviewing the itinerary for her next trip to the Far East—just finalised and emailed by Aoife, her PA. Dublin to Heathrow first thing tomorrow, then meetings in London for two days before catching the overnight Virgin Atlantic flight to Hong Kong, last thing Friday evening. Two nights in Hong Kong at The Mandarin Oriental, visiting suppliers' showrooms, choosing designs, fabrics and garment samples and agreeing tech-packs for next year's range of sportswear. Three nights at The Langham in Shanghai, auditing the manufacturers' outlying factories and employee facilities, then back via Paris with a one-night stay at La Tremoille, to visit the latest new store on the Avenue George V of the fashion-house, Cristiano a Fiorentina, acquired by Sportswear Inc. nearly twelve years ago and review the new Autumn/Winter collection with chief designer, Gabrielle Casteignede.

Aoife had added a footnote that she had booked Saoirse a room at her favourite London hotel—Brown's on Albemarle St in Mayfair tomorrow night and thoughtfully, a pre-flight massage in the Virgin lounge at Heathrow before the Hong Kong flight, in Paris, a lunchtime table for twenty at Laperouse with a list of acceptances and reserves. Aoife had become a close friend and confidante in the time since Saoirse had relocated to Dublin.

Saoirse would be away for nearly nine days so logged onto her account with HSBC to ensure there were sufficient funds for any impulse purchases of her own. Scrolling through the payments she noticed the standing order dated 2 January 2016 to the UK Female Clinic for £350.00. She paused and tried to remember exactly how many payments she had made—eight? Or was it nine?

If that was right, there were only one or two payments left. She got up from the sofa, went to her desk and searched for the folder with the contract and related documents which informed her that:

Ten annual advance payments of £350 for oocyte cryo-preservation will be taken on the 2nd of every month, commencing on 2nd January 2007, the tenth and final payment being due on 2nd January 2016.

So, the payment just made was not the eighth or indeed ninth but incredibly—the tenth and final payment. How could time have gone so quickly?

She realised too, with a sense of dismay, that this meant that she would soon be 40. She pressed the home button on her phone—it was 3.32 pm. She locked her laptop and stepped out onto the balcony and looked across Merrion Rd and the rooftops of Ballsbridge towards the Irish Sea.

The weather was bitterly cold but fine. A strong westerly wind was ushering white clouds with grey underbellies across a clear blue sky. She had not exercised in the last two weeks so decided to run out to Poolbeg Lighthouse at the end of the Great South Wall, a run she had done several times before, to clear her head and then do some serious thinking on her return. She went to her bedroom and selected some running kit.

As she stepped out of the apartment block, she felt the fresh air on her face, clicked her remote to open the wide front gates, pressed play on her iPod, pulled on her gloves and pulled down her bright red Munster bobble-hat—a Christmas present from Aoife.

Liam, the gardener, his back bent amongst the bare rose bushes, waved to her as she walked past. At the end of the drive she broke into a trot turning left out of the gates onto Merrion Road, and passing in front of the high railings and expansive front lawn of the British Embassy. The solitary representative of the Garda Siochana stamping his feet and warming his hands in the entrance to the Embassy gatehouse nodded to her and added a friendly salute.

It was a run which Saoirse had done several times before—the last stretch was along the top of The Great South Wall, reaching nearly two miles out into the Irish Sea. From the lighthouse, looking back, she would be rewarded with a breath-taking view of the Wicklow Mountains to her left—today, probably capped with snow—and the River Liffey and Dublin harbour on her right.

Saoirse crossed Merrion Rd. heading towards Sandymount Green. A train standing at Sandymount DART station—destination, "BRE / BRAY "—delayed her progress. It was the first day of the new school term. She stopped at the barrier with its red and amber flashing lights and jogged on the spot, with Jackson Browne's *Running on Empty* beating through her headphones, as chattering school-children in their neat uniforms swarmed excitedly off the train, heading homewards, their sonorous Dublin accents gently reminding her she was, despite her three years in Dublin, far from her Manchester roots.

Her run took her round the Green, across Sandymount Strand, along the south edge of Poolbeg Peninsula with a moderate climb through the Irish Nature Park, then past the landmark red and white hooped twin towers of the old generating station before emerging onto Pigeon House Rd. The final, straight stretch was along the top of the wide causeway—The Great South Wall—a good run of eight miles by the time she returned home.

The wind was welcome behind her as she climbed the grassy trail through the Nature Park then recovered her breath on the gentle descent but stiffened as she emerged from the shelter of Poolbeg Peninsula onto Pigeon House Rd. There, she got her first view of a swollen River Liffey and a choppy Dublin Bay Saoirse increased her pace—regretting that she had not put on another layer of kit—she would be running into the bitterly cold onshore breeze on the return leg.

She fixed her gaze on the stubby, rust-red shape of Poolbeg Lighthouse in the distance and settled into her stride, along the wide, black granite surface of the Wall, helped by the steady beat of New Order's *Bizarre Love Triangle*.

After covering about half a mile Saoirse became aware, in her peripheral vision, of the dark shape of a large container-ship on her left, slowly overtaking her, heading out along the Liffey into the open waters of the Irish Sea. She heard several loud, short blasts on the ship's horn but kept on running—looking resolutely ahead—assuming the blasts were the captain's noisy farewell to Dublin but also suspecting that if she turned to look, she would be the object of a rude gesture of some sort from crew members.

Several more short, loud blasts followed as the stern of the vessel came level with her. She noticed that the deck was heavily stacked with containers and the ship was sitting very low in the water, creating a deep, spreading wake. On the starboard stern she could now clearly see, as she had expected, three crew members—but realised that they weren't making rude gestures—they were waving and pointing frantically behind her.

Still lightly suspicious, she glanced over her left shoulder and was horrified to see the ship's wake, breaking and frothing over the top of the Wall, some twenty metres behind her—a solid wall of green and white, more than a metre high—surging towards her at speed, devouring the surface of the Wall and quickly gaining on her. Looking ahead she could see that alarmingly, the Wall began to dip sharply on the side adjoining the Liffey.

She realised she would be unable to out-run the wake but spotted a large mooring ring set in the surface about 10 metres away on her right and broke into a sprint but could run only a few paces before her feet disappeared below the leading edge of the wake. She splashed on, now unsure of her footing. In an instant her legs were struck by the full force of the displaced river. The freezing, heavy dark green and white waters swirled noisily around her, taking her breath away, engulfing her thighs and waist, pushing her forward. Suddenly her legs were swept from under her.

She was being propelled helplessly towards the right edge of the Wall and the jagged boulders several metres below. She managed to find her feet as the waters ebbed slightly, but the impact of the next wave threw her forward again. She stumbled onto her hands and knees as the sea began to break over her back. The surface of the Wall around her was now completely submerged—had become part of sea and river. She took a deep breath and forced herself flat onto the surface of the Wall, searching frantically, left and right for the mooring ring.

She managed to find and grip the ring just before the third wave broke—with such ferocity that she was swept around and over the edge of the Wall. Fighting for breath, she tightened her grip on the ring. Another three waves cascaded over her, but with lessening intensity, then the waters began to ebb, pulled backwards over the surface of the causeway by the invisible, indifferent forces of nature, back into the River Liffey.

Gasping, she remained, dangling from the edge of the Great South Wall.

Fucking Hell! Jesus Christ!

"Hold on! Hold on!"

She felt hands under her armpits and then on her thighs as she was hauled up. She crouched on all fours on the causeway, coughing and spluttering—the taste of salt water in her mouth. She glanced back at the granite rocks below her onto which she would have been thrown, but for the mooring ring. She shivered and carried on trying to spit the salty water from her mouth.

"Just take your time—get your breath back. You're safe now."

Her rescuers helped her to her feet—she recognised one of them—had seen him in the basement car park at the apartment block on Merrion Road.

"Are you OK?"

"Yes thanks, thanks. I'm just a bit shaken."

"Yes, another few yards and I think we would have lost you! We saw the wave coming up on you from behind and shouted but the ship's horn kept blasting away. I think they were trying to warn you. Then the wave hit you and I saw you fall over then completely disappear under the water. I thought you must have been swept off the Wall and onto the rocks."

He looked at her. "Don't I know you from the Merrion Rd apartments?"

"Yes." Saoirse coughed. "I've lived there for the last three years."

"I am Juan and this is Richard. Well, maybe you might like to run with us sometime—you might be safer!"

"You might be right. I'm Saoirse, Saoirse Fitzgerald." Saoirse coughed again.

Juan was well-tanned and had fine, symmetrical features. She thought his accent was Spanish—but with a hint of Irish.

"You're Spanish?"

"Yes—I work at the Spanish Embassy here in Dublin although I am away in Madrid and Brussels quite a lot—Richard works for Google in the Grand Canal Docks." Richard nodded to her.

"Hi—how ya doin? You were very lucky there now! I've seen this happen just once before—when the river is in full flow and the tide is high all you need is a big ship passing too quickly or too close to the Wall with a following wind and the wake breaks over the surface of the Wall."

Richard had a deep, rich voice and a strong Irish accent—not Dublin, Saoirse guessed Cork—like her father and Aoife. He had too, the darkest deep-blue eyes and a shock of thick, jet black hair.

Richard stepped back and pointed.

"You were just approaching the most dangerous part—where the causeway begins to drop—if you look you can see the dip—the foundations must have sunk into the sand at some stage."

Saoirse looked along the Wall and now appreciated how much the Wall dipped on the side by the Liffey. She began to well up and bit her lower lip. There were a few moments of silence as she composed herself.

Breaking the silence, Richard continued, "We've had a lot of rain up in Wicklow over the last few days so the Liffey is running very high."

Richard paused again, noting the tears in Saoirse's eyes.

"Are you going to be alright? You took a big tumble. Your knees are bleeding a bit—so!"

"I'll be alright."

"Why don't we walk you back?"

"No—thanks—I'll be fine thanks—thanks a million! I'll be fine in a bit—I'm just shaken—I really thought I was going over the edge onto the rocks."

Saoirse shivered again—she was soaked to the skin and the wind seemed to be getting stronger—and colder—her drenching didn't really matter—she'd been soaked on many occasions before whilst out running, but her fall had shaken her.

"Look, you guys run on—I'll be fine, really."

"Are you sure? You look like you've taken a bit of a battering—you're bleeding at the knees—let's just walk you back a bit to make sure you're OK."

"Thanks Richard—that's very kind of you both."

They set off walking—back along the Wall.

After 15 minutes or so they reached the start of Pigeon House Road and the shelter of Poolbeg Peninsula.

Saoirse was now more composed.

"Look—I'll be fine now—you two get going. I'll be OK."

"If you're sure?"

"Yes—I'm sure—there's no point all three of us getting cold—and thanks again."

Juan and Richard set off running and Saoirse began to walk slowly after them.

Her leggings had been torn at the knees and her knees and wrists, even though she'd been wearing gloves, were sore and grazed and bleeding. Her arms and shoulders ached with the sudden, intense effort of clinging onto the mooring ring. She had lost her Munster hat but her iPod was still clipped to her waist and after replacing the ear-pieces she found that surprisingly it had survived, although The Buggles and *Video Killed the Radio Star* had replaced New Order.

She broke into a trot—her left leg was stiff but she kept going—she looked up and noticed Juan and Richard looking back as they turned the corner ahead to check on her so she smiled and waved them on.

She retraced her route, crossing Sandymount Green as dusk was falling, and was again held up at Sandymount DART station—this time the train was enroute to NA CLOCHA LIATHA / GREYSTONES and the passengers were now early-evening commuters returning from their offices in Dublin city centre—the excited chatter of schoolchildren replaced by the more considered conversation of adults.

On Merrion Rd the guard outside the British Embassy gave her a quizzical look and another friendly salute.

Back in her apartment Saoirse slipped off her sodden trainers and overcome by a sudden thirst, gulped down two large glasses of water in the kitchen before going to her bathroom where she turned on the shower. With difficulty, she peeled off her wet running kit and gratefully stepped into the steaming cubicle, wincing as the hot water ran over her various scrapes, grazes and cuts and again as she washed her knees and wrists to remove the embedded grains of sand and gravel.

She closed her eyes and after several minutes relaxing in the warmth of the shower stepped out. Standing naked in front of the mirror she noticed that shiny, bluish-purple bruises had already appeared just below her left hip, on both knees and on each of her wrists. She gently applied an antiseptic cream to her wounds.

She looked again into the mirror and at her eyes and remembered her father Dermot and how he had adored her eyes. She recalled too, her early childhood memories of their small, but happy family home in Moss Side and then the sadness of his sudden death. Her mother had never recovered from his loss.

She looked at herself again and wondered about all the latent biological triggers within her—all the changes that pregnancy would bring. Would her eggs, separated from her so long ago, when fertilised and implanted, still trigger her body's hormones into pregnancy mode? She hoped all the running was going to be worthwhile and wondered whether she had made the right decision?

Now in her bathrobe, with a white towel wrapped, turban-style around her damp hair, she took a bottle of gin and a large high-ball glass from the freezer and chinked several ice-cubes into it. She splashed a generous measure of gin over the ice and watched as the chilled, viscous gin irrigated slowly to the bottom of the frosted glass.

As the ice noisily cracked and popped she rolled a lime backwards and forwards on the chopping board, gently increasing the pressure until she felt the fruit soften as the vesicles within ruptured. She cut the lime in two and held one half over the tumbler and twisted a wooden reamer into the flesh, allowing the juice and pulp to fall onto the gin and ice. She winced slightly as some of the juice splashed and trickled, stinging, into the graze on her left wrist.

Finally, she took a bottle of Indian tonic water from the fridge and avoiding the grazes on her wrists opened it with a twist and poured the effervescing contents over the combination of gin, ice, lime juice, and pulp in the bottom of her glass.

She carried the drink over to the sofa and after easing herself gently down, took her first sip and closed her eyes. She took a second, larger sip, which she flushed around her mouth, trying to rinse away the returning saltiness of the River Liffey.

She picked up the draft designs for Cristiano a Fiorentina's contribution to the "Fashion Against FGM" campaign—100 special edition Cristiano a Fiorentina T shirts, sweat shirts and wrist bands and a draft press release to be signed off by her CEO, Annette. She flicked through the various pages, ticking each if approved or adding her comments and suggestions for improvements if not.

She lost concentration—her thoughts strayed. She felt the ineffable urge, of which she wasn't ashamed and didn't wish to overcome, return—an urge which she desperately wanted to fulfil—to have a child, or better still, children with a caring and loving father.

Working in the fashion industry she had come to easily appreciate the allure of an attractive woman—in Milan several years ago, after a champagne-fuelled party at the new store on Via Montenapoleone, out of a sense of curiosity and not a little loneliness, she had engaged in flirting and then allowed herself to be seduced by one of the models and had indulged herself similarly, but discreetly on several other occasions since, but had no doubt about her true sexual orientation—she was instinctively attracted to men and wanted too, the physical fulfilment and companionship of a relationship which she had somehow allowed to pass her by—had failed to secure for the last fifteen years or so.

She thought about her eggs, harvested from her ovaries, in deep-frozen preservation in the UK Female Clinic in Westminster. Would it all really work? It seemed so scientific—robotic—unromantic, but if successful it would be far from scientific—it would be a miracle and she would be overjoyed. The answer was simple—she'd known it all along—she needed a man—to love—and to love her—it was, as Aoife had readily agreed, as simple, yet as difficult as that.

Suddenly she felt her stomach begin to turn. She clenched her teeth and clasped one hand tightly to her mouth as the last traces of the Liffey refluxed. She ran quickly to the bathroom and kneeling on the floor began to retch. A rueful thought crossed her mind—was this what morning sickness was like? Even so, she didn't care—it would still be worth it—it wouldn't last forever.

Her taxi was booked for 5.00am. She checked her inbox—there was an email of a copy letter from the UKFC, acknowledging her tenth and final payment of £350 which ended with the following endorsement:

IMPORTANT LEGAL NOTICE—PLEASE READ

UKFC is regulated by the Human Fertilisation & Embryology Authority (HFEA). It is currently the law in the United Kingdom that all human eggs remaining unfertilised on the tenth anniversary of being harvested must be destroyed. We are writing to confirm that in your case this date is the 6th March 2017.

PLEASE ACKNOWLEDGE RECEIPT OF THIS NOTICE BY SIGNING AND DATING IT WHERE INDICATED AND RETURNING IN THE PRE-PAID ENVELOPE—A COPY IS PROVIDED FOR YOUR OWN RECORDS

So, as well as her body-clock ticking away, there was now a legal deadline approaching. With a sigh, she packed away her laptop, placing it with her other luggage in the hallway of her apartment. Returning to her bedroom, she checked that her passport was in her shoulder-bag and setting the alarm for 4:15am, took off her bath-robe and slipped into bed.

As she collected her thoughts, she became slowly aware of the murmur of gentle conversation—*parlando,* emanating from the apartment above. Soon, this gave way to the sound of love-making—*pianissimo.* The tempo increased—*allegro con amore,* then—*allegro di molto,* groaning—*con brio e passione,* a climax—*crescendo*—gasping—*finale e diminuendo.*

For a few minutes, there was silence before she heard the *staccato* click-clack-click, of a pair of stilettos on the tiles of the bathroom floor above.

Saoirse stared at the ceiling for a while then closed her eyes. She heard the sound of water cascading and the stilettos crossing the bathroom floor again—then more conversation, giggling and laughter.

She was aroused and couldn't sleep. She reached into her shoulder bag and unzipped the inside pocket, then lay back. The gentle buzzing wasn't loud enough to disturb the lovers above who were now slumbering blissfully and Saoirse's solitary love-making lasted just a few minutes.

Only partially fulfilled she turned over and tried again to sleep—with Aoife's mantra running even more urgently through her mind—Be bold! Saoirse, Be bold!

Chapter Two

APARTMENT 26
31 MERRION RD
BALLSBRIDGE
DUBLIN 4

5:00am
Thursday 7th of January 2016

Saoirse locked her apartment door, then walk down the carpeted corridor to the lift. She pressed the down button and shortly afterwards, the lift doors opened, revealing an attractive young woman in her twenties, her mascara and make-up slightly smudged, wearing a long black trench-coat, its collar already turned up against the cold morning.

She smiled at Saoirse who smiled back. When they reached the ground floor, Saoirse left the lift and walked down the corridor, into the ground floor reception area.

As she crossed the hallway, she heard the familiar click-clack of stilettos following her out of the apartment block. The young woman took to the footpath, in the direction of the pedestrian exit.
Cristy's taxi, engine quietly idling, was waiting for Saoirse on the gravel driveway at the front entrance of the apartment block—white exhaust fumes swirling silently in the cold, early morning air. There was frost on the lawn and in amongst the rose-beds which Liam had been tending yesterday afternoon. Cristy had been her driver of choice from the day she had started working in Dublin. By chance, he had been first in the taxi-queue at the airport when Saoirse had arrived in Dublin, looking for accommodation and had endeared himself to her with his easy manner.

He was punctual and polite. She liked the old, large, black Mercedes he drove which was always scrupulously clean and didn't reek of stale cigarette smoke. Cristy made sure the service he gave was first class—he was grateful to Saoirse because following their first trip, when he had told her how scarce work was, she had arranged for Sportswear Inc to open an account with him. It had been an easy decision for Saoirse—she knew she would need someone reliable to collect and deliver prototype garments, designs and pre-production samples between the office and her apartment.

Cristy opened the rear door, took her luggage from her and placed it in the gaping boot. Saoirse slipped into the warm rear seat and fastened her seat belt. Cristy had all the heaters running and after closing the boot settled back into the driver's seat.

"Morning to ya Miss Fitzgerald! How ya doin?"

"Fine thanks, Cristy."

"Aer Lingus—Terminal Two, as usual Miss Fitzgerald, is it?"

"That's right, Cristy. Thank you."

This morning, of all mornings, she knew she had to make the customary small talk before she could settle back into her seat and be alone with her own thoughts.

They sped along the deserted streets of Ballsbridge past the sweeping, tessellated curves of a silent Aviva Stadium and the frozen GAA pitches at Irishtown before emerging onto the dock approach roads in Ringsend.

"How are you keeping Cristy?"

"Grand—thank God Miss Fitzgerald and great news last night—our daughter Shona phoned from Boston to say that she's expecting again—her fourth—maybe a little girl this time please God. That'll be eight grandchildren altogether now! So, all grand, thank you. And you, yourself?"

"Yes—I'm fine thanks Cristy—that's wonderful news."

"Where are you off to today then Miss?"

"Oh—London today for a couple of days then Hong Kong and China for a week or so."

"Ah sure—it's a woman's world these days—but you take care out there now. The stories you hear!"

Saoirse knew from her previous conversations with Cristy that Shona was just 32—seven years younger than Saoirse and a mother three times over already—and now another baby on the way. As they crossed the Tom Clarke Bridge Saoirse stared upriver towards the Samuel Beckett Bridge, spanning the now calm and tranquil Liffey. Looking the other way, out to the Irish Sea she could see **Shackleton** and **Beaufort**—the two Port of Dublin tugs, moored alongside each other like sleeping siblings.

She would be back in less than ten days and decided she would take up Juan and Richard's offer to go for a run with them. It would at least be a start and who knows what it might lead to? It couldn't be worse than online dating. She knew from her contacts at the British Embassy that there was a lively social scene amongst diplomatic circles in Dublin.

They had both seemed nice—her father had originally been from Cork—*Irish by birth—and Cork by the grace of God*—had been his favourite catch-phrase—she was just able to recall the evenings when he had returned home early from work, reeking of diesel and wet, excavated earth and played pat-a-cake with her as she sat astride his big, bony knees—his large roughened hands gently slapping her soft tiny palms.

They were now entering the Port Tunnel—the soft, incipient dawn and silent buildings of North Dublin gave way to the harsh artificial lighting and anonymous brown interior of the surrounding walls and the amplified purring of the tyres on Cristy's Mercedes as it raced towards Dublin airport. Just a few minutes later Saoirse sensed the taxi begin to climb as they approached the end of the Tunnel—the sky seemed much lighter as they emerged and looking eastwards Saoirse could see the bright landing lights of the early morning incoming flights hovering in a yellowing sky over the Irish Sea.

Cristy pulled to a halt outside Terminal Two, popped open the boot and removed Saoirse's luggage. She had mastered the art of travelling light many years ago—once she had realised that there were only a small number of essential items to pack—everything else was freely available these days wherever you were going in the world. Cristy placed her case on the pavement.

"On the company account Miss Fitzgerald?"

"Yes—please Cristy—Sportswear Inc." She signed his receipt book and slipped him a 20 Euro note.

Cristy doffed an imaginary cap.

"Thanks a million, Miss Fitzgerald—safe trip now—take care!"

"And you Cristy!"

Saoirse stepped towards the terminal building and the doors slid silently open—she crossed the spacious hall to the lifts and pressed level two for DEPARTURES. Before the doors closed a young couple stepped in, a JUST MARRIED sticker and a large red "L" plate were attached to their luggage. They were holding hands and so obviously in love. Saoirse looked away, lest her emotions got the better of her.

The lift doors opened, the newlyweds stepped out and Saoirse was surprised but delighted to see one of yesterday's rescuers, Juan, stood some 20 metres away, looking at his mobile phone. She remembered that he had said that sometimes he had to travel to Brussels or Madrid.

Saoirse started to walk over to him and then saw yesterday's other rescuer, Richard, approaching from the opposite direction—he walked up to Juan and embraced him and then they kissed—an unmistakeable lovers' kiss. She shouldn't have been surprised—they had seemed close.

Juan and Richard turned and walked away from Saoirse, arms around each other. Dispirited, Saoirse walked across the departure hall to join the priority queue for security screening and a few minutes later, having collected her bags from the scanners set off for the Aer Lingus lounge where she settled down with a coffee.

She noticed Gavin Thompson from the Embassy check in to the lounge and help himself to a coffee before sitting down in the armchair opposite.

"Morning Saoirse—I saw you setting off on your run yesterday as I was leaving the Embassy—where did you get to?"

"Out along the Great South Wall."

" Very impressive!"

"Well, not entirely!"

She turned her wrists to show him her grazes.

"Ouch! They look sore. Nothing broken though?"

"No."

"And I see no damage to those eyes of yours!"

"No." Saoirse blushed—Gavin was a terrible flirt and very handsome—even more handsome than either Juan or Richard, but—very happily married.

"Good! Where are you off to today?"

"London today, then the Far East. And you?"

"The Near-East! Edinburgh! Giving a talk to the newly formed British and Irish Chamber of Commerce. By the way, I'm glad I've seen you—Sir James and I were hoping that Cristiano a Fiorentina might be keen to repeat the fashion show at the ambassador's Summer Garden Party this year—it was a great success from our point of view and I hope yours?"

"I would think so. It was a success for us too—we made a few new contacts—not least at Brown Thomas—lots of positive publicity and also recruited a very talented new Irish designer on to the staff here in Dublin. In fact we've already been working on a few draft designs—with the emphasis on something pan-European. From what I've seen of the designs so far they look very exciting."

"Good."

"I'll need to speak to Annette—as you know, she likes to maintain a high profile for all her favourite causes, but it will be her decision."

"Of course. I didn't know, until James told me that her grandparents were caught up in the Birmingham pub bombings."

"Yes—they had gone to New Street to meet her grandmother's sister, off the London train, to swap Christmas presents, then have a meal together, but the train was delayed so they went for a drink at The Mulberry Bush—witnesses say that they had only just walked in when the bomb went off."

"How terrible!"

"So, as you can guess Annette is as keen, as I am to support you, and Sir James."

"Well, that's welcome news—we need as much support as possible if we're going to keep the Good Friday Agreement in place—I'll let Sir James know when I get back from Scotland. I'm sure in return he'd be happy to support Annette in her various campaigns in any way he can. Shall we keep in touch on that? I'll get Jenny to make an appointment for us to meet up in the next few weeks or so. We've got plenty of time—the Garden Party is not until September."

"Fine—I'll be away for a week or so but I know Jenny has Aoife's contact details—she has access to my diary."

"I'll look forward to that."

"Me too!"

"You know, my father always said his life was saved by a pint of Guinness. He was, is a vet and was a Prof at Glasgow University Vet School and an external examiner for Trinity College. He was here in May 1975 and had just finished a meeting with the Dean of the vet school. He was walking back to The Shelbourne Hotel through the grounds of Trinity and decided to call in at The Pavilion Bar for a drink. He had just sat down with it when he heard a loud explosion—it was one of the three car-bombs to go off in Dublin that evening.

"He ran around the corner into Leinster Street South and joined the medical and dental students giving first aid to the victims—he said it was utter carnage and indiscriminate slaughter—and but for stopping for that Guinness he reckoned he would have been walking right past the car-bomb when it was detonated.

"Not surprisingly his favourite drink is now a pint of Guinness!"

Gavin took a glance at the departure board—EDINBURGH—GO TO GATE.

"Looks like my flight's been called early and it's a long walk to the Edinburgh gate—I'd better get going. See you soon, Saoirse. Have a safe trip."

"And you, Gavin."

As Gavin gathered his belongings, his phone rang.

"Hi darling—no I haven't forgotten—navy blue cashmere—size 10—fine—and two medium for the twins. I'll see you later tonight. Bye, love." He ended the call and smiled at Saoirse. "Mrs T!"

Saoirse idly thought of discussing sperm donation with Juan and Richard when she returned from her trip. She assumed gay men would be more sympathetic and liberal-minded than most when it came to creating extended families. She wondered how shared parent-hood with a gay couple might work, but knew that whatever the arrangements, they couldn't provide her with a man to love and share her life with—not in the way she wanted.

Disheartened, she glanced at the departure board LONDON HEATHROW—GO TO GATE She stood up and realised how much she was still aching from yesterday's fall on The Great South Wall—she realised how close she had been to serious injury—if she had been swept off the Wall onto the unforgiving granite below that could have put an end to all her hopes.

Chapter Three

Brown's Hotel Albemarle St Mayfair
London

7:30 am
Friday 8th of January 2016

Consultant anaesthetists are reputedly a safe pair of hands—Volvo estate drivers and wearers of entirely suitable rainwear—both belted and buttoned and two umbrellas, at least, in the boot. Not so Dr Julian Bracken—his Aston Martin Vantage convertible was day-glo yellow—matching some of his silk ties bought at his shirt-makers, Turnbull and Asser of Jermyn Street, on his frequent trips to London.

His arrival in the consultants' car park at Somerford Royal Infirmary was usually announced by Bruce Springsteen, Ry Cooder or U2—having invested in a high-performance convertible, he was determined to get value for money—so provided it was neither raining nor snowing, the top was down and the music was up.

His self-confidence, to be fair, was in large measure justified—he was the "go-to" anaesthetist for spinal corrective surgery in the South West of England—his particular skill being to achieve and maintain surgical anaesthesia for the duration of the operation, whilst ensuring a swift post-operative recovery with few complications.

He was a regular contributor to *The European Journal of Anaesthesia* and had recently returned from **The 9th International Congress of Anaesthetists** in Santa Fe, New Mexico where he had presented a paper on *Post-Operative Complications In Spinal Corrective Surgery*. Amongst his colleagues he was tipped to be a future president of the Royal College.

His only serious professional embarrassment—one that he had never been able to quite forget—had taken place during his first year in post at St Bart's, when he had failed to supervise a nurse inserting a urethral catheter into a female patient. Two hours later the operating table began to flood with urine and the procedure was abandoned—he could still visualise the lead professor-surgeon's contemptuous glare through narrowed eyes above his surgical mask at the unnecessary and unwelcome development.

The prof had not needed to speak—the unspoken message *your responsibility—entirely preventable* was transmitted and received loud and clear—in the ten or so years since then he had been sure to eliminate any possibility of repeating the same mistake.

Julian was sitting at the desk in his hotel room scrolling through the PowerPoint slides for his presentation later that morning at the Royal College. He had participated in this lecture, *Safety in Anaesthesia*, for the last three years—he was scheduled to present his paper at 11.30 after morning coffee and would stay for lunch to catch up with colleagues—it would be no bad thing to be seen at the College and participate in a bit of "pressing the flesh".

At 3.00pm he had a meeting with Robert Morley, the senior partner at Morley and Casson, Wealth Managers and Tax Advisers on Stafford St, just around the corner from Brown's for an annual review of his financial standing. He would then have plenty of time to walk over to Jermyn St, pick up his new shirts—perhaps choose a new tie or two—collect the Aston and still get a head start on the rush-hour—hopefully he would be back in Bristol by 8.00pm.at the latest. He was not on call tomorrow so he could finalise his article for submission to **The British Journal of Chronic Pain Management**.

Unlike his professional life, which had had few set-backs, apart from the leaking catheter, Julian's personal life had not been without sadness. A sadness to which he had reacted by redoubling his commitment to his career in medicine and setting aside his earlier expectations of life—expectations he had by now all but given up on—despite having Eleanor's blessing. In one of her more grimly prophetic moods, she had made him promise that if anything should ever happen to her, he would make a new life for himself.

That prophesy had turned out to be chillingly self-fulfilling—no more than three weeks later, Eleanor had died instantly, less than a mile from their home, when a mini-cab driver, texting on his mobile phone, had failed to notice Eleanor's stationary car ahead of him, indicating to turn right. The resulting collision although not in itself fatal, shunted Eleanor's car into the opposite carriageway and the path of an oncoming lorry, fully laden with scaffolding poles.

Julian had immediately recognised one of the police officers—Sergeant Morrissey—from the hospital, as the police were often there, when he'd opened the front door to their house that evening. He was accompanied by a young female officer. With a feeling of dread, Julian realised that Eleanor had not, as usual phoned or texted to say she would be late home.

In the short interval between opening the door and Sergeant Morrissey speaking, Julian immediately knew, from their reverential demeanour—radios turned down, solemn-faced, and bare-headed, Sergeant Morrissey's whispered request to enter the house—that they were the bearers of bad news.

Facing him across the coffee table, Sergeant Morrissey had introduced his colleague as WPC Rosie Crossley, a family liaison officer and concluded with his apologies and regret that there had been nothing that either the two off-duty nurses who were first on the scene, or the emergency services, despite arriving within minutes could do to save her.

They had kindly driven him to formally identify Eleanor's body and he recalled bracing himself as the mortuary assistant had prepared to reveal Eleanor's face but, there had been no need—she looked serene—so serene that he could imagine her chest to be slowly rising and falling underneath the green sheeting.

He wondered, as he often did, how such a small movement, ethereally sustained, could have such significance and how easily his patients breathed, with no conscious effort—how often he had lain beside Eleanor at night, feeling her sweet breath, gently caressing his face, now gone forever. To the silent question he had nodded and bent forward to kiss Eleanor one last time, warm lips kissing cold.

Julian put his lecture notes down—time to finish dressing and go down to breakfast.

***

In her room at Brown's Hotel, Saoirse was thumbing through **The Financial Times** for any news of the Initial Public Offering of Sportswear Inc. When she had joined Sportswear Inc, her one and only job after graduating from Central St Martins 16 years ago, she had accepted a salary package which included share options which had increased considerably as the company grew—and would be of even greater value on flotation.

After her induction, she had achieved rapid promotion, becoming Chief Buyer at the age of 26 and had spent most of the time since, criss-crossing the globe, initially attending trade exhibitions in the United States, visiting suppliers and manufacturers in the far East and Turkey but following the acquisition of the fashion house, Cristiano a Fiorentina in 2004, also attending the four main fashion shows in New York, London, Milan and Paris.

Any prospect of sustaining a relationship had finally disappeared when she had been appointed Head of Visual Display, in addition to Chief Buyer, two years later, at the age of just 28, which meant that as the company opened a new store in another new country Saoirse and her NST—New Store Team—would spear-head the project with a deadline of three months from survey to launch party and first customer crossing the door.

Her life became even more hectic—but the work was enjoyable, although sometimes there was a thin line between euphoria and hysteria. It had always been her ambition to work in the fashion industry—it was what she had wished for from the age of twelve or thirteen.

Her friends from school and college had drifted out of regular contact until a wedding invitation would arrive out of the blue. One year she had received seven such invitations. She had tried online dating but had quickly realised it would never work. The men she had met in this way bore hardly little resemblance to their online profiles and even less to their photographs, and were for varying reasons, easily dislikeable.

Then came news about her friends divorcing, followed by bitter disputes over children, money and the matrimonial home—even the dog!

Just before her 30th birthday she decided with misgivings that she would put the "mating game" on hold and devote the next ten years to her career, then with her savings and whatever her shares in Sportswear Inc. would realise she would look at her options and perhaps take a position which was more conducive to meeting a suitable partner and starting a family—although she was concerned that becoming a mother in her forties might be difficult for her and present additional risks for the baby.

Some weeks later in the departure lounge at Heathrow, thumbing through her copy of UK Vogue she had noticed an advertisement for the United Kingdom Female Clinic—a fertility clinic offering:

Career women the opportunity to take control of your lives by choosing **elective egg-freezing,** *enabling you to preserve your fertility until* **you** *choose the right time for* **you** *to become a mother.*

Did you know that after the age of 35 a woman's eggs deteriorate, both in quantity and quality?

Eggs harvested at a younger age are healthier and more viable. Using the latest techniques we will harvest and preserve your eggs so **you** *can choose the time* **you** *want to start* **your** *family with confidence*

This seemed to serendipitously address her concerns about late motherhood so she logged on to the UKFC website and completed the online questionnaire, requesting an appointment at their Westminster clinic after her return from Milan. After an initial assessment, the procedure had been relatively simple and pain-free, apart from several days of feeling slightly unwell some weeks later because of the hormone injections required to stimulate "superovulation" to enable her eggs to be harvested.

The harvested eggs had then been flash-frozen by vitrification and could be fertilised whenever she chose—provided of course—that she had access to a source of healthy sperm. It had all seemed so simple then but the time had just flown by.

Saoirse gathered her FT, mobile phone and clutch-bag and went down for breakfast. After a brief wait at the restaurant entrance, George, the head waiter, escorted her through the busy restaurant to a table by a window overlooking Albemarle St. She ordered her usual Orkney kippers and decaffeinated coffee.

***

She noticed Julian as soon as he entered the restaurant.

"Good morning, Dr Bracken—would you like your usual table by the window?"

"Yes please—thank you George."

Saoirse watched as George escorted her fellow guest to the table in the opposite corner. Dr Bracken took the chair George eased out for him—he was not only handsome but smartly dressed. With her fashion brain, she guessed a size 56 / XL and some 6'2" tall. Saoirse guessed his age to be forty-something and although a little overweight he had a slim athletic frame.

His hair was dark, greying slightly at the temples and held a natural curl—hanging just on the collar of his shirt. His grey flannel suit was well cut but not bespoke—more Hugo Boss than hand-made on Dover St. A yellow silk tie was gracefully knotted, four-in-hand style over a powder-blue shirt. He had a healthy tan as if he had just returned from a Mediterranean holiday.

He settled down, placing a copy of **The Times** and what appeared, judging from the illustration on the cover, to be a medical journal on the tablecloth and picked up the menu. Saoirse noticed he wasn't wearing a wedding ring.

"Your breakfast madam—and your coffee."

"Thank you."

She continued her observations and wondered what Dr Bracken was doing in London and where he lived. Why he wasn't married? He must surely be in a relationship. With dismay, Saoirse recalled Gavin, then Juan and Richard—surely, that would be too much of a coincidence—and he didn't look gay.

A waiter went over to take Dr Bracken's order—Eggs Albemarle, toast and Orange Pekoe tea. When they were served, some ten minutes later, Saoirse got up and left the restaurant with no other intention, initially, than to linger in the lobby, but seeing a note on the concierge's desk addressed to Dr Bracken, she took a seat on an armchair opposite the reception desk from where she could see the restaurant exit. She opened her **Financial Times** and pretended to read.

Twenty minutes later, Dr Bracken emerged from the restaurant, with his copy of **The Times** and his medical magazine tucked under one arm, walking in the direction of the lift. As he passed the reception desk, Henry the concierge approached him.

"Good morning, Doctor Bracken—Mr de Gascoigne from Turnbull & Asser called—would you like him to arrange for your shirts to be dropped off for you here at the hotel?"

"No thank you Henry—could you please tell Charles that I will call in later this afternoon and collect them? I thought I would have a look for some ties to go with the new shirts. I'll be there at 4.30. Many thanks."

"Thank you, sir, and just to confirm—your car has been valeted and is ready for you. I need just 10 minutes notice and I will arrange for it to be at the hotel entrance on Albemarle St when you're ready to leave."

"Thank you, Henry, if the car could be there for 4.45pm that would be perfect. I'm hoping to get ahead of the week-end rush and onto the M4 back to Bristol before the traffic builds up too much."

Deciding that she had heard and seen enough Saoirse discreetly watched as Dr Bracken walked across to the lift and stepped inside. Saoirse knew Turnbull & Asser well—in fact she had an account there—from time to time she bought ties for her brothers.

Back in her room she decided it was time to follow Aoife's advice and "Be bold!" She first logged on to the General Medical Council website and completed the details required to "Search the Medical Register" entering the surname "Bracken" and ticking "Male"—the results showed there were four male Doctor Brackens on the GMC medical register—Bartholomew, Henry, James and Julian.

Further general internet searches of all four "Dr Brackens" revealed varying results but no pictures until she clicked on a link to—**Santa Fe—New Mexico—The 9th International Congress of Anaesthetists**. This website had profiles of the speakers and when she clicked on "Dr Julian Bracken" a picture and profile of her fellow guest appeared on the screen.

Turnbull & Asser was a stroke of luck—but how best to take advantage? She knew from her marketing training that she needed to create the desire in him—then prompt him into thinking he was making the first move—but most of all she needed to be patient.

Saoirse emailed Aoife:

Hi Aoife—the meeting with Croce Valentina—at 3.00pm today—something's come up and I need to be here in Mayfair this afternoon—can you arrange for me to do the meeting by 'phone conference? Tell them I'll call everyone in at 3.00pm and that it won't take more than forty-five minutes—could you please email me when you've done it Aoife?

She returned to the internet profile of Dr Julian Bracken. As she was reading more she noticed an incoming email from Aoife.

Hi Saoirse—all sorted—numbers and times to dial in are set out below.
Aoife
XX

PS Would that "something" be male?

**Might be—I'll tell you later
XX**

Well—don't forget your sample of the new perfume I gave you, on Wednesday before you left the office—it's pheromone based and supposed to work wonders!
Aoife.
XX
PS Be bold!

**I will!
xx**

Saoirse had in fact forgotten about the perfume but easily found it in her handbag. She took the package out and then opened her e-folder under ***Cristiano a Fiorentina—Pheromone Based Signature Perfume***

She began to read:

HIGHLY RESTRICTED—COMMERCIALLY SENSITIVE

To: All—Research Group
Cc: Annette Russell, Saoirse Fitzgerald

The so-called Athena Pheromone was first produced in the United States by Dr Winnifred Cutler and is still, today, marketed by the Athena Institute. Although the effect of female pheromones—airborne messengers that enhance sexual attractiveness—remains the subject of scientific scrutiny, many women have reported increased interest from male colleagues when wearing pheromone based perfume. In a double-blind placebo controlled test…

Saoirse wasn't entirely convinced by the science of pheromone-based perfumes herself, but it could surely do no harm. Her sample bottle had arrived, marked NOT FOR PUBLIC SALE OR SUPPLY from the Research and Development Team a few days ago and had remained unopened on her desk. She opened the box and sprayed her wrists and then her throat and let it settle—it was an attractive, powerful perfume. She pulled on her coat and left the hotel, heading in the direction of Piccadilly and the Burlington Arcade.

Chapter Four

THE ROYAL COLLEGE OF ANAESTHETISTS
CHURCHILL HOUSE
RED LION SQUARE
HOLBORN
LONDON

11.30 am
8 January

Julian's first slide on his PowerPoint display was a cartoon of a man and woman in bed snoring happily away—a bubble above their heads was filled with ZZZZZZZs.

This is not a drawing of me at work—his audience laughed—*it is a drawing of how we should all be sleeping, but I suspect we don't always sleep as well as these two people, here in the cartoon. This lecture is entitled "Safety in Anaesthesia—Avoiding Complaints—and the Police" and is about your safety as anaesthetists, because whilst we all have a paramount duty to our patients to ensure their clinical safety, we as a College want to ensure that you as College members remain professionally safe too.*

In an increasingly litigious world we are all too fully aware of the growing number of clinical negligence claims, which cost the NHS and our protection bodies many millions of pounds a year in legal fees and compensation, but perhaps more damaging and costly than that—certainly from a personal and professional point of view are investigations by our regulatory bodies and indeed even the police.

Julian clicked his PowerPoint control again and a cartoon of a police van skidding around a corner on two wheels, with flashing blue lights, heading past a sign pointing towards a hospital came up on the screen to his side—his audience smiled and some laughed.

This may happen where things have gone seriously wrong in theatre and a manslaughter investigation is launched, the result of which can mean not only an end to a career but if prosecuted and convicted a prison sentence measured in years followed almost certainly by erasure from the medical register.

He clicked again and another cartoon of an irascible judge in red gown and full bottom wig, pointing at a woman in the dock wearing scrubs, with a bubble saying, Nothing less than five years for you, doctor—take her down!

Regrettably, there will be very few of us who will conclude our professional careers without being sued, complained about to NHS England, referred to the GMC or investigated by the police and if we are fortunate enough to have survived all of these professional pitfalls also manage to escape criticism from the final investigator—one of Her Majesty's Coroners.

As it happens, the leading case on gross negligence manslaughter in the hospital setting concerns one of our colleagues, an anaesthetist by the name of Dr Adomako and sets out the test which the judge will direct the jury to apply in a criminal prosecution, when, after hearing all of the evidence they retire to consider their verdict.

This case is also very important because, before deciding whether to bring charges or not the Crown Prosecution Service will review all the evidence, including anything you say if you are interviewed, in the light of that decision.

Having said that, my purpose today is to reassure you that the degree of negligence required to justify a prosecution for gross negligence manslaughter must be very bad indeed—hence the description "gross"—effectively, so bad as to amount to "criminal conduct" in the minds of the jury.

The facts of the Adomako case were that during an ophthalmic procedure at the Mayday Hospital in Croydon, the patient's endo-tracheal tube became disconnected from the ventilator. There were several very clear clues that this had occurred, not least that the patient had stopped breathing…

He clicked again to reveal a cartoon of a ventilator from which was hanging an obviously disconnected tube with a large red arrow pointing to it. A cartoon bubble with a large question mark hung over the anaesthetist's head.

The other signs that things had gone wrong were…

Chapter Five

THE OFFICES OF MORLEY AND CASSON
WEALTH MANAGEMENT AND TAX ADVISERS
STAFFORD STREET
MAYFAIR
LONDON

3:00pm

"Good afternoon, Julian—how did the lecture go?"

"Oh—fine—just reassuring everyone that amongst other things, the nightmare of a prosecution for gross negligence manslaughter isn't going to happen, provided you do your job properly. It's got to be really serious negligence to come to that. I think everyone was reassured although it doesn't do any harm to keep people on their toes!"

"Absolutely, we've got the Financial Conduct Authority to keep us on our toes!"

"Well, it doesn't seem like a year ago since we last met."

"No, time flies."

"Take a seat Julian. Would you like some tea?"

"Yes please, do you have peppermint?"

"We do, I'll organise that. Richard walked silently across the office to his sideboard I've updated the spreadsheet with income and capital growth predictions for the next three years and printed off a copy for you to take with you. I've highlighted the relevant figures in red at the bottom of sheet 4. The pie-chart shows how the various investments are split."

Julian looked down the spreadsheet produced by Richard who was now sat across the desk from him. He was familiar with the lay-out from their previous meetings.

"I think you made a good choice of investments—a nice mix of equities, bonds, cash and alternatives. The bottom line Julian, as you can no doubt see, is that you could stop work tomorrow and still maintain your current lifestyle—if that is what you wished to do, but knowing you I doubt if you any such intention."

"None Richard, I think I would be bored stiff. I would miss all my colleagues and the challenge of the theatre, all the things I've grown accustomed to, and of course, I still miss Eleanor. She was a wonderful woman and wife and I think would have been a wonderful mother. What would I do with all that time on my hands?"

"I would be very lucky to meet someone like Eleanor—unless and until I do, I need something to occupy myself—after all, it's what I was trained for. Financial security is welcome but I would rather have her back than any amount of money."

"I'm sure."

Julian took a sip of his tea.

"It's surprising how cheaply a single person can live. My colleagues are always complaining about school fees or university tuition fees and wives who seem to order a new kitchen and bathroom every other year."

"Tell me about it! I've got three of those children but fortunately only one of those wives. Oh, that was a little undiplomatic, please forgive me!"

After a pause, Julian said, "Don't worry about it Richard."

"All the same, it must be reassuring to know that you are financially secure although I fully appreciate the tragic circumstances which brought us together."

"It seems to me that I will just get old and one day retire—they say nothing very exciting happens to anaesthetists—even those who drive Aston Martins."

Richard chuckled. "Well, they say the same about financial advisers who drive Porsches, but I think we're both happy and content. Anyway, I think we should just leave the portfolio as it is—if you have any views when you've studied my annual report just let me know. Please pass on my very best wishes to your brother Gerry."

"I will. Thank you Richard, I will see you in another 12 months or so."

"Yes and I'll keep sending you a monthly update."

Chapter Six

**TURNBULL & ASSER,
JERMYN STREET
MAYFAIR
LONDON**

4:25pm

Saoirse stepped ono the soft carpeting of Turnbull & Asser to be greeted by a smiling Charles St John de Gascoigne.

"Good afternoon, Miss Fitzgerald, what a pleasure to see you again. It has been some time and … may I say what a most alluring perfume. It really suits you."

"You may, Charles."

Saoirse allowed herself an inward smile.

"It's the new signature perfume from Cristiano a Fiorentina. Charles nodded in appreciation."

"How can I help you today Miss Fitzgerald?"

"I'm looking for a tie for one of my brothers."

"Well, we do have our new 2016 range just in. May I show you?" Charles began to drape a selection of silk ties over the glass-topped display cabinet between them. "These are all from the new range. You might recognise some of the silk as we used some supplied by the company you recommended in China."

After a few minutes consideration, Saoirse selected a blue and red tie and asked Charles to put it on her account. "I don't know if you have my up-to-date contact details Charles? Here they are."

She offered Charles one of her business cards. Charles carefully checked the details on his computer. "I'm afraid I have absolutely no knowledge of Chinese but I imagine it simply says the same as the English."

"That's right Charles."

Charles worked the keys on his computer and then looked up. "Well, that's done and here's the receipt and your card back Miss Fitzgerald."

"Oh, would you mind just stapling the card to the receipt as a reminder for me that you updated the details today? Perhaps you could then put it in the bag with the tie please?"

"A very good idea, Miss Fitzgerald."

Charles duly stapled Saoirse's business card to the receipt and put it, together with the chosen tie, into one of Turnbull & Asser's bespoke tie bags before placing it on the counter in front of Saoirse.

"There now Miss Fitzgerald, I've put your receipt with your contact details in the bag with the tie. Is there anything else I can help you with?"

"I wondered if I could have a look at some cufflinks please, Charles?"

"Certainly." Charles turned away bent down to open a draw and as he did so Saoirse took a quick glance at her watch—it was 4.29. Charles then placed a display tray containing several pairs of cuff-links on the counter in front of Saoirse who began to look through the selection.

"They are all sterling silver and mother of pearl, just let me know if you would like to see some more, Miss Fitzgerald."

***

As Julian emerged from Morley and Casson on Stafford St and waited for a gap in the traffic he glanced at his watch. It was nearly 4.30pm. If he was quick he could collect his shirts and be back at the hotel to pick up the Aston and be out of London before the rush-hour proper.

When he opened the door, and stepped into the shop he noticed the only other customer was a woman in a red trench coat, its collar turned up and belt fastened tightly, accentuating her narrow waist. She was standing with her ankles crossed and her slim Achilles tendons descended from shapely calf muscles into a pair of black, heeled court shoes.

He noticed that, intriguingly, one of her stockings was a deep purple and the other opaque black. His anaesthetist's brain assessed her height as 5'7" and weight at 45/50 kilograms. Julian breathed in her perfume—expensive and powerful.

Although she was facing away from him he could see part of her face in the mirror behind the display cabinet as, head bent down, she looked through a tray of cuff-links. Her sleek blonde, shoulder length hair was partly restrained by a pair of mirrored sunglasses. A pair of black ladies' leather gloves sat on the glass counter in front of her. The left-hand glove was embellished at the wrist by a silver and diamante cuff linked by silver chains to diamante rings on each of the three middle fingers.

He glanced again at the mirror and as he did so the woman looked up and their eyes met. She held his gaze for a few seconds and then smiled. Julian was taken aback. He had heard of heterochromia iridis during his ophthalmology rotation at Bart's many years ago and in fact had seen a few mild examples, but this was the first time he had seen complete heterochromia and eyes as striking as hers.

Her left iris was a very dark green and her right the palest of ice blue. The effect was mesmerising. He could see now that she had pronounced cheekbones. Her hair had an off-set parting and her eyes were lightly but well made up. She had a slim aquiline nose but the astonishing thing about her appearance was that, with her shoulder-length blonde hair, she bore a striking resemblance to Eleanor. He was inexplicably attracted to her.

Charles excused himself and moved over to Julian. "I have your shirts ready, Dr Bracken. I'll just go and get them for you. I understand you might wish to purchase another tie or two, so I have left some from our new range out for you to look at—mainly yellow—your favourite colour if I recall." Charles disappeared into the back of the shop.

When he had left, Julian pretended to study the ties and tried to avoid being seen as he glanced again at the woman again and again. He thought she was one of the most beautiful women he had ever seen—her eyes were entrancing. Charles returned with Julian's shirts, placing them on the counter close to the woman.

Julian lingered over his choice, dallying as long as he could, breathing in her perfume and hoping an opportunity to speak to the woman might arise but she appeared too engrossed in examining the display of cufflinks in front of her.

"Thank you, Charles, I'll take this one please."

"On your account, Dr Bracken?"

"Yes, thank you."

Charles slipped the tie into one of the shop's bespoke bags together with the receipt placing it on top of Julian's shirts.

"I'm just looking at some more ties. I may be some time—you can see to the lady if you wish."

"If you wish, sir. Your receipt is in the bag with your tie just there."

"Could I just look at that other tray of cufflinks, down there please, Charles?"

The woman pointed to the cabinet behind Charles who began to turn around. As she pulled her arm back her elbow brushed her gloves off the display cabinet and they fell to the floor. Julian bent down to pick them up.

"Thank you, that's very kind."

"You're welcome."

She smiled, again holding his gaze for just longer than usual, but before Julian could say anything, she turned away.

Julian could hardly speak. He was paralysed by her appearance and presence.

Perplexed, he picked up his shirts and his tie bag and said goodbye to Charles. He left the shop and the woman in red behind.

Chapter Seven

ALBEMARLE ST

4:00pm

Julian turned the corner into Albemarle St and could see his car, as Henry had promised at the front entrance of the hotel with hazard lights blinking. He had left the shop with reluctance and walked hesitatingly back to the hotel to collect his keys from Henry who told him his luggage was already in the boot. He gave Henry a £20 tip.

In a few minutes he would be heading back to Bristol but something inside of him was nagging away. For some reason, he hadn't been able to bring himself to speak to the woman in the red trench-coat—he'd not even had the sense to look if she was wearing a wedding ring.

He put his shirts and tie bag onto the passenger seat and within two minutes was on Piccadilly heading west to join the M4. However, he felt he had missed an opportunity—he simply couldn't get the woman out of his mind and on impulse, as he was stopped at traffic lights he turned right and began making his way back to Jermyn Street, eventually finding an empty parking bay around the corner on Bury St.

He stepped into the shop again. The woman had gone but her perfume lingered on. Charles lifted his head up from rearranging a selection of ties and greeted him with a smile.

"Dr Bracken, have you forgotten something?"

"Not really Charles…well, sort of—the lady who was here before when I called in to collect my shirts—is she a regular customer?"

"Well yes sir, the lady has had an account with us for some time. She works in the fashion industry."

"I don't suppose you perhaps have her contact details?"

Charles frowned. "Well we do have her personal details on file, yes."

Julian stood awkwardly for a few moments. "It's just that… I was wondering if you might possibly have her mobile number?"

Charles raised an eyebrow. "I see sir, well I hope you won't regard me as being unhelpful but—there is data protection legislation in place."

"Well, could you perhaps pass on a message?"

"Doctor Bracken, I'm sorry but I'm not sure that would be very appropriate. Quite apart from legal confidentiality issues, the lady might take offence—we have our reputation to protect, which we have done successfully since 1885."

"No, you're quite right Charles, I really shouldn't have asked. I'm sorry to have put you in such a position. It was most improper of me."

"May I assume then doctor, that our current excellent relationship is to continue?"

"Yes, of course Charles."

"Good and between us, doctor," Charles lowered his voice, "I can well understand why you might be keen to make the lady's acquaintance. She is a lady of quite exquisite appearance and taste. Although I would have to say, and I hope without sounding too discouraging, if I understand you correctly, very much totally dedicated to her career if you understand me—I'm afraid."

"Yes Charles, quite! Thank you. Good evening."

"Yes, good evening Dr Bracken. I hope you have a lovely weekend."

"And you too, Charles."

Despite this unscheduled visit Julian had still gained a head start on the London traffic. He pulled off the M4 at Leigh Delamere Services and visited M&S Simply Food and stocked up on essentials. It was Saturday tomorrow and he planned to review and finish the article he was writing for **The British Journal of Anaesthesia**.

On returning to the car he dropped the hood and re-joined the M4. He clicked on his iPod playlist shuffle, a Christmas gift from his teenage niece, Lucia, who seemed to have created an eclectic musical horoscope—*Kylie Minogue—Can't Get You Out of My Head* came up—Julian smiled ruefully. It was true, he couldn't get the woman in Turnbull & Asser out of his head. He couldn't help thinking he had missed an opportunity.

Julian accelerated to 100 mph and turned the volume up. He sighed. If only Charles had been amenable to disclosing the woman's contact details—or even passing on a message. He would simply have to try to forget her, however, Lucia's next choice was *Chris de Burgh's The Lady in Red*.

There was little traffic on the M4 that night and he took up a position on the inside lane. A little before Junction 34 he pulled out to overtake a slow-moving Renault Clio which was indicating to leave the motorway and leaving a strong smell of burning oil behind.

As Nurse Mary Keaveney steered her battered Renault Clio onto the slip road she easily recognised the yellow Aston Martin zip by.

"There's that arrogant, flash bugger! He's going to come a cropper one of these days if I've got anything to do with it" she muttered to herself as the Aston disappeared out of view under the flyover bridge."

A couple of years ago Mary had found herself alone in the recovery room with Dr Bracken—lots of nurses had "bagged" a doctor so why not her? Ever since she had paid £3,000 for a boob job, she had taken to wearing a quarter cup bra under her scrubs in order to display what she regarded as, and indeed was, her very appealing, enhanced profile. She had opted for the sub-fascial placement for extra perkiness.

She knew how most men and therefore most doctors thought and had been toying with the idea of making a pass at Dr Bracken for some time. The opportunity had just not arisen before, but the moment seemed right. It was the end of the list - they were alone in the recovery room.

Dr Bracken was wiping the Whiteboard clean. Mary stepped towards him, quietly breathed in and pulling her shoulders back so that her breasts became particularly pronounced. She touched him gently on his forearm, asked him about the line of incision and scarring left by spinal surgery and then turned her back ever so slightly towards him.

To her delight she felt him place a finger just above her buttocks, saying, "Depending on the severity of curvature, from here."

He then began to move his finger slowly upwards. To her surprise she felt a genuine thrill as his finger moved slowly upwards, with varying pressure, along her back towards her bra strap. She was hoping, now possibly expecting him to slip his hands round her waist, but instead he carried on tracing his finger up her back, flirtingly, she thought, stopping on the nape of her naked neck, above her scrubs top.

"…to here."

She turned around, running a moist tongue slowly along her upper lip, ready for anything but was exasperated and indignant to see that he had simply resumed wiping the Whiteboard clean.

"So that's the line, Susan," was all he had said, without even looking at her.

Although they had been alone, she felt utterly embarrassed and insulted as she had been sure he had understood that she wasn't really interested at all in the line of surgical incision and must have known it was a "come-on". How much more obvious could she have been?

She had never forgiven him for going along with her, raising her expectations and then carrying on as if nothing had happened and to make matters worse, calling her Susan. It was all so condescending. In fact, the more she had thought about it the stranger his behaviour had seemed, as if he'd taken advantage of the situation for his own reasons—been teasing her.

The next day she decided to complain to Julie Lightfoot the Deputy Head of Human Resources that he had touched her "inappropriately" but despite Julie's enthusiastic help and support, nothing came of it. He had just been informally "advised" about his behaviour—but there would always be another time!

Chapter Eight

THE BACKS
BRISTOL

7;30pm
Friday 8th of January 2016

When Julian arrived home, he left his shirts and tie in the hallway with his overnight bag and laptop. He then went into the kitchen and unpacked the shopping from M&S. He poured himself a cold beer from the chiller which he took into the lounge and settled down on the sofa with his feet up on the coffee table.

He looked across the room to Eleanor's photograph and was struck again by the likeness of the woman he'd seen earlier in Turnbull & Asser.

For Julian, the time after Eleanor's death had at first been long days of loneliness—even when well-meaning family and friends had called or visited, their departure only served to emphasise that he was all alone and that the reality was that Eleanor had gone for ever. In due course there had been some well-intentioned attempts at match-making by some of his colleagues' wives but Julian hadn't been ready for a new relationship—instead he threw himself into his work.

During the day, he was busy enough but when he returned, in the evenings grief still filled their home. Sergeant Morrissey had called again with WPC Crossley many months later, just before the taxi-driver's trial, to take a victim impact statement from him.

The jury had returned a guilty verdict of causing death by dangerous driving and the judge had imposed an immediate prison sentence of five years. The case was widely reported in the local press, amidst calls from politicians for increased penalties for using mobile phones whilst driving.

The conclusion of the trial triggered a decision in Julian to leave London—he realised that the house in Ealing only served as a reminder of what he and

Eleanor had shared and could have shared. They had talked, embraced, laughed, slept, made love there—and in time would have raised a family there. He decided to return to the West Country which was familiar to him and held happier memories—from his schooldays.

He resigned himself to never seeing the woman in red again but made a mental note to thank Lucia for her thoughtful, if innocently beguiling Christmas present.

TERMINAL 5
HEATHROW AIRPORT LONDON

9 pm
Friday, 8 January

Saoirse sat in the Virgin lounge, occasionally checking the departures board. HONG KONG—WAIT IN LOUNGE. The massage had been just what she had needed after her fall and had eased her shoulders and arms which had been aching for the last two days. She was looking forward to the inflight meal with a few glasses of champagne then a long sleep—hopefully waking as the plane started its descent to Hong Kong's Chek Lap Kok airport.

She could see the huge Virgin 747 at Gate 78 being refuelled and serviced. The various ground staff wore ear protectors as they went about their work but despite the departure and arrival of jets every few minutes, with a soft growl which faded as the departing jets lifted from the runway and a new growl as the arriving jets engaged reverse thrust, the lounge was almost completely silent, apart from the gentle murmur of occasional exchanges between the staff on the reception desk and travellers checking in and the clink of ice in glass tumblers as they helped themselves to drinks.

Some of the cleaners were pulling their trolleys around the cavernous room, clearing and polishing tables as they went.

She glanced at the departure board and noticed that her flight had jumped up the queue but the display still said, WAIT IN LOUNGE. Her phone blipped and she picked it up, wondering if her scheme had worked and it might be Dr Julian Bracken but it was just another incoming work email. She carried on indulging herself, scrolling optimistically through the flight times from Dublin to Bristol.

Chapter Nine

THE BACKS
BRISTOL

6.30 am
Saturday, 9 January 2016

Julian was still an early riser—a habit from his schooldays. After a shower, he made some coffee and returned to the hall to unpack his laptop and log on. After this he picked up the shirts and tie bag and returning to his bedroom began to unwrap his shirts and place them on hangers.

When he'd finished, he opened the tie bag to look at his new tie and was puzzled to see that it wasn't the yellow and blue tie he had selected, but a red and blue tie. Instinctively, he turned the bag upside down and out fluttered a receipt to which was attached a business card:

Saoirse Fitzgerald
Head of Global Display
Cristiano a Fiorentina
IFSC DUBLIN 2
EIRE

首席买方和团长全

球显示克里斯蒂亚诺 2

佛罗伦萨 IFSC 都柏林爱尔兰

And on the reverse;

Saoirse Fitzgerald,
Chief Buyer
Cristiano a Fiorentina
IFSC DUBLIN 2
EIRE

首席买方和团长全

球显示克里斯蒂亚诺 2

佛罗伦萨 IFSC 都柏林爱尔兰

There was also an email address and a mobile phone number. It could only belong to the woman in the shop. She had been the only other person there and Charles had told him that she worked in the fashion industry. He must have picked up the wrong bag.

Perplexed but delighted at being given an unexpected opportunity to make contact with the woman he picked up his phone to text a message but looked at the time—it was still only 06.50am—it was too early and this was a second chance he didn't want to lose. He decided instead to draft an email and sat down at his laptop.

Dear Ms Fitzgerald,

Please forgive me for this unsolicited email but I believe we may both have been shopping yesterday afternoon at Turnbull & Asser. Somehow, I appear to have picked up the tie you bought and I imagine, therefore, you may have picked up mine. The mistake was all mine. I am very sorry for any inconvenience caused—if I'm right, perhaps you could email me to let me know how we might exchange the ties.

Yours sincerely,
Julian Bracken.

He paused before pressing the SEND button. Nervously, he inserted the words '*for your husband*' after '*bought*'.

He read and reread the email and then made himself a fresh cup of coffee before sitting down to read it yet again. He looked at his watch—it was now

07.20am. He pressed **SEND** and wondered how long he would have to wait for a reply and more importantly—what would the reply say?

From: Saoirse Fitzgerald 2.20pm

Dear Mr Bracken,

Thank you for your email—forgive me for not replying sooner—I am in Hong Kong on business and have been in a meeting.

I did not realise that we had mistakenly picked up each other's ties but having now checked I see that I must have yours as it certainly isn't the one I chose for my brother, which was blue and red. The one I have is yellow and blue and I presume therefore yours.

I do not know where you live but if you can email me your address. I will post it to you as soon as I arrive back in the UK although, depending on where you live, it occurs to me that it might be better to meet up and exchange the ties?

Please let me know what you think.

Yours sincerely,

Saoirse Fitzgerald

Julian's mind began to race. He read the email again and noticed she had pointed out that the tie was a present for her brother, not a husband and that she had also suggested a possible meeting. He made himself another cup of coffee and began to think of the best way to respond. After several drafts, he gave up and made yet another cup of coffee. He then sat down and composed the following email

3.10pm

Dear Ms Fitzgerald,

Thank you for your email. I am going to be in Bristol with work for the next few weeks—but I wondered if you might let me buy you dinner as an apology for the mix-up, which I am sure was my fault.

Kind regards,

Julian Bracken.

From: Saoirse Fitzgerald 4.03pm

Dear Mr Bracken,

Thank you for your email. Dinner would be lovely although perhaps we should go halves as I think I may be as much to blame as you for the mix-up over the ties. I return from Hong Kong very late next Friday 15th January and am free most evenings the following week—perhaps the evening of Wednesday the 20th would be convenient? Would you care to let me know where we should meet?

Kind regards,
Saoirse Fitzgerald.

Julian could scarcely believe what was happening.

4.13pm

Dear Ms Fitzgerald,

There is a restaurant called Marckwicks in Bristol which is a favourite of mine. If you are agreeable, we could perhaps meet there at 8.30pm on the 20th January? I will reserve us a table.

Kind regards,
Julian Bracken.

4.26pm
From: Saoirse Fitzgerald

Dear Mr Bracken,

I can be in Bristol on Wednesday 20th January. I do not know Marckwicks but I am sure I can find it.

I shall bring your tie with me.

Once again, my apologies for the mix-up.

Thank you.

Kindest regards,
Saoirse.

In the Mandarin Oriental Hotel, Hong Kong, Saoirse, mildly euphoric, lay on her bed.

In the Backs, Bristol, Julian, mildly euphoric, sat at his desk.

Chapter Ten

Somerford Royal Infirmary

7:30am
Wednesday 20th of January 2016

Julian was in a very good mood—today would be fully occupied in a procedure to correct scoliosis in a fifteen-year-old female patient and tonight with dinner at his favourite restaurant, Marckwicks, on The Backs in Bristol, with Saoirse. The operation had been postponed from three days ago because during the pre-op assessment Julian had detected a slightly raised temperature and on auscultation some crackling, indicative of a lower respiratory tract infection in the inferior lobe of the left lung.

He was concerned about the risks of proceeding with the operation, bearing in mind the compromised efficiency of the lung, already somewhat compressed by the curvature of the spine. He had discussed his findings with James Broadley, the lead surgeon who had immediately agreed with his suggestion of postponing the operation.

The rest of the surgical team, the young patient and her parents had been disappointed but understanding, although there would be no such complications today. On re-examination yesterday afternoon, the airways assessment confirmed that the antibiotics had cleared the infection. He could detect no crackles or other sounds indicating any residual congestion. Her temperature was normal.

In these lengthy surgical procedures, the patient is prone on the operating table for several hours, presenting a risk of post-operative pain and tissue damage from sustained downward pressure. In order to minimise this risk, the patient is supported by padding at vulnerable areas—the eyes, all bony promontories, hips, knees, elbows, arms, the testes in males and the breasts in females.

With two minutes to go before "*knife to skin*" and the surgical team fully assembled Julian made one last check on the pressure points, working his way up from the patient's feet. He finally took up a position at the patient's head and in a moment of exuberance, which he would later find hard to explain, not least to himself, he spread his arms wide and announced to the theatre that he was going to perform the "Wonderbra Manoeuvre", slipping his hands under the patient's breasts, taking time and care to gently reposition them, in order to redistribute pressure evenly, in accordance with good medical practice.

Chapter Eleven

**THE MARRIOTT HOTEL
BRISTOL**

**12:30 pm
Wednesday 20th of January**

Saoirse had caught the 10.05 flight from Dublin to Bristol and in the quiet Arrivals Hall had easily spotted "Miss Saoirse Fitzgerald" on the taxi-driver's iPad held up at arm's length above his head. A short drive from the airport and they had arrived at The Marriott Hotel in Bristol city centre. Her room was ready for her when she had checked in.

She confirmed her appointment with the *Beauty Room* at the hotel spa for 6:30pm and then spent the rest of the afternoon replying to emails—checking, updating and then confirming the production schedules, shipping and delivery dates from the various suppliers and manufacturers she had met in Hong Kong and China, and her other suppliers in Istanbul and Izmir for Sportswear Inc, then reviewing the updated designs emailed by Aoife earlier that morning for the A/W collection for Cristiano a Fiorentina which she had reviewed in Paris last week.

She was, however, unable to devote her full attention to her work—only Aoife knew where she was and why. She logged off and shut down her laptop. She was too distracted to continue working.

She looked at her watch—3:30pm—and sauntered into the bathroom to run a bath, returning to unpack and lay out her clothes for dinner that evening—nothing too racy—although that might come later, when she knew Julian better.

Earlier that morning, in Dublin, she had chosen a purple mid-length shantung silk dress with a diamante and pearl embellished ruched waist and matching bolero jacket with three-quarter length split sleeves. She telephoned reception and ordered a taxi for 8.30pm so she would be at the restaurant just a little after 08.30pm. She certainly didn't want to turn up before Julian and give him the impression she was desperate, although, quite simply, she was.

She was not tired but undressed and lay down in her bathrobe, emperor-style, on her bed. She closed her eyes and contemplated her options, or more particularly her only current option—Dr Julian Bracken. Would he become her deus-ex-machina and make her dreams come true? She had "known" Julian for less than two weeks and not even had a conversation with him, but certainly found him attractive. She had never dated a doctor before but knew he should be trustworthy.

She picked up her phone and texted:

Hope your day has gone well—I am here in Bristol—arrived on time—I will meet you at Marckwicks, but I may be just a few minutes late. Work and all that! Saoirse. XX.

After a long, hot bath she wrapped herself in her bathrobe and made her way down to the *Beauty Room* in the hotel Spa Centre. The receptionist checked her in and confirmed her treatments—a full body massage—her bruises had now faded, shampoo and cut, facial and make-up. She decided to have her blonde hair put into a loose single French plait, which, she thought would make her look younger, yet still professional.

Returning to her room just after 8.00pm, she slipped out of her bath-robe and put on her underwear, one black and one white lace stocking, her purple dress and jacket, red suede court shoes, her black gloves with the diamante embellishments and her red raincoat. Finally, she took her "Signature" perfume and sprayed her throat and wrists. Her taxi was waiting for her. She was slightly, no, extremely nervous. She felt like she was going for an interview.

Chapter Twelve

Somerford Royal Infirmary
BRISTOL

7:00pm

The operation had gone smoothly with no unexpected problems. When Julian had reviewed the patient with the ward nurses, she was already showing signs of a good recovery. They had completed the Post Operative Handover Checklist and Julian had then gone to his office to check his messages—he was particularly looking for one from Saoirse—and was pleased to see a text message which told him she might be a little late but would meet him at Marckwicks as planned.

He was unsure how the relationship, which currently amounted only to a chance encounter in London, when they had hardly spoken and an exchange of emails resulting in tonight's "date" was going to proceed. He had thought Saoirse might have developed cold feet—might have called it off at the last minute—but to his relief, the text message confirmed that she was in Bristol—had made the trip from Dublin, as arranged and would be meeting him at Marwick's at 08.30—as arranged.

Despite his reputation for calmness and confidence in theatre he hadn't felt so nervous since his teenage years. But, looking at the worst-case scenario, as Saoirse was based in Dublin, if for some reason the "relationship" didn't work out, there would be little chance of any awkward and embarrassing chance meetings and at the very least he would have the company of a beautiful woman for an evening—which hadn't happened in a long time.

Julian stepped out of the hospital and took a long, welcome breath of fresh air as he walked to his car. Settling into the soft leather of the driver's seat he dropped the hood and clicked on his iPod play list, waiting for Lucia's next choice—it was Diana Ross—*I'm Going to Make You Love Me*.

He smiled and looked up at the stars, twinkling above him and admired the pink and orange of the lingering mid-winter sunset. As he reversed away from his parking space, and steered the Aston towards the car park exit, he felt the heated seat begin to warm his back and legs.

He pulled out into the light stream of early evening traffic, put his foot down and headed homewards to The Backs. Ry Cooder's *I think It's Going to Work Out Fine* came up next. He felt, as he had felt all day, slightly exuberant.

He was home in under 15 minutes, showered and changed and flopped into an armchair from where he could see Eleanor's picture on the credenza across the room. It was his favourite picture—un-posed, catching her in a moment's natural laughter—her head slightly back and her long, blonde hair falling to her shoulders.

A few days after Eleanor's death, Julian's university colleague Francis Beaumont, one of the local pathologists had been in touch. He had phoned to ask if he could call to pay his respects that evening.

On arrival, Francis settled down on the sofa and looked at the many cards and bouquets of flowers arranged about the house and noticed, oddly, a *Congratulations* card addressed to *Julian* and next to it on the coffee table a bottle of expensive champagne.

"I've brought you a copy of the post-mortem report, carried out by my colleague Johnny Drinkwater." Francis eased forward and placed an envelope on the coffee table.

They were silent for a few moments—both doctors knew exactly what a post-mortem involved.

"Thank you, Francis. I'll read it later? It's not as if it's going to change anything is it?"

"No, of course not."

"Are you sure you won't have a drink?"

"No thanks Julian. The coroner had no objection to me giving you a copy of the report, provided you keep it confidential, but there is another reason I wanted to call round—something I wanted to tell you face to face—although I'm not sure whether you might already know."

Julian nodded sadly.

"If you mean that Eleanor was expecting, I do know, but I only found out about two hours ago—Sergeant Morrissey called round to drop off Eleanor's belongings which the police found in her car boot—her laptop, handbag and other things—including some shopping, amongst which were a receipt for a pregnancy testing kit and these."

He pointed to the card and the bottle of champagne on the coffee table. We had only just started trying for a family.

Francis picked up the card:

Congratulations!
You're going to be a father!
We're going to be a family!
All my love!
Eleanor
XXX

He looked at the bottle of champagne—Perrier-Jouet, 2002.

Eleanor always did have good taste.

"Julian, there's something else—as well as confirming that Eleanor was about eight weeks pregnant, Johnny was able to note the presence of Mullerian ducts—we thought you would want to know rather than find out when you read the report." Julian nodded again.

"That's very thoughtful of you both—so I knew Eleanor was expecting but I didn't know she was expecting a little girl—our little girl."

"Yes, I'm so very sorry, Julian."

Julian remained silent for several minutes.

"Everyone's been so kind—you, Sergeant Morrissey—I've had a card from the two off-duty nurses—our neighbours—and the taxi-driver's insurers have written a letter to say that they will not be contesting liability and asking me to appoint a solicitor—but I can't think straight just now."

"There's plenty of time for that Julian. I'm sure your brother Gerry will know a good solicitor. Why don't we go for a walk? Get some fresh air? You look as though you need it."

They didn't talk—just walked through the fresh night air together as they had done many years before, when they were medical students along Ealing Green and through Walpole Park.

That night seemed such a short time ago, the intervening years had slipped quickly by.

He checked the time—it was already 8-15pm—he got up and looked across at Eleanor's picture again before picking up the Turnbull & Asser bag and leaving for Marckwicks.

Chapter Thirteen

MARCKWICKS RESTAURANT
THE BACKS
BRISTOL

8:30pm

It was only a short stroll to Marckwicks. Julian cut through Queen Square and onto Welsh Back and within two minutes he was ascending the stairs to his favourite restaurant.

Waiting at the front door of Marckwicks was Marcello who greeted Julian with the graceful deference of an accomplished front of house—reinforcing his sense of well-being and his hopes of a pleasant end to a successful day.

"Good evening Dr Bracken—please follow me."

Marcello escorted him through the already busy restaurant to his usual table and gently eased his seat forward as Julian sat down. Julian was quietly pleased that tonight he didn't recognise any of the other guests in the restaurant.

"So lovely to see you again, Dr Bracken and as you are not dining alone tonight, I make this special table for you and your guest—the flowers are with my compliments un regalo si? It's a special occasion, si?"

Marcello chuckled as he placed two menus and a wine list on the crisp linen tablecloth. "I've asked Giulia to bring you over your usual Campari con lemonade—was I right?"

"Yes Marcello—you were—all perfect."

Shortly the bright red aperitif was presented to him. He took his first sip of the ice-cold drink. He began to relax and look forward to Saoirse's arrival.

Julian picked up the menu, which he knew by heart but was in fact contemplating neither the menu nor the wine list.

Although he had become content with his own company, could please himself about everything, if he was honest with himself, he missed company—especially female company. He missed the simple things—sharing conversations, meals and holidays—the lecture trips, however exotic, were no substitute for those and although he was only 42, he knew that in retirement, which would soon come around, he would be lonelier still.

His emotional debate was interrupted by a pleasant fuss at the restaurant entrance and he looked up to see Saoirse being greeted by a smiling Marcello, Saoirse's red raincoat already draped over his arm as he began to guide her to their table. She was wearing a purple dress and a short jacket and Julian couldn't help noticing—one white and one black lace stocking.

Julian stood up to greet Saoirse who embraced him and offered her cheek for a brief kiss and then sat down opposite him. She placed her leather clutch-bag on the table cloth—her black gloves with the diamante embellishments on top. Julian breathed in her perfume and felt unusually helpless—pleasantly out of control. She smiled and her eyes held his gaze for a few seconds.

Julian handed Saoirse a menu—she was still studying it when Marcello returned. "Marcello, this is my friend, Saoirse Fitzgerald."

"Delighted to meet you Miss Fitzgerald, would you care for a drink?"

"Yes please—I'll have a gin and tonic. Bombay Sapphire and slim-line tonic please."

"Certainly Miss Fitzgerald. Dr Bracken—another Campari and lemonade?"

"Yes please"

"Straightaway."

Saoirse looked up from her menu. "Is there anything you would especially recommend?"

"Well, I tend to be a creature of habit, so I normally have the King Prawns Pil-Pil followed by the Braised Ox-Cheeks in Barolo sauce. It is one of Marcello's best dishes."

"That sounds perfect. I always follow the local advice although I might need a Peroni to go with the prawns—just to take the fire away—if that's possible please?"

"Of course. Red or white wine?"

"Red for preference please."

Marcello returned with their drinks.

"Marcello, we're ready to order. I think we're going to have the same—Prawns Pil-Pil to start and the Braised Ox Cheeks to follow."

"Certainly, Dr Bracken, and some mineral water? Frizzante?"

"Yes, please and two glasses of Peroni and a bottle of the Number 34, the Chateau Cantemerle please."

Marcello nodded his approval. "Bene!"

Saoirse took a sip of her gin and tonic.

Marcello hurried off with their order.

"So, you're a doctor?"

"Yes, an anaesthetist, at the Somerford Royal Infirmary, here in Bristol."

"How did you get interested in that?"

"Well as a kid I was bought a chemistry set one Christmas and began messing about with it—creating all sorts of smells and other noxious substances—I think I was hoping to discover a new element all on my own."

"I think I had one of those chemistry sets too!"

"One of my father's friends who was a surgeon told me about Theodoric of Lucca who wrote one of the first text books on medieval surgery—**The Cyrugia**—he would use sponges soaked with a solution of opium, mandrake and hemlock to induce unconsciousness in his patients, one of whom was the pope—Pope Innocent IV—at that age I rather liked the idea that I might grow up and have the Pope as one of my patients—although I haven't yet!"

"Well, I'm sure there's still time! It must have taken you a long time to qualify Yes, the degree plus ten more years of training before I got my first consultant's pos.'""

" And has it lived up to your expectations?"

"Yes, and it's a little more expansive than most people think—not confined to the operating theatre—anaesthetists are involved in chronic pain management and sedation for some imaging and scanning procedures and of course pain relief in the maternity wards when necessary."

"I can imagine that's necessary all the time—you must be very popular with expectant mothers—I've never witnessed a childbirth—is the pain that bad?"

"Well, all I would say is—it certainly looks very, very bad."

Saoirse pulled a face, but seemed keen to add, "But apparently, soon forgotten when the mother holds her baby for the first time."

"I believe so."

Their eyes met briefly.

Giulia appeared with two glasses of chilled Peroni.

"Thank you Giulia."

"Prego, Dottore."

"Have you always practised in Bristol?"

"I did my consultant's training at St Bart's in London and then got my first post there."

"So, how did you end up here? You fancied getting away from London, did you?"

"Yes, at the time. The move was really brought about by events out of my control. Sadly, my wife was killed in a car accident—the other driver was prosecuted—sent to prison. After the trial I decided I wanted a change of scene. We had been living in West Ealing and the accident happened at a junction within a mile of the house—every time I passed there it brought back memories. I was born in Bristol and went to school down here in Somerset, so the West Country seemed a good option—a fresh start—with happier memories."

"I'm sorry to hear about your wife—she must have been quite young."

"Yes, just 28."

Marcello quietly placed their King Prawns Pil-Pil on the table and then unfolded and draped their napkins over their knees. "Please—the plates are very hot!"

"Thank you, Marcello."

"You're welcome, Dottore."

"What did your wife do?"

"She was an economic journalist, with the foreign news agency Reuters, but based in London, on Fleet St. What about you? Do you spend a lot of time in the Far East?"

"Four or five trips a year. The last one, just after we met had to be done before Chinese New Year which this year starts in about three weeks' time because everywhere in China basically closes down for the best part of a month—while all the workers return to the country from the cities—similar trips to Turkey, then trips to the States—there are trade shows in New York and Las Vegas—and whenever we take on a new manufacturer in China I have to audit them to ensure that the factories are compliant with EU and WTO working standards. So it can be quite hectic, especially as about three years ago the company relocated to Dublin for tax reasons, so I've been based there since then."

"And where are you from?"

"From Manchester but I studied merchandising and fashion at Central St Martins College, then after graduation got my one and only job with

Sportswear Inc. I've been travelling the world ever since. It sounds glamorous but most hotels look the same and the constant travelling means that you, well, you never get a chance to have a meaningful relationship—except with your PA!"

Saoirse paused, wondering what reaction her statement would have on Julian. He seemed to be thinking carefully, before he asked, "So, you're not married?"

"No—and never have been—as I say it was difficult managing a relationship with all the travel, so I finally gave up, which sounds a bit drastic but after so many attempts you do just give up." She smiled at Julian.

"But, not forever?"

"No, of course not forever—there must be someone out there." She looked at Julian again and held his gaze for a few seconds. Julian felt a pleasant lightness spread across his chest.

Marcello returned with the bottle of Cantemerle and presented it to Julian who touched it with his hand.

"Just right Marcello!"

Marcello uncorked the wine and poured for Julian who tasted and nodded his approval, then poured a glass for Saoirse and added to Julian's glass before placing the bottle on the table and retiring.

"Do you have any siblings?"

"I have one older brother Gerry who lives in London. He works for an agency taking care of high net-worth sports personalities—everything from handling their PR to arranging house moves and holidays. They have two daughters—Lucia and Cecilia."

"And how old are they?"

"14 and 16—they're delightful."

"I can imagine."

"How about you?"

"Three older brothers, Patrick, Kevin and James. Patrick is, like you a doctor—at Leicester Royal infirmary—he specialises in leukaemia—mainly treating children which can be very sad. Kevin organises tours for rock bands so he is away a lot—all over the world, a bit like me and James works for a large pharma company near Princeton, New Jersey."

"A brainy family then! Your job sounds interesting—apart from the odd lecture I spend most of my time here in Bristol—it must be nice to see the world."

"It is, but after so long it has become a little routine, apart from when we open a new store—then it's three months hard work away from home, but normally it's all about good decision-making and diary management. You need to have the right kind of garments, in the right numbers, in the right place at the right time at the right price so, really it's a little like being a glorified market-stall trader."

"I'm sure there's more to it than that—you certainly don't dress like a market-stall trader."

"I'll take that as a compliment."

"It was meant as one—actually, you look stunning."

"Thank you."

They both blushed.

Marcello returned with Giulia and they replaced their empty first course dishes with the main course of Braised Ox Cheeks.

"There are some vegetables here too Doctor Bracken."

"Thank you, Marcello - the prawns were perfect."

"Buon appetito!"

"Sportswear and fashionwear are worth billions of dollars to the global economy and generate significant profits, which means at the top-end that the fashion industry can influence politicians and governments and change the world for the better—and it's not just the money talking, 65% of 18-24 year olds and 75% of social class ABs, the "fashionistas" turned out to vote in the 2015 UK general election, so fashion can have a big influence on the make-up of governments and their policies, not just domestic governments but global entities—the EU and UN—many UN Special Ambassadors have come from the fashion sector.

Annette—the CEO's—current big causes are fashion against FGM, modern slavery, sex-trafficking, increased sentences for acid attacks, LGBT rights and the environment—saving the planet—so that keeps her busy! I just make sure the profits keep coming in by hopefully getting everything right."

"Well, you seem to be doing a good job so far.

" I really enjoy that sort of thing. Last year—our second based in Dublin we were asked by the British Embassy there to collaborate with new Indie British and Irish designers and produce a fashion show based on traditional Irish and English materials—linens, tweeds, wool, and cotton designs based on the leine—

the traditional Irish tunic or shirt, to support the British and Irish Chamber of Commerce's promotion of trade between the UK and the Republic.

"We had a six-month schedule to get everything up and running in time for the Ambassador's Summer Garden Party—this year we've been invited to do it again—it will be even bigger. This time, we've tried to emphasise the commonality of European fashion by asking our designers to produce a modern version of the surcoat—a kind of open tabard, popular throughout Western Europe from the 13th century onwards using the same traditional Irish and British materials. We're flying in twenty-eight models—one from each member state of the European Union. We're thinking of adding a lingerie range."

"Well—it makes my world seem a bit parochial."

"It is part of a long-term diplomatic strategy to promote trade between the UK and Ireland following the Queen's visit to the Republic in 2011, Michael D's state visit to the UK in April 2014—to improve relations ahead of the centenary of the Easter Rising scheduled for later this year and indirectly support The Good-Friday Agreement—the thinking is that if there is more wealth, co-operation, trade and business between the two countries, then peoples' life-styles change—and so does their outlook on life."

"That must be very worthwhile if you're helping to keep terrorism off the streets."

"That's what Annette thinks—and she's right."

"But how do you have any idea what people will want to be wearing next year? Or do you control the market through advertising?"

"Nothing like that—we employ trend predictors—they forecast what styles, fabrics, textures will be "on trend" for Spring / Summer and Autumn / Winter each year, so it gives me the confidence at least for sportswear, to order up to two years in advance. High fashion, less so—I like to trust my own judgement more."

"What about your parents?"

"My mother is still alive, but my father was killed in the Tenerife air crash in April 1980, when I was four. He'd gone on a golfing trip with three friends—the plane crashed into a forest on the side of Mount Esperanza—the pilot was told to go into a holding position, but for some reason didn't realise how low he was and flew straight into the side of the mountain. There were no survivors, everyone on board was killed. The strange thing is that according to my brothers, my father was terrified of flying. He would always take the boat back to Ireland to visit his parents in Cork, so they could never understand who could possibly have persuaded him to go on the trip.

"In the end they put it down to a stupid dare or bet after too many pints of Guinness in Chorlton Irish Club one Saturday night and I suppose the sad thing is that whoever dared him was probably on the plane with him and so that's one secret I'll never get to the bottom of."

"I'm sorry. That's tragic. You must have missed him."

"Yes. I was the youngest in the family by a long way and the only girl, but my three older brothers looked after me."

"Your mother must have been devastated."

"She was. She never really got over it—she was never the same—would never even talk about it—they were both devoted to each other—Mum's in a care home in south Manchester now, suffering from Alzheimer's—very sad really, because she was always so sharp—always had her wits about her."

"Did you go to school in Manchester?"

"Yes—St Cuthbert's—just a mile from where I lived in Moss Side—I was about to start at the Infant Prep School—my father had already bought my school uniform just before he was killed and ten my mother told me that she couldn't afford the fees—even with some assistance from the school—but a few weeks later, completely out of the blue the headmaster wrote to my mother saying that my fees—all my fees—right until the end of the Sixth Form had been paid in advance—I would guess somewhere near £250,000."

"That was very generous of someone. Did you ever find out who it was?"

"No, that was something my mother wouldn't talk about—ever—just forbade all talk of it and muttered threats about taking me away from St Cuthbert's if I kept asking questions."

"And you have no idea to this day who it was?"

"No, that's another secret—all these years I've wanted to thank them—I owe them so much. I don't even know if they are still alive or why they did it. I don't think I'll ever find out now. Mum's memory's gone completely and I feel I've got to respect her wishes. I wouldn't know where to start. I was very lucky the fees were paid, otherwise I wouldn't be sitting here today."

"Well, in that case, maybe I should thank whoever it was too."

Saoirse smiled. Julian returned it.

"I've always suspected it was someone from the Irish community—someone who knew my father, but he was a very popular man so it could have been several people, but it's not the sort of question you can really put to people out of the blue."

Marcello returned to clear the table.

"Dessert? Coffee? Miss Fitzgerald."

"Just coffee please Marcello. Thank you."

"Dr Bracken?"

"Yes please, just coffee too, Marcello."

"And you—where did you go to school?"

"In Somerset, Downfield—a big rugby-playing school."

"I've heard of it, so you're a public schoolboy?"

"Yes."

"And you survived—you seem quite normal!"

"I'll take that as a compliment."

"It was meant as one!"

Saoirse smiled and Julian laughed.

"So, did you have fags and all that?"

"Yes."

"You didn't! That's so non-PC! Why did you do it?"

"Well—you had no choice—and it wasn't all one way—you usually got a big present at the end of every term—and anyway, after three years, you then got someone to fag for you!"

"What was the worst thing you had to do?"

"Are you sure you want to know?"

"Yes, we're both grown-ups! Or is it that bad? I hope it's nothing really bad! I hope nothing sexually inappropriate?"

"Well, since we've both finished eating."

"This doesn't sound like it's going to be very nice."

"Probably not as bad as you think—and it explains how I got my nickname. At Downfield, the lavatory blocks were unheated and in the winters, they were simply perishing. You can imagine the cold winds blowing in off the Mendips—so all the fags had to go and warm up the seats by sitting on them for twenty minutes or so."

"How horrible! That's like serfdom!"

"I was fagging for the captain of the 1st XV—obviously it was a 'No-No' to actually use them but one morning, it was the last day of Short Half and we were finishing for Christmas—I'd had a stomach upset for days—and even on a good day you can only sit on a toilet for so long without getting a kind of Pavlovian urge. I managed to resist for nearly twenty minutes but then just as I heard him coming into the lavs, I gave in. Of course, he thought I'd timed it on purpose!

"He went mad—so, this is your idea of a Christmas present is it Bracken? You little stinker!"

"He put me on triple detention for "Showing disrespect" and so I got the nickname "Stinker" after that. Everyone at school thought it was funny, but it took me years to shake off the name Stinker. I've never told anyone outside school about that and only my brother still calls me Stinker!"

Saoirse was shaking her head. "Gruesome!"

"But then, the really annoying thing was that the school abolished fagging the year I would have been able to have a fag of my own—so I fagged for three years—all for nothing!"

"Ha! How about your parents?"

"Still both alive—they live in Spain—a place called Ronda—about two hours' drive from Malaga. So, did you have a nickname at school?"

"Yes."

"And?"

"Well, it was Posh, but a sarcastic Posh—you know—the way they call tall people Shorty and short people Lofty."

"Explain."

"Posh came about because when I was very young, I overheard one of my father's comments—he would say to my brothers when they told him some of their friends at St Cuthbert's lived in Cheshire."

"Sure now—they're all posh in Cheshire—they even wear matching socks!".

"I decided I didn't want to be posh so I would deliberately put on socks that didn't match. My brothers teased me about it and the more I got teased the more I carried on—I was quite wilful as a child—even a very young one and the habit stuck—it became a bit of a family joke but now it's a way of remembering my father every day when I get dressed. He would make me put on matching socks and as soon as he left the room I would change them."

"I think he must have secretly admired your wilfulness. So is that why…"

"I sometimes wear different coloured stockings? Yes—except sometimes the difference is only quite small—at work—not so anyone would notice—not a distraction—but sometimes it's a way of sending a message!"

Saoirse smiled at Julian.

"So, sometimes quite striking—and sometimes hardly noticeable?"

"Yes—sometimes!"

"So, flirting? In a way?"

"I suppose so—sometimes—and of course there are my eyes which are very different colours—as I'm sure you will have noticed but been too polite to yet mention. My father said I was one in a million—he made me feel very special because of that so I decided I was special and shouldn't be ashamed of it, so I've always liked being different—mixing things up—I especially like garments and designs that juxtapose strong contrasting colours—block colours that give you retinal rivalry."

Saoirse smiled, widening her eyes slightly. The effect on Julian was bewitching.

"I did notice—when you glanced at me in the mirror for the first time—in Turnbull & Asser, I think your father was right—they make you look very special. One in a million—he was certainly right. And… are you flirting right now?"

"I might be." She smiled and laughed. "Can't you guess?"

Julian could only smile.

"My eyes have also helped me in my career too."

"I imagine that's right—I would have thought there are a lot of men who would find them well, rather persuasive and—seductive!"

They both smiled.

"Well, maybe but I meant dealing with the Chinese—you know how superstitious the Chinese are—they call my eyes 'Gwei' eyes—not that they are saying I am a ghost but that I have the ability to see ghosts—there are lots of ghosts and spirits in Chinese culture, some good, some evil and they can have a huge influence on business decisions. I think they treat me with a lot more respect and trust—especially when they ask me whether I can see any evil spirits near them—and of course I say I can't see any—which of course I can't—that seems to make them trust me more."

"Didn't you get teased or bullied at school?"

"No—St Cuthbert's was an independent school—not a public school—we were all very civilised."

"Very funny! What I meant was kids can be cruel—especially young kids."

"Yes—I was called a witch once or twice but fortunately I became captain of the school hockey team—it's surprising how a little bit of status can turn things around—not to mention carrying a hockey stick around a lot—I also had three older brothers and grew up in the "Moss"—so that toughens you up."

Marcello appeared with their coffees and two glasses of prosecco. "Miss Fitzgerald, Dr Bracken—please—compliments of Marcello. I hope to see you both again soon!"

"Thank you, Marcello, the food was wonderful."

"You're both welcome."

Saoirse sat back and enjoyed the closeness of a man she had missed for so long.

Julian paused—thinking—he was overwhelmed and felt his earlier exuberance welling up inside him and looked for a few moments at Saoirse. He wanted to reach out and embrace her.

"I know we've hardly known each other for very long, but people say that you know within a few seconds of meeting someone whether you will get on—like them—I felt like that in Turnbull & Asser but for some reason couldn't bring myself to speak to you."

"Well, it's a good thing we got our ties mixed up then, isn't it? I feel the same—sometimes things like this happen—perhaps finally we've been lucky. I've enjoyed the evening so much."

Julian paused.

"Would you like to do this again?"

"That would be nice. I've enjoyed the evening very much too—the food and the company was excellent. Have you ever been to Dublin?"

"No, but I think I'd like to!"

"Perhaps you might like to come over—soon—and we can have dinner at my favourite restaurant. I've got a spare room at my apartment—Dublin's a lovely city but there would be a lot to talk about—I mean—I live in Bristol and you in Dublin—and we've both got our respective jobs."

"But there are direct flights—it doesn't take long—and we're both mature people."

"I was going to say I was sorry I caused this mix-up with the ties but I'm not—if that's what was needed to bring us together but let's not make the same mistake tonight—here's your brother's tie."

"And here's yours—I'm sorry about the mix-up too."

"It was all my fault—honestly." Saoirse smiled at him again.

They raised their glasses.

"To the future!"

"To the future!"

"Are you ready to go?"

"Yes—I just need my raincoat."

"Can I walk you back to your hotel?"

"Of course, that would be nice."

Outside Marckwicks, Saoirse linked Julian's arm and they set off walking slowly. At some stage without speaking Julian put his arm around Saoirse's waist and Saoirse around Julian's.

They reached Saoirse's hotel, embraced and then kissed—it seemed to Julian—and Saoirse, that whilst it wasn't a fully passionate kiss, it was a meaningful one.

"I am on leave tomorrow, but I'll look at the roster first thing on Friday. I'll look forward to Dublin and seeing you again."

"Yes—me too! I fly back to Dublin first thing tomorrow morning and will be there until I go to New York next Tuesday."

They kissed again.

Saoirse smiled. "Goodnight, Stinker!"

"Goodnight Posh!"

Chapter Fourteen

The Backs
Bristol

23:45

The evening had surpassed Julian's expectations—the food had been excellent—Marcello had not let him down—and Saoirse's conversation had been exhilarating—after a life devoted to medicine Julian found Saoirse's career in fashion refreshing and interesting. They had agreed to meet again—in Dublin—he would check the roster and speak to his colleagues to see how soon he could arrange a few days off—he was owed a few favours for helping out, covering at critical times during the summer holidays although he didn't expect to be able to go soon—unless he was very lucky and could arrange a swap at short notice.

Julian felt that he had finally met someone who could fill the void in his life left by Eleanor—with at least the possibility of fulfilling something that he thought he had lost forever—a chance to have a child—maybe a daughter who would embody the memory of the daughter he had lost, but Saoirse was, quite clearly a dedicated career woman—off to New York next week—perhaps it would be too much to ask of her?

Given her high-powered career, he thought it unlikely she would share his dreams. Charles had remarked that she was committed to her career. Perhaps he would have to settle for something just a little less than perfect happiness.

He opened his iPad and Googled "flower shops Dublin". There was one on Talbot St not far from the International Financial Services Centre.

He ordered the largest bouquet and filled in the message box: *Dear Posh, I truly enjoyed this evening—I will check my roster first thing Friday and let you know when I can make it over to Dublin. Love, Stinker.*

In his apartment in the Backs Julian lay in his bed—euphoric.

In the Marriott Hotel Saoirse lay in her bed—euphoric.

Chapter Fifteen

SOMERFORD ROYAL INFIRMARY
The Nurses' Station
Tiverton Ward

10:30 am
Thursday 21st of January

After thinking about nothing else overnight and most of the morning, Nurse Helen Griffith stared at her unfinished coffee and decided she needed to unburden herself to her colleagues. She had found it difficult to believe what she had seen Dr Bracken doing yesterday—and to an anaesthetised patient too!

All the other theatre staff had been occupied with their pre-op tasks when she heard Dr Bracken say something about a Wonderbra and looked up to see him with his hands under the patient's breasts jiggling them about—that couldn't be right.

She hadn't been able to see his face fully, but she had been sure there was a glint in his eyes and also sure he was smirking to himself. She had glanced quickly round the theatre but had not caught anyone's attention. She seemed to be the only one who had noticed or cared about what Dr Bracken was doing. She glanced at him again but just then the lead surgeon Mr Broadley had announced the time and leaned forward over the patient with scalpel in hand.

She turned to Sister Jean Harrington who was busy reading some patient records.

"Jean—you'll never guess what happened yesterday morning in theatre."

Jean's eyes widened in mock surprise. "Go on—tell me!"

"Well, a few minutes before the operation started, I heard Dr Bracken say something about a Wonderbra and when I looked up I saw him with his hands all over the patient's breasts—he was giving them a right good feel and it looked like he was getting off on it."

"I bet I know who you're talking about—the flashy doctor with the sports car? Julian Bracken."

This wasn't Jean asking but another sister, Rachel Johnson, who had recently moved from Cardiff to work at the hospital, who had overheard.

"That's right—Dr Bracken—how did you know?"

"Well, I guessed, see—because on Monday of last week I was helping him prep a female patient. I was placing a urethral catheter and the next thing he was standing by me looking over my shoulder. I told him I'd done this loads of times before and could manage without him but he just stood there staring. It felt really strange. He didn't say a word as if I wasn't there and do you know what he did next, mind?"

"No."

"He only got hold of one of the theatre spotlights and turned it on her vagina—as if he wasn't getting an eyeful anyway! And guess who the patient was?"

"Don't know."

"Do you remember the young blonde glamour model who was in the bad car accident? Multiple fractures—including her ankle—thought she was never going to be able to walk again."

"Yes."

"Well, it was her."

"Really? That's so pervy!"

"And I can tell you—she's had a little bit of work done down there—she must spend quite a bit of time taking care of her Lady-Garden! A couple of very pretty tattoos as well—a serpent and an apple! All very tasteful mind!"

"No wonder he was having a good look then! A free peep-show!"

"I told him again to get back to his end of the table, but he just ignored me. I was really annoyed but couldn't think of anything else to say. Anyway, I managed to finish off as quickly as I could and I covered the patient up. It was only then that he turned away—real arrogant—as if nothing had happened—completely ignored me—didn't say a thing even."

"Very, very pervy or what? I'd keep an eye on him if I were you, I never liked him—he's not married either."

"That's what happens when you live on your own for too long—can't be getting any!"

"Men! They're all the same!"

"Even so—he shouldn't be allowed to get away with that!"

"Get away with what?" Nurse Keaveney was now leaning over Helen's shoulder. "Go on! You've started—so you've got to finish!" She gave Helen a friendly push on her shoulder.

Helen was now embarrassed—she wasn't sure what she had started—she had meant only to confide in Jean Harrington and was reluctant to respond to Mary Keaveney who was known around the hospital as a gossip and a flirt.

"You might as well tell me—I'll find out anyway!"

She gave Helen a wide smile. "Come on—cough it up," and sat down opposite her.

"You won't believe this," said Rachel Johnson. "Go on, tell her Helen!"

Mary Keaveney listened with interest as Helen Griffith repeated her story about the Wonderbra manoeuvre, then with even more interest at Rachel Johnson's story about the model with the tattoos.

"Well, I must say, I'm not surprised—he came on to me once—touched me up when we were alone in the recovery room—he just put his hand on my bum and then ran his finger very, very slowly all the way up my back, twanging my bra-strap as he went! Then he started feeling my neck above my scrubs - then—like you just said Rachel—just pretended nothing had happened. They think they can get away with anything, some doctors."

"Dirty so and so."

"He's a sex pest—you should complain to HR—they'd sort him out—they wouldn't let him get away with it. I'll come with you if you like Helen."

"Would you Mary?"

"Course I will. Do you know Julie Lightfoot? She's just been promoted to Head of HR—she's very nice—are you free now?"

"Yeh, I'm on my break."

"Well, why don't we go now?"

"Thanks Mary."

"Come on," said Mary, "no time like the present!"

As they walked along, Mary added, "By the way—Julie might ask you if you're interested in joining a thing called WAMP—I think that stands for Women Against Male Patriarchy—she asked me last time and I looked it up—it was all about "male patriarchy" and the "gender war against men"—stuff like that—I mean some of them are a pain in the arse, but I most of 'em are alright. Just tell her you'll think about it—that's what I did last time!"

"OK—thanks again, Mary."

That'll teach him, thought Mary Keaveney.

Chapter Sixteen

Somerford Royal Infirmary

7:30am
Friday 22nd of January 2016

As planned, Julian had got in early to check his roster, speak to colleagues and try to arrange a few days off to go to Dublin and spend more time with Saoirse—to get to know her. He logged on to his inbox and was making his way through his emails. There was a large number but what caught his eye immediately was an email from the Medical Director's secretary.

When he opened it, he saw that it was entitled:

MAINTAINING HIGH PROFESSIONAL STANDARDS IN THE NHS

…and referred to **a meeting scheduled for a time to be agreed as soon as possible and within the next 24 hours at the latest.** It was timed yesterday at 16.25.03—on Thursday 21st January 2016 At first, he thought Sebastian wanted some advice but to his concern he saw that the email was subtitled **COMPLAINT IMPORTANT—YOU MAY WISH TO BE ACCOMPANIED BY A COLLEAGUE, A REPRESENTATIVE OF THE BMA OR YOUR MEDICAL DEFENCE ORGANISATION.**

He looked at the extension for Sebastian's secretary and keyed in the number. There was a recorded message—"This is Jenny Bishop, secretary to Professor Sebastian Somerville, Medical Director, Somerford Royal Infirmary. I am on annual leave now until Monday 1st February, please leave a message or if your call is urgent, please contact my colleague Susan Middlehurst on extension 3656. Thank you."

Exasperated, Julian quickly keyed in 3656.

"This is Susan Middlehurst, secretary to Mr Johnson, Mr Thomas and Mr Shaw in the Ophthalmology Department, Somerford Royal Infirmary Bristol. I am currently unavailable—please leave a message and I will return your call as soon as possible."

He left a message: "Dr Julian Bracken here—please call back as soon as possible."

Julian was racking his brains trying to think what the complaint could be about—he had been in theatre all day on Wednesday and everything had gone well—he tried but couldn't recall anything controversial—nothing came to mind.

Susan Middlehurst returned Julian's call some 15 minutes later—she could not say what the meeting was about but told him she had just spoken to Professor Somerville who asked that he come to his office at 8.30am.

***

Professor Somerville motioned Julian to take a seat.

"Morning Julian, can I effect some introductions? This is Julie Lightfoot, our new Head of Human Resources—Julie Lightfoot nodded but didn't smile. I think you know Nigel Thomas. Nigel has been appointed as Case Manager. I've asked Martin Doyle to be Case Investigator. Julie will be making notes and you will be provided with a copy to review and confirm as a true record. I see you're unaccompanied—are you sure you don't want a colleague to be with you? I'm afraid, Julian, we have some serious issues to discuss."

Julian shook his head. "Case Manager? Investigator? What case? What's all this about Sebastian?"

"OK—I've called this meeting after Julie came to see me yesterday afternoon. Julian, I'm afraid yesterday morning Julie had a serious complaint, initially from Nurse Helen Griffith, raising concerns about your behaviour in theatre on Wednesday morning, which is of an inappropriate and sexual nature and since then another, from Sister Johnson, who recently joined the staff here. She also alleges that you acted in an inappropriate and sexually motivated way when she was placing a catheter on a female patient a week last Monday and thirdly, you may recall this—Julie, as Head of HR has advised me that we now need to re-open the complaint regarding your touching of Nurse Keaveney, some two years ago—because we now have three complaints on three separate occasions from three different members of the nursing staff—all alleging inappropriate and sexually motivated conduct.

"Here are copies of the two statements taken yesterday afternoon from Nurse Griffith, Sister Johnson and. Julie managed, very helpfully, to retrieve Mary

Keaveney's statement from the previous incident too—from her HR file. They're not very long but it's all the information we've been able to gather, given the short time we've had.

"Unfortunately, James Broadley is away for two weeks—gone climbing in Nepal—he left yesterday morning. What we need now are your comments before we decide the next steps. These are copies for you to keep—take your time—as much time as you like."

Julian read and then reread with mounting astonishment and indignation the handwritten statements of Nurse Griffith, Sister Johnson and Nurse Keaveney, then put them back on Sebastian's desk.

"Do you need some time to consult the BMA, a colleague or your defence organisation? Or some further time to think about these matters? I would strongly suggest you do."

"No, I'm very clear about what happened. I remember exactly what happened and what didn't—I've done nothing wrong. This is surely some kind of mistake. I accept that the events happened, but I do not accept that any of them were inappropriate—and certainly not sexually motivated."

"Nevertheless, Julie here, as our new Head of HR has taken advice from the National Clinical Assessment Service and also consulted the Trust's solicitors. Subject to obtaining your comments, which we are now doing, I have been advised to consider making a referral to the General Medical Council and also excluding you from work.

Given the seriousness of the allegations and the fact that there are now three, all of a similar nature, immediate, temporary exclusion for two weeks is being considered. I stress that no decision has yet been made and won't be—until we know your version of events. You will recall you were advised about your conduct in relation to Nurse Keaveney just over two years ago."

"Yes, and I have not touched another nurse since—ever! The rearrangement of soft tissues—especially breasts—is necessary to avoid post-operative discomfort and possibly permanent harm and catheters, unless placed properly, can result in the bladder leaking its contents during an operation and soreness from tears and infection. You know that!"

"Julian—I do know that but you're missing the point—it's not what you did but the way you did it—and the things you said—or didn't say. I don't know what you were thinking of but was there any need to use the expression "Wonderbra manoeuvre" when repositioning the patient's breasts in the manner

Nurse Griffith describes? And certainly not for as long as she says.

"She says that you were touching the patient's breasts for a long time—as long as two minutes—much longer than was necessary to simply reposition them and Sister Johnson who is an experienced nurse of sixteen years in surgery says she told you that she could manage and yet your response was not only to remain there but to put a spotlight on the pubic area of the patient—a young female patient who just happens to be a glamour model and I understand has had cosmetic surgery and tattoos in the most intimate of places! Did you not think of explaining what you were doing?"

"No—I was concentrating on what Sister Johnson was doing."

"Did you know the patient was a model?"

Julie Lightfoot was staring at Julian but remained expressionless.

"Yes—but it has nothing to do with it! You know as well as I do that a patient is a patient is a patient—gender doesn't matter—or her occupation—the procedures I undertake are all clinically justified—and necessary."

"So, you deny that you acted inappropriately?"

"Yes—of course I do—I was discharging my professional responsibilities to my patients and as far as Nurse Keaveney is concerned—as I told you two years ago, I was responding to her question—this is a teaching hospital after all!"

Julie Lightfoot looked up, still expressionless.

"Is there anything else you want to add?"

"No, except that I completely deny any wrongdoing."

"Ok. Finally, Julian, can I ask you about your health—is everything OK?"

"Yes. I'm fine."

"Are you sure? Is there anything you'd like to tell us?"

"Yes, of course I'm sure. I've never felt better actually."

"You've not consulted your GP in say, the last three years?"

"No."

"Is there anything else you feel we ought to know?"

"No."

"Anything happened to disturb or interrupt your usual routine?"

"No."

"OK, thanks Julian. Will you take a seat outside please? I'm sure Susan will get you a tea or a coffee. Julie will give you a copy of the notes she has just made. Perhaps you could read them through whilst you wait and if you are happy that they are an accurate record of what has been said sign each page at the bottom and date them. I will now consider the position in the light of your comments and response. Could I ask you to take a seat in Susan's office?"

Julian sat in Susan Middlehurst's office and read the notes provided to him by Julie Lightfoot and then signed and dated them. He then had to wait for 30 minutes until Susan Middlehurst showed him back into Professor Somerville's office.

"Julian, I've reviewed all the information we have managed to collect in the time available to us, and of course taken into account your comments but these are serious matters. I've discussed them with Julie Lightfoot who has had to get away to another meeting. I have to tell you that I've decided, despite hearing what you've had to say and after considering the legal advice obtained by HR that I need to refer these concerns to the GMC for further investigation, including the "old" one of two years ago since it now appears to possibly form part of a pattern of behaviour.

"We also need to investigate fully, but in the meantime, I'm afraid that, given the need to protect patients and staff and to protect the integrity of the investigation which is now under way, I'm afraid that I have concluded that you need to be excluded from work and the hospital premises—initially for the next two weeks."

"What?"

"Julian, it would be a temporary, neutral step and would in no way be considered as a disciplinary sanction—simply for the sake of expediency—we need to sort things out, which I'm sure we'll do when James Broadley returns. I will arrange cover. You will be on full pay."

"Sebastian—are you serious? You say it's a neutral step, but the rumour machine will be working at full speed and within hours my reputation will be gone—completely. Whatever you say everyone will think I'm guilty when they find out I've been excluded?"

Sebastian thought for a few minutes. "Julian, you know how it is—it's not like the old days—if I don't play a straight bat on this HR will be having me up on a charge next!

"But I understand your point about the rumour mill—what if you were to take a couple of weeks' leave—that would mean I wouldn't need to formally exclude you—just take a couple of weeks off, while we sort it all out. Don't you think that would be the sensible thing to do?

"I'll tell HR, Julie Lightfoot that you're taking a break—God knows how hard we all work. I'm sure the GMC will see this for what it is, but you might want to speak to your defence organisation about this to put them in the picture and get some legal advice. I strongly suggest you do that Julian—it's for your own good. You know what it's like these days!"

"This is totally ridiculous."

"I'm sorry Julian. I can see you're upset, but don't blame me—blame that bastard, Shipman—everyone is looking over their shoulders now and covering their backs—you understand my hands are tied—I've got to do something but I'm sure it will all blow over once you've explained everything to the GMC. Shall we say two weeks "compassionate" leave?"

Julian thought for a few moments.

"There's no alternative, is there?"

"I'm afraid not Julian, but at least this way there's no formal exclusion—you're right—you know how people talk—it would spread like wildfire and soon reach the Royal College—even when it's supposed to be a neutral step. Would you like Julie or one of her colleagues from HR to drive you home? It might be for the best."

"You must be joking. I can drive myself. thank you."

"Julian, I'm sure it will all blow over, but for God's sake can you avoid any more compromising positions. You understand what I'm saying."

"Sebastian, do you remember who you're talking to? Do you really think I'm capable of all this?"

"Well, Julian it's not a question of what I think anymore—it's what other people think!"

"Just remind me Sebastian—when we were training—it wasn't me, was it, who ran a daily book on the colour of each nurse's knickers?

"Oh, come on Julian that was years ago—just a bit of harmless fun—you know trainee doctors and all that!"

"Or remember the jackpot prize – for guessing which nurse was wearing no knockers at all? Try telling that to your new Head of HR—I doubt if she'd think it was a bit of harmless fun!"

"Two weeks leave then?"

Julian stared at Sebastian and nodded.

"I'll sort it all out—you see Julian—you'll be back here in no time."

***

Julian reached the end of Hospital Road and was about to pull out when a juggernaut blasted its foghorns at him. He instinctively stamped on the brakes and flinched as the tractor and trailer passed within inches of his bonnet—buffeting the car with its tailwind—foghorns still blaring.

Jesus!

He checked the traffic again and then again. He pulled out slowly and drove joylessly home. The drive seemed much longer without the music which he couldn't face—he didn't want to discover what Lucia's next random choice might be and he had none of his usual enthusiasm for putting the top down.

When he finally arrived at The Backs, he parked the car and took the elevator to the third floor. He was relieved to walk into his own familiar private space and closed the door behind him to collect his thoughts. He looked at Eleanor's photograph and slumped onto the sofa to take stock.

Surely the GMC would understand his position? Any expert would confirm his version of events and James Broadley would support him. He had nearly 20 years clinical experience and apart from the incident with Nurse Keaveney, an unblemished record—surely no one would regard that as anything other than an innocent misunderstanding?

He had thought that had been dealt with—indeed, had forgotten about it. His defence organisation would surely be able to resolve everything with the GMC and then he would be back at work. He looked up the helpline and dialled the number.

"Good morning, Doctors' Protection Union—can I take your membership number please?"

"Yes 2878736/C/JB."

"And your name please?"

"Dr Julian Bracken."

"Could you just confirm your date of birth please Dr Bracken?"

"Yes—it is 07 06 1974."

"And how can we be of assistance to you doctor?"

"I've been referred to the GMC for alleged misconduct."

"Can you tell me the nature of the alleged misconduct?"

"Sexual misconduct—alleged, which I deny."

"I am very sorry to hear that, Dr Bracken. Can I assure you of our support throughout this stressful time? The lines to the medico-legal advisers are all busy now so I'm going to arrange for one of them to call you back. They will take all the details and put you in contact with our solicitors who are experienced in defending proceedings before the GMC. Together we will ensure the very best possible advice, representation and support. Is this the mobile number you would like us to use? Ending in 854?"

"Yes please. Thank you."

"You're welcome, in the meantime, if you are approached by the media, would you please make no comment and refer them to our Press Officer on this number."

"The media? Is that likely?"

"It's our standard advice in these circumstances—especially with sexual misconduct allegations. I'm afraid the press seem to find out about these sort of cases very quickly."

"Ok, well, thank you for that."

"Thank you, Dr Bracken, you're welcome. Someone will contact you very soon."

"Thank you."

He ended the call and again glanced at Eleanor's photograph. They had been so happy together—the photograph confirmed that. He slumped back in the sofa and closed his eyes."

A text alert sounded:

Thanks for the flowers—they're absolutely beautiful. Did you get a chance to book some time off?
Saoirse. XX

Saoirse! What was he going to tell her? And when? And how? Just when everything was going so well. How would she take it? She would surely end the relationship—such as it was—before it had really started. God—what a mess!

He now had another chance of happiness and Eleanor had in some way been prescient: "Make a new life for yourself".

He calmed down—began to think—the sooner he told Saoirse, the better—rather that, than she finds out by chance from the media—but it would be best done face to face. She had told him she was in Dublin until she went to New York next Tuesday. He logged onto the Aer Lingus website—the 3.45 pm flight from Bristol was fully booked but the Manchester—Dublin flight departing at

18.30pm had seats available. It took him just 3 minutes to book a seat on the flight.

He texted Saoirse:

Hi—yes—I've arranged some time off; are you still in Dublin?

Hi Yep—in Dublin—only just arrived at the office—the flowers are really beautiful. I was going to call you this evening to thank you.
XX

Good—I'd like to come and see you.

So, you've sorted your roster out? When were you thinking of?
X

Well, there's an Aer Lingus flight this evening—arriving about 19.30 from Manchester. Would that be alright?

Well, yes—of course—I'll send my driver Cristy to pick you up—I'll give him your mobile number? You can't miss him—drives a big black Mercedes—Dublin plate—ends in 7638. See you tonight then!
X

Yes—see you tonight!

Saoirse looked across the office at Aoife. "That was Julian—the doctor I had dinner with on Wednesday evening in Bristol—he's coming to Dublin—tonight."

"On business, or to see you?"

"Yes! To see me!"

"He seems keen—flowers delivered first thing after dinner on Wednesday and now flying over to see you specially—I told you he was the one—he sounds perfect—looks like the "Signature" perfume worked—shall I give him the once-over for you?"

"Well—as the doctors say, I wouldn't mind a second opinion! Are you free tonight?"

"Sure, I am—until about 8.45—James is away with the 'Rock rugby team in Galway and I've got a ticket for a late showing of "Calvary"—part of the Brendan Gleeson retrospective at the Irish Film Institute—I missed "Calvary" first time round—do you want me to arrange for Cristy to pick him up? Terminal Two, is it?"

"Yes—he's arriving about 19.30 on the Aer Lingus flight from Manchester—give Cristy this number and tell him to bring him to The Palace Bar on Fleet St—ask him to text before he leaves the airport—we can introduce him to some Guinness and proper Irish music while you give him the once-over!"

"OK—and now Saoirse," Aoife giggled, "I hope you've not been too "Bold"?"

"No—I haven't! But, "Bold" enough by the looks of it!"

It took Julian just a few minutes to pack an overnight bag and five minutes later he was in the car, heading for the M5 and Manchester.

Shortly before the Cheltenham/Gloucester junction his mobile rang.

"Hello? Is that Dr Bracken?"

"Yes."

"I'm Dr Goddard from the Doctors' Protection Union—I understand that you've been referred to the General Medical Council…"

Chapter Seventeen

DUBLIN AIRPORT TERMINAL TWO—ARRIVALS

7.:35pm

Julian was trying to arrange his thoughts and then in turn his explanation to Saoirse as he felt St Columba begin its gentle descent into Dublin airport. From his window seat, he caught his first glimpse of the Irish coastline and then playing fields and modern housing estates scattered in the countryside, north of Dublin.

His composure was interrupted as the aircraft's engines were suddenly powered up to full thrust as St Columba turned sharply upwards and to starboard accompanied by shrieks and streams from the large hen party at the rear of the cabin. The plane shook and shuddered as it climbed steeply upwards through the low clouds.

"Ladies and gentlemen, this is your captain—can I please apologise for that sudden manoeuvre—the aircraft ahead of us was struck by a bird as it touched down and the ground crew need to inspect the runway for any debris before we can land. We have been asked to take up a holding position, but should have you safely on the ground in no more than a few minutes."

Despite the captain's explanation Julian's heart was pounding and his nerves were frayed. He closed his eyes and tried to recover his composure, until several minutes later, he felt The engines fade and a gentle bump as St Columba touched down.

Following the ARRIVALS signs after disembarking from Aer Lingus Flight EI 1304, St Columba, Julian made his way through Dublin airport and as he did so turned on his mobile phone. He had been allocated a seat near the front doors and had only a small overnight bag which had been stored underneath the seat in front so was one of the first off the plane and well ahead of the other passengers.

As he followed the signs, turning corners and riding up escalators, he encountered a succession of giant photographic portraits of typical Irish faces—

some old and lined—some in the first flush of youth—some with the Irish red hair in its many forms—tumbling curly locks on a young woman and the last flush of rust-red yielding to steely grey in an old man's beard and eyebrows.

He recognised some—the rugby players, Paul O'Connell and Brian O'Driscoll, actors Gabriel Byrne and Pierce Brosnan—politicians—Presidents Mary McAleese, Mary Robinson, Michael D Higgins and the Taoiseach Enda Kenny and singer Sinead O'Connor.

As he was waiting in the queue for the EU passport immigration channel, he felt his phone vibrate with an incoming message.

You missed a call from me. Timed at 19.28—to return the call press 3.

As he passed through Immigration Control and entered the cavernous baggage reclaim hall, he pressed 3 on his keypad—after a short while an Irish voice answered, "Now! That'll be Dr Bracken, will it?"

"Yes."

"It's Cristy here sir—If you follow the sign for taxis out of the Arrivals Hall and down the escalators then I'll be at the very bottom there outside on the left—a black Mercedes—Dublin plate—the last four numbers are 7638—I'll be flashing me lights."

"Fine, thank you Cristy."

Julian passed through the green customs channel and then the small duty-free shop towards the EXIT sign. As the doors slid silently apart hysterical screaming broke out in the Arrivals Hall. Julian was confronted by a crowd of female teenagers—he looked round as the doors closed behind him—the screaming stopped as quickly as it had started. He was stranded in a no-man's-land between the closed doors and a crowd of perhaps two hundred highly excited young females.

The girls were pressed up, eight or ten deep behind the barrier preventing his exit. He could see three members of the Garda Siochana, arms folded, nodding and chatting amiably behind the girls. He stepped forward, towards the girls, expecting them to part and allow him through, but they were too excited about the arrival of their idol or idols to notice him—he didn't seem to exist to them. He looked beyond the girls at the guards and recalling Sebastian's exhortation to avoid compromising situations, raised his arms up, holding his overnight bag aloft so it was clear to the guards where his hands were and stepped forward, pushing his way through.

The girls wouldn't move and so he had to push harder, pressing himself up against and squeezing through the crowd of scantily dressed teenagers, involuntarily touching their bodies—a succession of breasts, buttocks, bare thighs, backs, shoulders and arms pushing back against him. Still holding his arms aloft, with an effort, he finally pushed through and with relief, passed the guards and started to walk towards the down escalator and TAXIS.

As he reached the top of the escalator, he heard a loud Irish male voice shout out a command, "Stop! Hold on! You!"

At the same time, the screaming started again. He turned to see two of the guards hurrying towards him and behind them the other guard—the more senior bending down and talking to one of the girls from the crowd. He had one hand on her shoulder as if comforting her and Julian saw that she was pointing directly at him.

Julian's heart surged—as they approached him the first guard said something, but Julian couldn't hear for the screams. Both guards had now caught up with Julian and one of them gripped him by the elbow and bent forward.

"Just hold on there, sir, please."

The third guard started to walk over to Julian and when as he approached, he nodded at the younger guard. "Thanks Seamus," he looked at Julian, "can you tell me your name please sir?"

"Yes—Julian Bracken—Dr Julian Bracken."

"Is that our man?" Asked one of the younger guards.

"I believe so," answered the sergeant, with a smile.

Julian was feeling faint—his mouth had suddenly turned dry, adrenalin was coursing through his body and he was feeling nauseous. Insanely, he momentarily thought of running off.

What could she possibly have said to make them detain him? His mind raced back to the morning—with allegations coming out of nowhere—how could he explain another misunderstanding?

"Is there a problem of some kind?"

The sergeant stepped up and took a good look at Julian. "So, we caught you just in time—before you disappeared."

Julian felt light-headed—as if he was going to faint.

"It appears you dropped this, doctor"—the sergeant had Julian's passport in his hand and was looking at the picture in the passport, comparing the likeness.

"It must have fallen out of your bag as you were getting through the wee girls back there and one of them handed it in—we were lucky to catch you."

The sergeant handed Julian his passport, still smiling.

"Thank you—thank you very much." Julian took the passport, but immediately dropped it through his trembling fingers. One of the guards picked it up and handed it back to him.

"Are you alright doctor?"

All three of the guards were now staring closely at him.

"Yes—yes—I have never liked flying very much."

"Me too," said one of the guards, now smiling. "If God had wanted us to fly, he would have given us wings now for sure. Take care now, Dr Bracken, sir."

"Thanks, and you."

Julian turned away and stepped onto the down escalator—his legs were shaking.

It wasn't hard to spot Cristy's big black Mercedes with the headlamps flashing every few seconds. Cristy, was out of the car straightaway to open the nearside passenger door, allowing Julian to slip into the rear seat with his overnight bag. He tried to compose himself as the Mercedes sped towards the motorway, passing through the airport complex of hotels, multi-storey car parks, fast food restaurants and car-hire offices. He was still shaken by his brief detention by the guards.

As the Mercedes picked up speed Cristy looked over his shoulder.

"Did yer come in on the same flight as Jedward?"

"Who? I'm not sure?"

"You were on the Manchester flight?"

"Yes—I'm sorry—who is Jedward?"

"You've never heard of Jedward? The TV stars—dancers—entertainers—they're brothers."

"So that's who all the teenage girls were waiting for?"

"Sure. They'd be as mad as a box of frogs, just to catch even a sight of 'em!"

Cristy drove on, negotiating the roundabout exit from the airport to join the M1 motorway to Dublin city centre. He took another look over his shoulder at the small overnight bag on the seat next to Julian.

"And it looks like a flying visit so to speak?"

"Yes—possibly just overnight."

"Ah well that's the business world for you these days—all go, go, go and is it your first time to Dublin sir?"

"Yes."

"Ah well you're in for a treat—Miss Fitzgerald says I've to drop you at The Palace Bar for a "welcome" pint or two of Guinness. And Miss Fitzgerald says you're a doctor now—what kind?"

"I'm an anaesthetist."

"You mean the fella that puts people to sleep before the operations?"

"Yes—that's right."

"Well, there's a few fellas I know around Dublin who would run you close on that one—without any of yer fancy drugs either and there'll be a few in The Palace Bar tonight mind you! Talk the hind leg off a donkey!"

Despite himself Julian smiled—when bad things happen, they certainly come out of the blue with no warning, but he was on his way to meet Saoirse and that was something to look forward to—at least for the time being.

As they left the airport behind and accelerated along the motorway Julian saw a jet scream by just a few hundred feet overhead, its high intensity landing lights illuminating the night sky and its red and green strobe navigation lights slowly blinking. He could clearly see the landing gear—the thick, black, nitrogen filled tyres, hanging, waiting to thump onto the runway. In the distance, he could see the lights of another incoming jet making its descent, suspended over the Irish Sea, imperceptibly moving along the same flight-path.

Julian had decided to tell Saoirse the complete truth about the allegations at work. If there was to be a relationship it had to be based on trust and honesty. Just a few days ago everything had been so promising but if Saoirse decided that she needed time to think about things that was fine—all he would and could ask was that she listened to what he had to say and didn't come to a sudden decision—but then how could he stop her?

She would surely send him packing. Why wouldn't she? She had no reason to be loyal to him—stick by him—he had never felt so vulnerable—his reputation, career and now a relationship that he'd waited for, for nearly 10 years were all in jeopardy.

Julian had been hoping to have gone straight to Saoirse's apartment so he could have explained immediately and if necessary, book a room at a hotel and take the first flight back the next day—perhaps a quick drink and then he would get the opportunity.

"She's a grand girl, Miss Fitzgerald. Yes, she's here, there and everywhere, all over the world and there's no side on her—her mother must have put some manners on her."

"Yes—I'm sure she did Cristy."

"Did you know her father was from Cork? It beats me why a lovely girl like that hasn't been snapped up! If I was a few years younger I'd be up the aisle with her tomorrow, if I wasn't already spoken for and my Kathleen being a bit too handy with the auld frying pan!"

Cristy certainly had a knack of unwittingly torturing his passengers.

"Well now doctor—what with all this work on the LUAS, I'm going to pull up alongside the front of The Westin Hotel here, but if you look over there you can see the start of Fleet St and The Palace Bar is just a few strides down on the right. You can't miss it alright—flower baskets all over the front for them as likes that sort of thing. Mind how you go now!"

"What's the fare Cristy?"

"All taken care of Dr Bracken—I told you she was a grand girl didn't tell yer?"

Julian looked left and saw the sweep of Trinity College's grey granite walls and heavy black railings and then right to O'Connell Bridge and the breadth of O'Connell St beyond. As Cristy had said the traffic was still heavy and clusters of pedestrians passed to and fro.

He sighed and eased himself out of the taxi and began crossing the road allowing, matador-like, two yellow and blue Dublin City buses to glide by, after which he walked quickly across to the opposite pavement and turned the corner into Fleet St.

There across the street, its front festooned with colourful hanging baskets of geraniums, coxcombs, fuchsia and trailing ivy above its frosted and stained-glass windows, stood The Palace Bar.

A couple were stepping out of the front door—from inside came the welcoming murmur of conversation and the chink of glasses. The man held the door wide for him and so Julian stepped inside. Although the facade of the bar was narrow the interior was tall and deep.

Amongst the general murmur of conversations Julian could hear fiddles being tuned somewhere towards the rear and Julian began to manoeuvre towards the back room, past the patrons stood or seated on stools along the bar or standing along the wall opposite, catching as he moved the Dublin accents engaged in relaxed early evening conversations—everyone putting a hand on their weekend.

As he reached the entrance to the back room the violins struck up a mournful melody in a slow 6/8 time and a male voice began to sing a lament about the Great Famine of the !9th Century.

As most of the room joined in the chorus, Julian spotted Saoirse sat at a table adjoining the panelled back wall of the bar—she smiled and pointed to a small armchair beside her, at the same time moving a coat and handbag from it onto the floor. Julian nodded and pushed his way gently through the bar and eased himself down into the now empty seat beside her.

She squeezed his arm and bent forward to kiss him on the cheek. She whispered, "I didn't expect you over so soon—but I'm so glad you came—I really enjoyed Wednesday night. This is yours," she said as she slid a pint of Guinness across the table towards him and at the same time gave him another kiss. Her perfume filled the air around them.

"Welcome to Dublin, Dr Stinker—Cristy texted when you were leaving the airport—plenty of time to pull a perfect pint of Guinness. This is my PA Aoife—Aoife—meet Julian."

"Pleased to meet you," whispered Julian.

Introductions over, the three of them settled down to listen to the remaining verses of Dan O'Hara. As the music ended the bar broke out in applause at the end of which the lead fiddler placed his fiddle on a chair and announced a 15-minute break.

Aoife leaned forward with a knowing smile. "So, what brings you to Dublin, Julian?"

"Well, just a flying visit." He felt compelled to return the smile.

Aoife's profiling assessment was nothing if not speedy.

"Well, I hope to see you again soon Julian, but I have a ticket for the Irish Film Institute's showing of "Calvary" It's due to start in just five minutes and it's at least a five minute walk to Eustace St."

Julian presumed that Aoife had stayed either to see him for herself and satisfy her own curiosity or to give Saoirse her opinion about him—or more likely both—in other circumstances that would have been good news, but now "He didn't look like a pervert" might be one dismissive comment when Saoirse and Aoife finally discovered what had happened.

"See you Monday Saoirse—have a great weekend, you two." Aoife gave Saoirse a kiss on the cheek, quickly whispering "Be bold, but not too bold!" and giggling, stepped around the table and was off, carrying her coat over her arm.

As Aoife made her way through the bar towards the front exit Julian looked around with envy at the easy conversations taking place amongst the patrons of The Palace Bar—all no doubt with their work done for the day and unlike Julian, work to return to. His thoughts turned back to the sudden and unexpected events of this morning and the reason he had had come to Dublin.

"I've booked us a table at The Cliff Townhouse on Stephen's Green in an hour. I hope you like seafood. I think you'll like it as much as Marckwick's—although it's very different."

She squeezed his arm again and gave him another kiss. A barman was taking advantage of the break in the music to collect empties. Saoirse's phone lit up with an incoming text which she read with a knowing smile and showed to Julian:

He's passed—enjoy your weekend! Aoife. XX

"Could we have two more pints of Guinness please?"
"Sure—I'll bring them over."
Saoirse gave him a E10 note. "Keep the change."
"Thanks a million!"
She looked at Julian and smiled. "This is a nice surprise—we've got the whole weekend and the whole of Dublin to ourselves and you're at least 300 miles from Bristol so you can't be on call! And Guinness is good for you! We've got all weekend to get to know each other better." Saoirse hesitated. "I take it you're not on business?"
"No."
"So, Dr Bracken, did you come just to see me?"
"Yes."
"That's lovely!"
Julian smiled, weakly as Saoirse leaned forward and gave him another kiss.
"And it's so nice to see you—I wondered whether you would come—I've been disappointed so many times before—I knew I could trust a doctor—I'm so glad you're here."
"Me too."

The band returned and immediately sprang into a fast-moving traditional jig for fiddles which caused Julian, despite his mood to begin tapping his feet. He looked at Saoirse and she widened her eyes then smiled at him—a beautiful smile.

They had another drink on the way. It was Friday night in Dublin—the last of the daylight had disappeared a long time ago, creating a snugness about the bar which was filling up with more Dubliners and tourists. The fiddles raced on.

Saoirse was in such a good mood—had utterly no idea of the purpose of his trip. This wasn't the time or place to tell her. He resigned himself to postponing the discussion and enjoying, as far as he could the evening.

He surveyed the room, noting the portraits of authors and journalists—Oscar Wilde, Patrick Kavanagh, Seamus Heaney, Flann O'Brien and W B Yeats, were the ones he immediately recognised. He sat back, exchanging smiles with Saoirse who was caressing his hand.

Thirty minutes later in a break between songs Saoirse and Julian stepped out of the warmth of The Palace Bar and onto Fleet St. and the fresh night air. The Guinness had had its effect on Julian. Saoirse linked his arm and they set off to Stephen's Green.

They crossed over Dame St, along the front of Trinity College and were soon passing the brightly lit shops on Grafton St. Julian looked in the windows of Brown Thomas as they passed and saw in the reflection Saoirse and himself, arm in arm. They were soon on Stephen's Green and ascending the double flight of steps to The Cliff Townhouse.

"How ya doin' Miss Fitzgerald? it's nice to see you here again—back from your travels? Your table's nearly ready—would you like a drink at the bar?"

They sat at the bar on high stools. Julian began to read the menu.

"We entertain some of our main contacts here, but there are so many lovely places to eat in Dublin—depending on how long you can stay we could catch the DART at the week-end, along to Gibney's in Malahide and eat there—or at The Bloody Stream in Howth or one of the restaurants by the quayside—Aqua is nice at the end of the quay. Sorry—I'm running away with myself—aren't I?"

"No—that would be wonderful."

Julian could only return her smile.

Champagne appeared.

"Compliments of the house Miss Fitzgerald—we hope you both enjoy the champagne and our food."

"Thank you, James—that's very kind."

The waiter took the bottle of champagne from the bucket and carefully wiped the beads of icy water away—he removed the foil—six turns and then the cage and gripping the cork, twisted the bottle slowly until there was a loud controlled pop—he filled two glasses and replaced the bottle in the ice-bucket. When he had disappeared, Saoirse lifted her glass so they could see the fine, swirling bubbles.

"Here's to us! Welcome to Dublin and—my life!"

She kissed him yet again. Her dreams were finally beginning to take shape.

Chapter Eighteen

Apartment 26
31 Merrion Rd
Ballsbridge
DUBLIN 4

9:30am
Saturday 23rd of January 2016

Julian woke with a slight headache and only a vague recollection of the evening before. It wasn't that he had drank excessively, simply that with being on call so often he was not used to an excess alcohol and its effects and had never had Guinness, champagne, red wine and cognac together before.

He gathered his thoughts—the first of which was to have a shower, to clear his brain and try to exercise some control over his emotions. As he showered, he acknowledged how perfect Saoirse must have thought last night had been but the black dog of the GMC kept padding back into view—right now it was sat just outside the shower cubicle staring silently—bothering him.

Showered, refreshed, dressed but anxious, he found Saoirse in the lounge, curled up on the sofa, in her dressing gown, with her laptop open, working.

She stood up and walked across to kiss him. He embraced her, guiltily feeling her breasts against his chest. He held the embrace until Saoirse whispered, "I'll make us some coffee."

Saoirse left for the kitchen and Julian settled onto the sofa, deep in thought and waiting for his moment. It wasn't long before Saoirse returned with a cafetiere and two large mugs on a tray. She settled down beside him, tucking her legs underneath her—he could feel her soft body-warmth as she leaned in against him. She looked at him.

"There's something I need to tell you. I enjoyed Wednesday night in Bristol and of course last night and although I haven't known you very long I have come to the conclusion that I'm really attracted to you—I can't explain—it's not capable of explanation—it's just that every time I see you I feel happy—in fact, being entirely honest, I believe I've fallen in love with you—I don't know if you feel the same way or could in time feel the same way, but I need to tell you what has happened and it may mean that you don't want to see me again—that you feel you're better off without me."

Saoirse sat up, took his hands and stared into Julian's eyes.

"This all sounds very serious—go on."

"The reason I'm here is to tell you what happened at work yesterday morning—and I wanted to be here with you—not at the end of the phone. I'll answer any questions and you can see all the statements and documents—I've nothing to hide. I only ask that you'll hear what I've got to say and not come to a quick judgment. I assure you I have done absolutely nothing wrong—nothing at all."

"Ok."

Julian took a deep breath. "Yesterday morning, I was called to a meeting with the Medical Director at the hospital because of an allegation that I acted inappropriately—used inappropriate language when I was repositioning a patient's breasts—which must be done to avoid pain and discomfort and possible tissue damage—I've done it many, many times before. You should also know that the allegations are also that my conduct was sexually motivated."

"And what was it you said?"

"I said—I am now going to perform the "Wonderbra manoeuvre"."

Saoirse laughed. "That doesn't sound that bad, but, why?"

"Well, because it describes the position of the breasts I was trying to achieve—if the breasts are symmetrical then it means there is equal downward pressure on the breast tissue."

"And where did you get that expression from? Did you make it up?"

"No—I heard it at a lecture many years ago, but I can't remember where. I've tried but I can't."

"But presumably you use it all the time?"

"Not really—from time to time—usually when teaching medical students."

"Then why on this occasion?"

"I honestly don't know—it was on the spur of the moment—it was a lovely day—this Wednesday—I was surrounded by colleagues—good friends—I was looking forward to having dinner with you that night—at Marckwick's—and I felt a little bit exuberant—exhilarated—and it just came out."

"OK, go on! What happened next?"

"Nothing as far as I was concerned—the operation went ahead as planned, except it appears one of the nurses thought that what I'd said and done was odd and inappropriate and it appears she reported the incident the next morning, but not before she'd discussed it with a number of her colleagues—including a theatre Sister who had been helping me prep a female patient a few days earlier.

"I was checking that she was placing a urethral catheter correctly because you don't want urine leaking onto the table during an operation—it's more difficult to correctly place a urethral catheter in a female—more difficult to locate the tip of the urethra—she must have resented me supervising her so closely, but it is my responsibility and once, about 10 or 11 years ago I didn't check and urine leaked out onto the table and the operation had to be abandoned. I can remember the name of the prof operating at the time and I'm sure he'll confirm all of this."

"Is that it?"

"No—there's a third incident, about two years ago when, to illustrate the answer to a question from a nurse I traced a line of surgical incision along her back with my finger. I can't have been thinking at the time, we'd just come out of theatre so I was probably a little tired—not alert—it didn't cross my mind that doing that would be inappropriate, but she apparently did. I had thought that was all over and done with—it was dealt with informally at the time. I was advised to consider my actions which I did but now that's adding fuel to the fire, making things look really bad for me.

"I'm so sorry, especially because after Wednesday night I thought there was a future for us. I was thinking things through all day Thursday—I know that you're away a lot, but I've lived alone for 12 years now—we're not teenagers. I thought everything would work out—then yesterday morning I went in to work early to try to arrange some time off, as we discussed after dinner and an hour or so later, I was on my way home!"

Saoirse seemed to be lost in her thoughts.

"What are you thinking?"

"Can I ask you some questions?"

"Of course, anything, anything at all."

"I presume you had seen the two patients before?"

"Yes—I would need to examine them—to assess them and advise them—get their consent and so on So—the first patient—the Wonderbra incident—what was she like—pretty?"

"Well, she was 15 and yes—she was a pretty girl—but only 15."

"Presumably, she had developed her breasts?"

"Again—yes—otherwise there would have been no reason to be concerned about tissue necrosis."

"Ok I understand—and the second patient?"

"She was, is a model."

"So, very attractive?"

"Yes—how can I deny it? It goes without saying."

"And the nurse—was she attractive too?"

"I honestly can't remember, she may well have been—assume she was—but it wouldn't have made any difference to what I did, I don't even remember touching her back."

"So, apart from the nurse's back incident, you needed to do these things, so what they are saying is not so much what you did but what you were thinking when you were doing these things?"

"Yes, exactly and the way I did them—the expression I used—body language I suppose Saoirse was silent for a while and then looked at him—tell me—I will only ask you this once—only you know what was in your mind and if you've done what they say you did—did you?"

"No, I swear not."

"OK—I believe you—so what do we do next?"

"We? You mean you don't want me to leave—go back to Bristol?"

"No, don't be silly! I've dealt with enough chancers, dodgers and divers all over the world for the last 15 years to be able to tell when someone is lying to me. And I have been thinking things through too—I was also thinking that we could have a life together."

"Saoirse, I'm so relieved! I spoke to my defence organisation yesterday and they called me back as I was driving up to Manchester. We had a long chat and they've appointed solicitors to represent me. As soon as I receive any communication from the GMC, I need to forward it to them and they will advise me further. They said the GMC should normally write to me within 14 days, asking for my comments so I'm hoping it will all be resolved fairly quickly.

James Broadley, the lead surgeon will be back soon—I'm sure he will support me."

"OK, so it seems we can only wait to hear from them, but as I see it, when they've had your explanation, it will blow over. I'm off to New York on Tuesday for a week, for a trade fair but we can keep in touch by email."

Saoirse paused before carrying on as if picking her moment.

"But, since we're being honest with each other there is something I need to tell you. I haven't been entirely honest with you—for what you may think are selfish reasons of my own."

Julian looked at her. "Is there someone else? Here in Dublin?"

"No, nothing like that—it's about how we first met."

"What do you mean?"

"I sort of set it all up."

"I don't understand. How?"

"Well, I was also staying at Brown's that day too. I noticed you in the restaurant at breakfast and when I finished, as I was passing through hotel reception, I saw a note on the concierge's desk addressed to "Dr Bracken" so I waited around, sat in a wing-backed chair hiding behind a newspaper initially. I didn't really know what I was expecting to happen, but I overheard you tell Henry, the concierge that you would collect your shirts from Turnbull & Asser at 4.30 because you wanted to choose a new tie, so I waited for you go into the lift and then went to my room.

"As you know by now—by sheer good luck I have an account at Turnbull & Asser, so I know Charles very well. I gave him some advice about silk merchants in China a few years ago.

"I logged onto the GMC website and spent some time searching the internet generally—there aren't many Dr Julian Brackens in the world—you're quite famous, aren't you? Anyway, as you now know I liked the look of you—you dressed well, didn't smoke, were polite, spoke well, so I decided I would be at Turnbull & Asser at 4.30 too—to buy my nephew a tie."

"OK. Go on!"

"I assumed you weren't attached as there was no wedding ring. My first rule of marketing is to create a desire and the second is don't expect instant success, so I made sure I was well dressed to make an impact, demurely of course—there's a very nice lingerie shop in the Burlington Arcade where I bought pairs of black opaque and purple stockings which I thought were the finishing touch—

we've already spoken about them over dinner at Marckwicks—you told me how you'd been intrigued by them so that part of the plan worked."

"And your perfume?"

"Yes, that was on Aoife's orders I was splashing it all over—it's £350 a bottle, but looks like it was worth it! It's a pheromone-based perfume—it's not just junior fags at Downfield and doctors who know about Pavlovian reflexes—it's our in-house parfumiers too!"

"So, are you going to say next that it was no accident that I took home your nephew's tie with my shirts?"

"Of course, it wasn't. I purchased a tie just before you arrived and asked Charles to staple my business card to my receipt before putting it into one of their bespoke bags.

"When Charles put your bag with your tie in it on top of your shirts, if you remember, I asked Charles if I could look at some more cufflinks from the display cabinet behind him and when Charles turned away, I "accidentally" knocked my gloves to the floor and as you were picking them up, as I assumed you would, I switched my tie bag for yours."

"That's thoroughly scheming! And some people might say a little desperate?"

"Well, I hope you won't think exactly desperate, more determined, what Aoife calls "Being Bold!" Anyway, you don't seem to be complaining."

"No, I'm not."

"So, when I'd swapped the bags I knew that you had my contact details and hoped you would email or call at some stage so when your email arrived I was so pleased I very nearly replied by return but didn't want to seem too eager. I couldn't wait to meet you properly—to find out more about you. I just started ticking off the days. The flight back from Hong Kong is always a drag but it seemed endless, especially as I had to stop over in Paris."

"Have I lived up to expectations then? Until this morning?"

"You have." She squeezed his hands. "But it doesn't matter because I believe you and I—we can and will sort all this out—together Saoirse paused and continued. But there's something else I need to tell you and the reason I haven't told you before is that I was worried that you may think I'm too desperate or determined. Have you heard of a clinic called UKFC on York St in London?"

"Are you going to tell me there's some part of you that's not completely original? I'm not bothered about that and if so, it was certainly money well spent."

"No, it's not that—I'm all real! UKFC is a fertility clinic. Just before I was thirty, I decided I would have some of my eggs frozen and as you may know, being a doctor, 10 years is the default period for storage when all my eggs will be destroyed. The clinic wrote to me confirming this earlier this month. I'm 39 now so there's not much time left—just a little over a year if I'm going to use those eggs and realise my ambition of finally having a baby—a family. That's also why I run—to keep my body in reasonable shape for what I hope will be the most wonderful experience of my life—but I want to share it with the right person—someone I know to be kind and caring and who'll be a good father—and I think you are that man."

"Despite what I've just told you?"

Saoirse nodded and smiled. "Yes—you said earlier that you've fallen in love with me, well, I've fallen in love with you! It does happen, if you wait long enough! I've noticed you keep fit and are in great shape. So, not only were you looking for a man but one who like you is still completely original, as my urologist colleagues would say still has his vas deferens connected. I don't think you'll find that information nor my sperm count on the internet."

"Put like that it sounds so scheming and desperate, but you need to do this online dating thing to appreciate that it's the absolute pits. I'd had enough by the time I was twenty-eight—I was travelling the world and never seemed to be in one place for very long. I would go away on business for a week or two and return to find my boyfriend had found a new girlfriend. One even wanted me to share him with her. The things men think they can get away with! Most of the men in the fashion industry are gay so there's little chance of hooking up there. Don't get me wrong, I'm not an erotophobe but for me there must be a relationship too."

"Well! Don't keep me waiting!"

"As it happens, I'm pleased to tell you that I am, like you, completely original—no snip!"

Julian sat in silence, unable to speak as he thought things through.

"So, despite everything I've told you, you still want to have a relationship with me?"

"Yes! Don't you? With me?"

"Yes! Saoirse—I'm so relieved!"

"I'm relieved too! It's Saturday and we have the whole week-end to ourselves. We just need to get this GMC business out of the way. I'm off for a shower—it's a beautiful day—let's go for a long walk—Sandymount Strand is just a few minutes away. Did you bring many clothes with you? Saoirse disappeared to the bathroom without waiting for a reply."

As Saoirse showered Julian went to the balcony to get some fresh air. The clouds were intensely white, scattered against a deep azure sky. As he looked eastwards over Merrion Rd and across the rooftops of Ballsbridge he could see to his left the upper profile of a cruise liner moving imperceptibly along the River Liffey, towards the open expanse of the Irish Sea.

He stepped back into the living room and looked around at the paraphernalia of Saoirse's life—which she had talked about so enthusiastically over dinner in Bristol and now it seemed a life that might become partly his. On the coffee table were piles of fashion magazines and draft sketches of garments. There was a rack of garments of all kinds in the corner. A T shirt was draped over the back of a chair. He held it up and saw the front bore the repeated slogan CHRISTIANO A FIORENTINA—FASHION AGAINST FGM he replaced the garment on the back of the chair.

When Saoirse returned to the living room Julian grinned at her.

"I didn't bring many clothes—I was so worried that you would not want to know me after I explained what happened in theatre that I really thought I would be booking into a hotel and on the first flight home today!"

Saoirse stepped forward and embraced him.

"We can always pay a visit to Brown Thomas but for now—let's go for that walk!"

Chapter Nineteen

SANDYMOUNT STRAND

10:00am
Saturday 23rd of January 2016

Sandymount Strand stretched, crescent shaped, along the south perimeter of Dublin Bay. It was flanked to the north by Poolbeg Lighthouse, standing at the very end of the Great South Wall and Merrion Gates to the south. The two towers of the old generating station, hooped in red and white, their navigation lights slowly blinking stood in the centre of Poolbeg peninsula like two giants of the Tuatha De Danann, guarding Ireland from hostile invasion.

Occasionally a DART could be seen in the distance silently threading its way through the suburbs of Blackrock and Seapoint, heading further southwards towards the pretty commuter villages of Killiney, Dalkey and Bray. Just visible, above the horizon, a small procession of yacht sails pointed skywards, beyond the Pier of Dun Laoghaire Harbour. The sea was a good mile offshore, but Julian sensed the tide was on the turn. The cruise ship he had watched earlier, slowly inching its way down the River Liffey was now just a vague, grey, misty shape slipping through the haze and over the horizon.

They walked as one, along the edge of the beach, crunching the remains of countless white shells under their feet. Small family groups had seized the opportunity to enjoy the unexpected January sunshine and joggers were passing to and fro along the esplanade and the edge of the beach where the sand was firm. Someone inspired at Dublin City Council had managed to secure a budget to have erected several sets of outdoor gym equipment at intervals along the wide grass verge between the beach and the wall running along Sandymount Rd, where joggers and some pedestrians would stop and cross-train.

They had walked in silence nearly the full length of Sandymount Strand—almost as far as Merrion Gates and instinctively turned to start the return walk along the beach. They were both lost in their own thoughts about their revelations earlier that morning and how their future together might take shape.

Julian paused. "There's something I want to tell you about my wife, Eleanor."

Saoirse looked at Julian, nodded and smiled.

"Eleanor was expecting when she was killed. The post-mortem examination revealed that she was about eight weeks into her pregnancy, which meant that the pathologist was also able to determine the sex of the baby. We would have had a daughter who would have been eleven by now—obviously I don't have her birthday to celebrate but I think of her or at least the girl I imagine she might have been every day—and of course, Eleanor."

"I'm so sorry, Julian."

"I suppose I have always hoped to find someone else with whom I could have a family, perhaps a daughter for the one I, we, lost and about whom I never knew anything. I never held her hand, dressed her, spoke to her, heard her voice, lifted her up into my arms and watched her fall asleep at night after a bedtime story and thought until this morning that there would never be that opportunity again. So it appears we have both been secretly hoping for the same thing and miraculously, we have found each other.

"Although I was instantly attracted to you, until this morning, I thought you were a dedicated career woman and I would have been happy enough with that but thought the last thing you wanted was to start a family."

"Julian, having a family is what I've wanted for such a long time. It's wonderful to think it can now actually happen."

Saoirse pulled him closer. "Shall we have a late breakfast?"

Julian nodded. Saoirse wrapped her arms round him and he held her tighter than ever.

"Come on! I know just the place—Browne's Brasserie on Sandymount Green. It's like a little piece of Paris in Dublin."

They strolled back along the strand in silence, seagulls wheeling and screeching in the sea air above them whilst gold-crests and dunnocks flitted about in the sand around their feet.

***

Sandymount Green was a verdant oasis of an acre or so surrounded by heavy gauge black iron railings containing several gates allowing access to the paths which criss-crossed the Green.

Although there were no children's attractions there were many benches, most of which were occupied with mothers, fathers, other carers and nannies and their young charges and since it was a Saturday older siblings—at least those who were not yet old enough to be exploring the Irish Nature Park on Poolbeg Peninsula, playing games of Gaelic football or hurling on the Irishtown pitches or just playing on Sandymount beach.

This picture of familial contentment was not lost on either Saoirse or Julian. They took it in as they walked along, arm in arm.

The North side of the Green was dominated by a well-proportioned Georgian townhouse of three stories with four sets of basement windows. The brass door-furniture was highly polished and complimented the rich black lacquered finish of the door.

Facing this small mansion on the south side of the Green was a stuccoed Victorian Gothic residence. The house and its castellated walls were painted a light pink. On the west and east side of the Green were variously shops, restaurants, a doctor's and a veterinarian's surgery and an "apothecary" whose entrance was graced by full height, quarter-turn antique glass.

Browne's Brasserie was situated on the south easterly corner of the Green and as Saoirse had said was a little piece of Paris transported to Dublin—mosaic tiled floors, a flow of tables both outside and inside with a flank of private wood-panelled booths at the rear, opposite which was a bar which would not have been out of place in Montmartre.

They chose a private booth and ordered a large bottle of sparkling mineral water. Both ordered poached eggs with flaked smoked fish and two cafes au-lait.

"I suppose that like you I was looking for that special person but thought time had passed me by. I felt that there was something unseemly about a man of my age going around "dating" and I've been living alone so long that I had an anxiety about how to start a relationship, so the days just run into weeks and then months and you throw yourself into work and deny that deep down you're lonely and hoping for a miracle. It becomes easier to just carry on pretending. You slip into a self-justifying and perpetuating routine." Julian paused for a moment. "Sorry—you didn't tell me."

"Tell you what?"

"The 10-year deadline—when does it expire?"

"On 5 March 2017—my eggs were harvested on 6 March 2007—after I was assessed as suitable, I had to return to the clinic several weeks later for a course of hormone injections so it wasn't until after super-ovulation that my eggs could be harvested."

"Well—that's plenty of time."

"That's what I thought—but that was nearly nine years ago! From what I was told at the clinic the eggs I'm ovulating currently will not be as healthy or viable as the harvested eggs, so it would make sense to use the frozen eggs, but you're the doctor—what do you think?"

"Well, I'm an anaesthetist but from what I know that seems right—your harvested eggs will be younger and healthier so carry less of a risk of any congenital abnormalities."

"So, once we get the GMC problem resolved, we can start to plan ahead?"

"Well, I'm hoping that the GMC complaints should be resolved in the next few weeks."

Saoirse pushed her breakfast plate away and leaned forward to look across the table at him. She widened her eyes and smiled. "But that doesn't mean we can't…you know…enjoy ourselves in the meantime—does it?"

She pulled her mouth to one side, in mock guilt, her eyes alive, bright and sparkling. She smiled again—a deep, powerful, penetrating smile that moved Julian both emotionally and physically.

"There now, I've said it!"

"Well, as long as you remember—I've been living a somewhat monkish existence for the last few years."

"OK, I will, because I've been living more or less like a nun for the last few years!"

"Does that mean we have some lost time to make up?"

The waiter approached their table. They asked for their bill—and a taxi please!

***

It was 2.30pm. Saoirse's arm was draped over Julian's chest. She stirred and gave him a long kiss.

"Well, I did tell you—I wasn't an erotophobe!"

He could feel her so soft skin on his body. She slipped out of bed and for a few moments stood naked before pulling on a satin dressing gown. "Would you like some coffee?"

"Hmm—lovely—thanks."

Chapter Twenty

Sunday 24th of January
5:30 pm

TERMINAL TWO
DEPARTURES
DUBLIN AIRPORT

Cristy pulled in and turned around.
"The fare?"
"All taken care of." He smiled. "Well, I trust I'll be seeing you again Dr B?"

"I hope so Cristy. By the way, who was that on the radio?"

"Ah—the great man himself—Finbarr Furey—he was singing his latest, *The Last Great Love Song*"—did yer like it?"

"Yes—it was beautiful. Will you do a favour for me?"

"Sure I will."

"The next time you're passing Merrion Rd, will you drop this off for me please?" Julian handed Cristy an envelope addressed to "Saoirse" and a E20 note.

"Thanks Dr B! Take care now—don't be a stranger!"

***

"Ladies and gentlemen welcome to Aer Lingus flight EI1003 to Manchester.

"Our flying time today will be a little bit over 30 minutes—the weather in Manchester is similar to here in Dublin—my name is Breeda O' Leary and together with my colleague, Bernadette Fagan I will be flying you to Manchester today. In fact you have an all-female crew and cabin staff today but even if you are a frequent traveller, please listen to Concepta, who is just about to outline the very important safety features on this aircraft.

"I hope you enjoy the fruit the cabin crew were handing out today as we were boarding—to mark two years since Aer Lingus introduced its very own "Five-a-

Day"—that's five flights a day between Dublin and Manchester!

"Ladies and gentlemen, we have a very special guest on board today could I welcome Bernadette O'Hara and two of her 18 great-grandchildren, Maura and Eoin—Bernadette is celebrating her 95th birthday today and this is the first time Bernadette has flown—Maura and Eoin are taking her to Manchester to their brother's wedding. Happy Birthday Bernadette, from the flight deck and all the cabin crew."

There was a round of applause for Bernadette before the cabin crew began the safety announcements as Captain O'Leary taxied the Airbus towards the runway, stopping every few minutes as the plane worked its way up the unseen queue of jets ahead of them. Julian finally felt the plane turn sharply and saw the black and white stripes underneath him marking the start of the runway, where for several seconds, the engines idled. Julian could see the steady blink of the navigation lights flashing on the tarmac underneath him and at the starboard wing-tip.

The plane began to move imperceptibly and then suddenly the engines roared into life, thrusting the plane forward and Julian back into his seat. As the plane accelerated along the runway Julian looked across the aisle and saw Bernadette O'Hara cross herself, kiss her rosary beads and then clasp the hands of her great grandchildren sitting either side of her.

He looked along the cabin and after several seconds saw the front gently tilt upwards and a few seconds later the rhythmic thump of the undercarriage wheels suddenly stopped as they were lifted from the ground. The whine of hydraulics took its place until Julian felt the clunk of the undercarriage doors closing.

The engines were still at full thrust as the jet continued to climb steeply through patches of low-lying clouds which caused the fuselage and the two long strips of overhead lockers to shudder and the wings to vibrate slowly, then the whine of the engines dropped and the plane gently levelled out.

Julian looked out of the window—through the evening haze and the broken clouds to his right he could see the city of Dublin, its lights twinkling and beyond, the red and white hooped towers of the old generating station on the Poolbeg Peninsula and just beyond them, the crescent of Sandymount Strand, where just yesterday morning he and Saoirse had been walking. He could just make out the long black stretch of the Great South Wall and at its end Poolbeg Lighthouse.

Chapter Twenty-One

**APARTMENT 26
31 MERRION RD
BALLSBRIDGE
DUBLIN 4**

8:15pm

The intercom buzzed in Saoirse's apartment. On the small CCTV screen she recognised Cristy's distorted face at the front door of the apartment block, so she clicked the "open" button and told Cristy she would be right down.

Cristy was waiting for her in the ground floor lobby. "Hi Miss Fitzgerald, I've just dropped Dr B off at the airport and he asked me to give you this." He handed over a letter and smiling, turned away.

"Be seeing you now, Miss Fitzgerald. Yer man is a lovely man Miss Fitzgerald and I've been telling him what a grand girl you are—a fine catch for any man!"

Saoirse smiled.

"Away with you Cristy—but thanks a million." She laughed to herself and hurried back upstairs, excited.

She sat down and opened the envelope.

Dear Saoirse,

The last few days are days I never thought would return to my life. You have been so kind and understanding but more importantly, you have believed me when I needed someone to believe in me, when I was beginning to doubt myself.

Saturday morning was the first time I have slept with a woman since Eleanor died. In truth, I would now have had two women in my life but for the accident. I couldn't bring myself to hope that there could have been a third, but you have magically arrived.

I have never mentioned this to anyone, but Eleanor once said that if anything should happen to her I was to make a new life for myself but until now I have never had the opportunity.

When you read this, I shall probably be on my way back to Bristol but I want to either have you there with me or be back in Dublin with you—I don't really mind where—if I am with you.

I hadn't realised how much I had fallen in love with you until Saturday morning—it wasn't just the lovemaking though that was special—it was as if I had found another perfect partner.

I know that the next few weeks or so will be the most uncertain in my life—to face allegations of such a kind when I know that what I was doing was practising good medicine is sickening but you have given me the confidence to believe in myself when my employers and some of my colleagues and friends seem to have turned their back on me.

I can barely bring myself to ask this question since your response is out of my hands, but would you at least tell me what your hopes are? I heard what you said over the week-end, but sometimes we get carried away with an idea—a wish—so can I ask you what you really wish for yourself and if I can dare to ask it—for us?

In short, after we have resolved all this mess, hopefully quickly, can we together, fulfil our dreams? It would be a great comfort to know for certain. I'll understand if you say you are having second thoughts—if so, far better to say now.

All my love,
Julian.

Chapter Twenty-Two

**THE BACKS
BRISTOL**

**22:45
Sunday 24th of January**

Julian saw the email notification fade onto his screen—**From Saoirse Fitzgerald**. He quickly opened it.

Dear Julian,

Forgive the email—it's not the most romantic form of communication—nowhere near as romantic as your beautiful letter—but it is the quickest—and I wanted to respond as quickly as possible. In short and first and foremost—I want you—and to be with you. Perhaps, if we're lucky we can have a child, or children and you may find in them the daughter you never had the chance to get to know and perhaps also a son you never had.

Secondly, I want to settle down—with you, and stop flying all over the world—it sounds glamorous and it is, for a while, but when you need to take a five-hour taxi ride out of Shanghai with a driver who speaks no English through countryside ravaged by serious air pollution—so bad it turns the vegetation yellow—amidst poverty you and no one in the developed world cannot begin to understand or even address then you just feel so helpless and want out.

I have savings and I have share options to exercise—something I could only have dreamt about, growing up in the streets of Moss Side and I imagine you are a man of independent means too, so together, if you wish, we can do it—and—I think—I know—we can be happy, truly happy.

I too would rather be with you but for the time being I am committed to be here in Dublin, but is there any reason why you cannot join me here and find a position in Dublin? It has its attractions—the people and the music and the wonderful countryside, but it's not home—it's just an apartment—and I want to make a home—with you and children—I have always wanted that, but now I want it with you.

Is there any reason you need to stay in Bristol? Can't you come over and the two of us live here in Dublin, once you've resolved all this business with the GMC? Let me know your thoughts!

I hope, truly hope, you will say Yes!
Saoirse.

Wednesday 27th of January
1:30 pm
The Backs
Bristol

Julian collected his morning post from his letter-box in the lobby. After Sunday night's exchange with Saoirse he wanted to get on with clearing his name and was hoping to receive a letter from the GMC soon so that he could explain the allegations away, but none had arrived yesterday or the day before. This morning there was the usual junk mail and unsolicited letters amongst which was one forwarded on from the hospital, in handwriting addressed to *Dr J A Bracken c/o Somerford Royal Infirmary, Hospital Rd, Bristol. Please forward.*

But there was also an envelope bearing the words in authoritative bold blue type **General Medical Council**. He wrapped it in his copy of The Times and pressed the up button for the elevator to the third floor.

Over a cup of coffee, he began making his way through the small pile of letters, leaving the GMC letter to the last.

When he came to the letter with the handwritten address, he opened it and read:

Dear Dr Bracken,

The hospital contacted us last week and asked us and Samantha to attend a meeting with Professor Somerville. He told us about what was supposed to have happened when Samantha was in the operating theatre—when Samantha was anaesthetised and that he has had to start an investigation and refer you to the General Medical Council.

He said he would keep us informed about the case against you. We wanted to write to you to say that we and Samantha do not believe that you would do what the nurse said you did as you have always been very kind and considerate to her and us whenever we have met. We hope you can return to work very soon.

Yours

Mr and Mrs Brown (George and Elizabeth) and Samantha

PS Samantha is planning to do a 10-kilometre sponsored walk as soon as she is more mobile—to raise funds for the Spinal Unit. We will always be truly grateful to you.

Julian sighed and smiled to himself and put the letter to one side. At least the Brown family were on his side. He opened the envelope from the General Medical Council and spread the letter out on his desk.

GENERAL MEDICAL COUNCIL HARDMAN STREET
SPINNINGFIELDS
MANCHESTER
26 January 2016

Dear Dr Bracken,

I am writing to inform you that the General Medical Council has received information which may call into question your fitness to practise.

We are investigating these allegations. If you feel that there is any information which may assist us then you are free to write to us although you are not obliged to do so.

We will take into account any information you provide.

If you have a defence organisation or have instructed solicitors to represent you, you should immediately forward a copy of this letter and its enclosures to them.

I shall write to you again in accordance with the Fitness to Practise Rules, once our investigations have concluded, inviting your comments.

Julian next read, with surprise and shock.

REFERRAL TO AN INTERIM ORDERS HEARING.

The Case Examiners considering your case have decided there are grounds for referral to an Interim Orders Tribunal, which will take place at the offices of the Medical Practitioners' Tribunal Service, Oxford Street, Manchester at 12.00 noon next Monday 1st February 2016.

The Interim Orders Tribunal will consider whether it is necessary to restrict your practice while the allegations about your conduct are resolved. The Tribunal has the power to impose conditions on your registration or suspend your registration if it finds it necessary

- for the protection of patients and members of the public
- in the public interest
- in your interests

The public interest includes preserving public confidence in the regulation of the medical profession and maintaining good standards of conduct and performance.

The procedure at the Interim Orders Hearing is outlined in the enclosed leaflet and further guidance is on the GMC website. Please let me know if you propose to attend.

EDF

Please complete and return the enclosed Employers' Details Form before Friday 29th January 2016.

DSS

I appreciate that these hearings can be stressful—you may wish to seek support from the Doctor Support Service—the contact information is at the end of this letter. If you have any questions, please call me on the telephone number at the foot of this letter.

Yours sincerely

William Wood
Assistant Registrar

There was a small bundle of documents attached to the letter which contained copies of the statements of Nurse Griffiths, Sister Johnson and Nurse Keaveney, which Julian had already seen, together with notes of the meeting with Sebastian, bearing the signatures of both Julian and Julie Lightfoot and a GMC Case Summary. A total of just 47 pages.

Julian picked up his mobile and keyed in Saoirse's number on his speed dial—after a few rings, her calming voice answered, "Hi!"

"I hope I've not woken you up?"

"No—it's 7.30am here in New York—I've been up for an hour already."

"I've heard from the GMC—and they've decided to call me to a hearing next Monday in Manchester where they will consider whether to suspend me from practising. I never dreamt they would do that!"

"It surely won't come to that I hope not! This is the first time anyone has mentioned suspension. I just thought I could explain everything and get back to work."

"What time is the hearing?"

"Noon on Monday."

"Ok—is there anything new in the papers?"

"No—it's basically what I told you."

"I'm sorry I can't be there—I'm stuck in New York until next Thursday evening."

"I'll email the papers to you as I said I would—I would appreciate a woman's view on things. You'll see things differently."

"Well, I do have a vested interest in keeping you sane and healthy."

"That might prove difficult. I feel so helpless—it's one thing lecturing about how to avoid being sued and complained about and another when it happens to you—you just don't see it coming."

"Look—email me the papers to me as soon as you can—I must go—taxi waiting—can we speak later tonight? I'll read the papers and let you know what I think. In the meantime, get the papers over to your lawyers."

"Yes, I will—love you!"

"You too!"

Julian picked up the phone and dialled the number of the solicitors Dr Goddard at his defence organisation had given him—Cavendish and Beauchamp.

Chapter Twenty-Three

Barristers
St James's Buildings
Oxford Street
Manchester
The Medical Practitioners Tribunal Service

8:30 am
Thursday 28th of January 2016

The ground floor lobby of St James's Building teemed with office workers and, unnoticed, several barristers, waiting politely for one of the four lifts to transport them to the seventh-floor reception of The Medical Practitioners Tribunal Service, where they would sign in and obtain their passes and swipe cards to access the secure area where the hearings and conference rooms were located.

They were all known, or if not actually known, easily recognisable to each other because, in this highly specialised area of law, their professional paths would often cross.

One month, they might be representing PIPS—*properly interested persons* at a multi-party inquest into a hospital death before Her Majesty's Coroner for the City of Newcastle upon Tyne and a few weeks later be re-united in a criminal trial at The Old Bailey—co-defending different members of a surgical team against charges of gross negligence manslaughter arising from the abbreviated, euphemistic soubriquet, SUI—*sudden untoward incident*—or, like today—representing a doctor—summoned by the General Medical Council to answer allegations of misconduct before an *Interim Orders Tribunal*—or a *Fitness to Practise* hearing of the medical profession's disciplinary body—the Medical Practitioners Tribunal Service.

Between hearings they would return to London and their various chambers amidst the historic cloisters, colonnades, halls, libraries and gardens of the Inns of Court—Inner and Middle Temple, Gray's and Lincoln's Inn—where they would devise their strategies for forthcoming hearings by drafting and deploying a discrete selection of weapons from their legal arsenal—Skeleton Arguments, Submissions of No Case to Answer, Advices on Appeal against Sanction, Closing Speeches, Submissions on Impairment, Applications for Judicial Review and avidly add to their already extensive knowledge of the law—for they belonged to the only profession that attempted, albeit of course, discreetly, and usually, but not always, with unfailing courtesy, to outwit each other in public.

The Inns of Court, despite their ancient origins, were now nothing less than twenty-first century intellectual "boot-camps", which was just as well because intellectual athletics were often required when defending the medical profession, for misconduct by doctors took many forms—dishonesty, sexual misbehaviour, bullying, drug or drink addictions and criminality, or sometimes a little and occasionally a lot, of all six.

Nor was a doctor's misconduct limited by geography, for the GMC's writ was global—the internet and the media were regularly scrutinised by the GMC, so that any deplorable behaviour—even if unrelated to medicine—a drunken indiscretion on a visit to Bondi Beach or on a salmon-fishing trip to the remotest parts of Alaska might result in an investigation by the GMC and an appearance before the MPTS, where the alleged misconduct would be scrutinised, with all the precision and detail afforded by a leisurely and exacting application of forensic objectivity and its omniscient sister—the benefit of hindsight—to establish whether and if so, how seriously, that misconduct fell below the standards set out in *Good Medical Practice* and its many *Guidelines*.

There was no one more capable or skilled in the exacting application of forensic objectivity and the benefit of hindsight than Connie Cornwall QC, the doyenne of GMC prosecuting counsel and the scourge of misbehaving doctors everywhere. Always impeccably dressed, her severely cropped blonde hair, gamine appearance and slightly petite stature provided the ideal camouflage for her fierce intellect and comprehensive mastery of her chosen area of legal warfare.

Although never formally tested Connie was thought to be able to recite all eighty paragraphs of *Good Medical Practice* and related *Guidelines* by heart—an ability which combined with her formidable legal weaponry made being cross-examined by Connie akin to a solitary re-enactment of a D-Day landing.

On her appointment to silk, her head of chambers had sent a congratulatory card which bore, light-heartedly, a long line of stethoscopes struck through with large red crosses—redolent of the "kills" on the fuselages of World War fighter aces. Connie had been greatly amused, indeed flattered and began, privately, to keep the score—43 erasures to date since becoming a QC prosecutrix—Connie didn't bother to count mere suspensions.

The assembled, august members of the bar observed a professional silence until all the non-lawyers had exited the lift and then, in their own exclusive argot observed the morning's ritual niceties and, as barristers often do, adopted their lay clients' personae.

Barrister 1: Saw you at Oxford Crown Court last month—did you get back in time for Mess?

Barrister 2: Just about – my jury came back in with a verdict, just after I saw you.j

Barrister 1: What was the verdict?

Barrister 2: Not Guilty! I don't know who was more surprised—me, prosecuting counsel, the judge or the defendant!

Barrister 1: Well done! What ya got today?

Barrister 2: IOT—I'm alleged to have falsified patient records, by adding a reference to a potential side-effect of paraesthesia following a surgical procedure. As it happens, completely unnecessarily as there was a full note I had already made in the pre-op assessment about all the potential side-effects—including paraesthesia—I'd just forgotten about it!

Barrister 1: Bit of a bugger! Who's batting for the GMC?

Barrister 2: Michael Rankin.

Barrister 1: Oh, Mike's a good guy! Scored a couple of very good tries for the Northern Circuit against the Irish Bar in Dublin last year.

Barrister 2: And you?

Barrister 1: Second day of the first week of four—I've been having, shall we say, *a very full relationship* with a *vulnerable* female patient—the problem is—she filmed it all. The press are absolutely loving it! I'm still at Stage 1, Patient A is starting her evidence today.

Barrister 2: Who's for the GMC?

Barrister 1: The Divine Suzanne!

Barrister 2: Oh well—a bit of eye-candy is always welcome!

Barrister 2: And you?

Barrister 3: IOT as well—I've been signing off fictitious medical reports for a firm of solicitors to pursue fraudulent personal injury claims—allegedly!

There were a few moments of silence as the four barristers reflected on just how ow members of the *other side of the profession* could sink.

Barrister 2: Anything interesting?

Barrister 4: IOT too—I'm a consultant surgeon in emergency medicine. I suspected my wife of having an abortion to cover up an affair and attempted to access her medical records, looking for evidence.

I telephoned the clinic, pretending I was her *treating psychiatrist* and that I *needed the information urgently to decide whether I should section her under the Mental Health Act.* Bit stupid really, as the clinic captured my mobile number and, well you don't have to be a genius to work out what happened next! I'm listed at 12 noon for half a day—so we're straight into con—I've got the smiling assassin et femme fatale—Connie!

Barrister 2: Good luck with that one!

The lift doors opened, and the cohort of legal fire-power stepped forward to sign in and start another day's work.

After accessing the secure area with their newly issued swipe cards, they swept past the GMC witness waiting area and a seated young woman who, on another day could have featured on the front page of Vogue fashion magazine. She was accompanied by an equally attractive woman, who might easily have been mistaken for her elder sister, but whose body language suggested that she was almost certainly her mother. Both were dressed in demure black, as if, somewhat appropriately, for a funeral.

"Crikey!" whispered Barrister 2, "Is that Patient A?"

"Yep! She would turn up for an appointment to see me at the surgery wearing heels and just a leather corset and black stockings under her raincoat! Then she started asking if I did home visits!"

"Well, I can certainly see how you ended up here! Just as well you've not got Connie against you! Good luck!"

They arrived at the conference rooms, some already occupied by their instructing solicitors and client-doctors, where introductions were politely and professionally effected.

Chapter Twenty-Four

**Cavendish and Beauchamp
Solicitors
Spring Gardens,
Manchester**

**10:30 am
Thursday 28th of January 2016**

Sarah Thompson put her head round Eugene Kennedy's office door.

"Ever heard of the Wonderbra manoeuvre?"

Eugene eyed Sarah quizzically. "I'm not sure I ought to comment."

"It's a new GMC case with an IOT next Monday morning 1st February at 12 noon—the papers have just arrived—I've printed them off for you. Sounds like one for Jonathan Bliss—just up his street." Sarah placed a small bundle of papers on Eugene's desk. "Will you deal with it?"

"Of course, sounds interesting."

Eugene settled down with a coffee to read the papers and began with the statements of Nurse Griffith, Sister Johnson, Mary Keaveney and supporting documents. Ever since reforms addressing the "old boys" culture and fitness to practise procedures recommended by The Shipman Inquiry had been implemented, corresponding with the GMC had to be done with the utmost care. Every word in every line of all communications was scrutinised for inconsistency, error or worst of all lack of insight.

After he finished reading the GMC Case Summary, Eugene picked up the phone and called Jonathan Bliss's chambers. The ever-cheery Danielle answered and put Eugene through to the Clerk's room. Lee, the Senior Clerk answered.

"Morning, Mr Kennedy."

"Morning Lee, I don't suppose Jonathan Bliss is free next Monday for an IOT?"

"Mr Kennedy, you're in luck—Mr Bliss has just had a three-week General Dental Council case come out of the list at short notice and is therefore free on Monday—I can look at other diaries if you wish but from memory the other counsel you have worked with before are all pretty much booked up and as it happens Mr Bliss is in chambers so if you are OK with that I can put you through and perhaps you can give him an outline of the case?"

"That's fine Lee."

"I just need the name of the doctor."

"It's Dr Julian Bracken."

"Thanks. I'll put you through to Mr Bliss now."

"Morning Jonathan, I understand you're free to take this new case. I'll email a brief and the papers later this morning and perhaps we could have a detailed discussion on Monday first thing, when you've had a chance to study them, but here's the "heads-up"—the doctor is a consultant anaesthetist at Somerford Royal Infirmary in Bristol—there is an IOT listed for next Monday at noon. Can I suggest the two us meet at say 9.30am for a pre-hearing con at the MPTS and then with the lay client at 10.30am?"

"Fine—what's it about?"

"Sex—unfortunately, there are three separate incidents, including one described as "The Wonderbra Manoeuvre". I don't yet know who GMC counsel is but I've put a call out to GMC Legal so I'll let you know as soon as I do."

"I will arrange for the client to join us in conference at 10.30, if that's OK with you. I know it will mean an early start for you but I think this doctor is in trouble. There was an incident two years ago and the other two took place more recently—all sex related."

"Well I will probably come up on Sunday afternoon—it will be quieter on the train and we can start with fresh heads—we might need them by the sound of it, particularly if Connie gets her hands on him."

"Fine, I'll get an email off to the client confirming all this now and will forward a copy to you."

"Yep, see you on Monday."

Dear Dr Bracken,

I refer to our recent telephone conversations and confirm that I have been appointed by your defence organisation to represent you at the forthcoming Interim Orders Tribunal on Monday next. I have instructed Mr Jonathan Bliss of counsel to appear on your behalf and arranged for a pre-hearing conference to take place with counsel at 10.30am at the offices of the MPTS next Monday. I shall meet you there.

Would you be kind enough to confirm you will be in attendance?

I would be grateful for a copy of your current CV, any testimonials you can obtain between now and Monday and any further information you feel would be helpful.

Please call me if there is anything at all you wish to discuss arising from your case.

Kind regards,

Eugene Kennedy

CAVENDISH & BEAUCHAMP SOLICITORS LLP

Chapter Twenty-Five

**THE HILTON HOTEL
DEANSGATE
MANCHESTER**

**8:00pm
Sunday 31st of January 2016**

Julian stared out of the window at the city below—different worlds. He wished Saoirse wasn't in New York and was here with him—he felt utterly alone—couldn't even talk to colleagues. He had been allocated a room on the 18th floor overlooking the city centre but was too tired to spend much time star-gazing—in any event the skyline was largely hidden behind an unusual soft Manchester drizzle.

He ordered room service for an hour's time and left the hotel for a walk, taking one of the hotel's umbrellas, killing time until tomorrow's hearing. He returned to his room almost an hour later, having wandered aimlessly through the wet Manchester streets. He was finding all the time on his hands difficult to fill.

When he returned to his room he began reading the statements yet again.

His phone rang—it was Saoirse.

"Hi—how are you?"

"Ok."

"What are you doing?"

"Reading the GMC statements—again—did you get them?"

"Yes."

"What do you think?"

"Well, in a way I can understand the allegations about the Wonderbra and the catheter—they are I think, as you say unfortunate misunderstandings, but this Nurse Keaveney—are you sure you can't remember what she looks like?"

"I can't remember at all except she was thirty something and blonde. Why?"

"Well, putting it bluntly, I would imagine a high-flying consultant would be quite a catch for a nurse in her early thirties?"

"Well it does happen—quite a few of my friends have married nurses although I'm not sure they've been hunted down—it's the life-style as much as anything—working shifts together under pressure—lives in common—same interests—that and being in regular close contact."

"But you can't think of anything she said or did when you were alone together in the recovery room?"

"No—I've tried and wish I could, but I can't. A little bit of good news is I received a letter from the family of Samantha Brown and her parents in which they say they don't believe the allegations about me."

"That's nice of them! That will surely help. Remember to take it along with you tomorrow. What time do you have to be there?"

"I'm meeting my lawyers there at 10.30 tomorrow morning—the hearing is at 12.00 noon."

"I'll be thinking of you—sorry I can't be of more use. I'm sure you'll be fine—be sure to let me know what happens"

"Thanks."

"Love you."

"You too."

Chapter Twenty-Six

MPTS
CONFERENCE ROOM THREE

9:00am
Monday 1st of February 2016

"Good weekend Eugene?"

"Yes thanks—and you?"

"Yes—thanks for the papers you sent on Thursday—I had a good look through them on Friday and then again yesterday afternoon on the train. Do we know who the GMC have briefed yet?"

"Yes."

"Is it Connie?"

"Yes."

"Oh well!"

"Dr Bracken will be here at 10.30 so that gives us time to go through the papers together, but first of all let's go and see if Connie is here and ask her what Order she's seeking, although I've got a pretty good idea it's bound to be Suspension." The two lawyers went off to the GMC Counsels' Room.

***

Julian had walked the mile or so from the hotel to Oxford Rd, although it seemed much longer. It was in fact a fine, bright Manchester day, yesterday's drizzle having disappeared overnight, and he arrived in good time. He took the lift to the MPTS reception on the seventh floor and gave his name to the receptionist who ran her finger down a long list and looking up, informed him that both his solicitor and barrister were already there. He was then escorted to the conference room area.

As the door was opened for him the two lawyers got to their feet. "Good morning, Dr Bracken—I am Eugene Kennedy—we spoke last week and this is Jonathan Bliss of counsel—we've just been going through the papers."

"Good morning."

"Well let's sit down."

"I received this from Samantha Brown and her family this week—the patient in the Wonderbra manoeuvre allegation. It's also signed by her parents. I hope it will help."

Julian handed the letter over and Jonathan read it, then passed it to Eugene.

"We'll talk about this later in more detail because in fact it raises some important issues which Eugene and I have just been discussing and which we'll need to advise you about in a little more detail after the hearing.

"Now, as I understand it, from the notes of the meeting with Professor Somerville taken by Ms Lightfoot, you deny any inappropriate conduct?"

"Of course! Absolutely!"

"And therefore, any sexually motivated conduct?"

"Yes, indeed."

"Fine, we do need to get your detailed instructions on all three incidents, starting with the first, and I'm sorry but we're going to be asking you some difficult questions—in fact it may seem to you that we're not on your side, but I can assure you, we are. So, tell me something about the first incident with Nurse Keaveney."

"I really cannot recall anything about it other than vaguely remembering that I did trace a line along her back, but my intention was to help answer her question. She didn't say anything at the time So, you admit touching her back?"

"Well, yes, as far as I can remember."

"Doctor—can I ask you to think very carefully about your answers? She says you did—can you think of any reason why she would lie about that?"

Julian thought for a few moments. "Not really."

"What does not really mean?"

"No, I can't."

"That's better—we want to be decisive."

"The better answer to the question is, of course, only Nurse Keaveney can answer that question" observed Eugene.

"So, did you touch her with your finger?"

"Yes."

"Was she still in her scrubs?"

"Yes."

"And were you?"

"Yes."

"And you were alone?"

"Yes."

"How old would she be?"

"Thirty-something."

"Did you work together often, sometimes or hardly ever?"

"No more than with any other nurse."

"Can you think of any reason why she would complain about the way you touched her?"

"As I said before, no, but can I make it clear? I don't feel any sexual attraction for any of the nurses in the work place—the work is very demanding, without introducing unnecessary complications and when Nurse Keaveney showed an interest in the surgery, I suppose I responded in that way, but there was no sexual motive."

"Do you recall touching her bra-strap?"

"If she says I did then I must have—I just can't remember the detail."

"From your memory—can you recall touching her bare skin—as she alleges?"

"Well—I think I must have—just at the top of her back—at the nape of her neck—all I remember is being with her in the recovery room."

"Just the two of you? On your own?"

"Yes, Yes, and she asked me the question."

"In her statement she refers to a Whiteboard—wouldn't it have been better to illustrate the answer by a diagram? You know how touching can be misinterpreted these days."

"Well, looking back that would have been the sensible thing to do, but I just didn't think—it was entirely innocent."

"Well—you must have known you were going to touch her all along her back and her bra, even if through her scrubs top and you accept you touched her near her natal cleft, then her bra strap and bare skin between her shoulder blades and her hairline."

"Well, I suppose so, but it was only for a few seconds."

"Well, not according to her statement—she says the touching lasted for nine or ten seconds, which doesn't sound long but if you count it out, it is!"

"I can only tell you what I remember, although my partner is of the view that things happened differently—that she might have been making a play for me."

"You mean she was inviting you to touch her in a sexual way?"

"That's what my partner thinks."

"Why does she think that? I mean if you can't recall anything, other than what you've just told us then on what could she properly base that view?"

"I think it's a woman's intuition."

"Well, we need to be careful before we start launching that sort of missile at a crucial witness. I can't suggest anything like that unless we have something to justify it—something a little more concrete than intuition—it could back-fire on us significantly."

"I'm sorry, I can't recall any more details."

"OK, can we move on to the second allegation? The incident with the catheter. We'll need to see what the experts say in due course, but would you really become involved in checking the placing of a catheter? Especially with an experienced theatre sister like Sister Johnson—she says in her statement that she has 16 years' experience in surgery and has successfully placed hundreds of catheters in both males and females with no problems."

"At the time, I didn't know how experienced she was, but I had a bad experience once when I didn't check and the surgery was interrupted and eventually had to be abandoned because the table started to flood with urine—as you can imagine the lead surgeon wasn't very pleased at all. I was just in post and it was very embarrassing."

"Who was the surgeon? Can you remember?"

"Oh yes, very well—Professor Hunter—at Bart's."

"And do you have Professor Hunter's contact details? Is he still practising? Eugene will need to get a statement from him."

"He is still at Bart's—you can get hold of him there. I remember he was quite young for a prof—I saw him at a function about three months ago—I'm sure he'll be happy to confirm everything."

"Good—that will be a big help. Now, the third allegation—the "Wonderbra manoeuvre"—is this your own phrase?"

"No—I first heard it years ago in a lecture—it's a phrase that's bandied about a bit, but I can't recall exactly where—I've been to so many lectures and seminars over the last twenty years—it would be either here or in the States—I'm not being much help, am I?"

"Well, as I said, although it may not seem like it now, asking all these awkward questions, but we are on your side and if we don't ask the awkward questions now and the first time you are asked them is by GMC counsel in the hearing you'll be all over the place and you won't be creating a very good impression with the Tribunal."

"You keep referring to "the hearing" does that mean that it's not going to be over in the next few weeks.

"Our task is to ensure the best possible outcome for you—both at this hearing and at any fitness to practise hearing. There is a clear difference between what the three complainants are saying and what you're saying so those differences can only be resolved at a full hearing which will regrettably take many months to come around, but that does mean we will be able to have the best possible answers to these difficult questions well prepared and in good time.

"Now, it's nearly 11.30 and we start at noon. Earlier, we had a chat with the GMC barrister, Connie Cornwall, who has indicated to us that she will be asking the Panel for an Order of Suspension."

"Suspension?"

"I'm afraid so and I have to say, having seen the allegations and the statements that's no surprise and would be normal, given the guidelines—and to be honest with you—we will be doing rather well to avoid such an order—given that there are three separate allegations, but we will oppose the Order sought on the basis that you have an answer for all the allegations in that your actions were clinically justified in relation to both Patient A and Patient B and whilst on reflection your conduct towards Nurse Keaveney could be regarded as inappropriate, it was certainly not sexually motivated, and of course none of the allegations are yet proven so we will ask for no order—which will enable you to return to work."

"That would be a relief. This has all come completely out of the blue! I never thought I could be suspended.

"We will do our best to avoid suspension, but I cannot guarantee the outcome."

"Now, I just want to tell you about the procedure today—you will not be giving evidence—this hearing is dealt with *"on the papers"* that is the Tribunal will reach their decision after reading the papers and hearing Submissions from

GMC Counsel and then from me on your behalf—any member of the Tribunal can ask questions but they will be directed to me. I hope that makes it a little more bearable for you. They will retire to make their decision and then write their "Determination".

"The maximum length of the Order the IOT can make today is 18 months—during that time the GMC will need to conclude its investigations into your conduct and if necessary, hold a fitness to practise hearing, but even the 18 months can be extended by application to the High Court."

"And in the meantime, the GMC barrister is asking that I be suspended? For 18 months? Or even longer? Not able to work? At all? But they can't have taken a statement form James Broadley because he's mountain climbing in Nepal. He would have supported me, I'm sure. Does this hearing have to proceed today?"

"I'm afraid so—adjournments are hardly ever granted at this stage."

There was a knock on the door. It was the Tribunal Secretary.

Eugene opened the door.

"The Panel are ready for you. Would you all like to follow me?"

4:00 pm

Determination

"Dr Bracken, yours is a new case before the Interim Orders Tribunal of the Medical Practitioners Tribunal Service. We have listened very carefully to the very able and eloquent submissions made on behalf of the GMC by Ms Cornwall and those of Mr Bliss on your behalf, which were equally able and eloquent.

"Ms Cornwall began by outlining the case for the GMC—she informed us that these incidents all took place at Somerford Royal Infirmary, (SRI), where you have been in post for just over 10 years as a consultant anaesthetist. She submitted that the allegations, of which there are three, are very serious allegations indeed, all involving inappropriate and sexually motivated behaviour spanning some two years and that our responsibilities to maintain patient safety, uphold proper standards and public confidence in the regulation of the medical profession are engaged. She submitted that each allegation alone calls into question your fitness to practise and that when added together they present an even more serious pattern of sustained and pre-meditated misconduct.

"She informed us that there are two allegations of inappropriate and sexually motivated touching—one of an anaesthetised teenager—Patient A's—breasts for a prolonged period of time—and the second involves unnecessary touching of a young nurse, who the GMC says was at the time a junior colleague of yours and so especially vulnerable. There is also an allegation of voyeurism in relation to Patient B, being once again an anaesthetised female patient—we noted this time the object of your attention was the patient's pubic area. SRI is continuing to investigate the concerns raised about your conduct.

"Ms Cornwall submitted that an order of suspension is necessary under s.41(A) of the Medical Act to protect members of the public and patients and to uphold proper standards and maintain public confidence in the regulation of the medical profession—that if no action was taken and you were allowed to continue working without restriction, public confidence in the regulation of the medical profession would be seriously undermined. She further submitted that an order was necessary in the public interest.

"Additionally, Ms Cornwall submitted that if these allegations, each of which she reiterated, calls into question your fitness to practise are proven, they involve a serious breach of trust and that given the apparent lack of insight demonstrated by your denial of these allegations, there is a real risk of repetition and it is therefore not only in the public interest but also in your own interests that an order be made.

"Mr Bliss, on your behalf, told us that the allegations are all denied and that no order was necessary or desirable and reminded us that the evidence is, as yet, untested and that it is not our task to make findings of fact. He informed us that the practice of re-positioning soft tissue, particularly breast tissue, is clinically necessary in order to avoid tissue necrosis and that you have practised as a consultant anaesthetist for nearly twelve years without criticism of your clinical skills, judgement or integrity.

"He informed us that, once anaesthetised, the patient was your responsibility and submitted that it was good medical practice to check that catheters were being correctly placed in the urethra to avoid leakage from the bladder, accidental tears, post-operative soreness and infection. He outlined a previous incident in which you were involved when you say you were severely criticised, for failing to ensure a catheter was properly placed.

"He submitted that all the allegations needed to be considered separately on their own facts and warned against, at this stage where the allegations remain unproven, from aggregating them and thus adversely and unfairly affecting your position. He pointed out that the allegation regarding Nurse Keaveney is in an entirely different category from the other two allegations although he conceded on your behalf that this touching could well be regarded in retrospect, as inappropriate.

"He drew our attention to three testimonials from eminent colleagues who are all aware of the nature of these allegations and yet spoke as to your integrity and professionalism. He reminded us that we need to balance the public interest and your interests—particularly two things—the de-skilling which will inevitably take place and the irreparable harm that would be done to your reputation if an order of suspension or indeed conditions were made.

"He submitted that, balancing your interests and the public interest that no order was necessary or indeed desirable."

Decision

"We have exercised our own independent judgment. We first considered whether to make no order but concluded that the allegations are so serious that public confidence would be seriously undermined if a doctor, facing these three allegations was allowed to practise unrestricted, pending the conclusion of the GMC's investigation.

"We then considered whether an order of conditions would be appropriate, bearing in mind that any conditions should be proportionate, measurable, workable and enforceable. We noted, with considerable concern, that one of these allegations, involving Patient A, took place in the presence of several colleagues, including two surgeons and another, relating to Patient B, in the presence of an experienced theatre Sister, which leads us to conclude that conditions aimed at introducing a regime of supervision of your work by colleagues would be unworkable and unenforceable.

"We further noted that there are three separate allegations and that two come from experienced nursing staff and the third from a very experienced theatre sister.

"We therefore concluded that the only appropriate order we can make is an order of suspension. An order of suspension is desirable and necessary to mark the seriousness of these allegations, to protect patients and the public and to maintain public confidence in the regulation of the medical profession and is in your own interests. We reiterate that this order is not meant to be punitive and is a neutral step pending the outcome of the GMC's investigation and any fitness to practise hearing.

"Ms Cornwall asked for an order of suspension of 18 months duration, but we agree with Mr Bliss that this investigation is one that ought to be concluded within a shorter period. We therefore make an order of suspension of your registration for 12 months, during which time we hope that the GMC will conclude their investigations as soon as possible and if there is a referral to a fitness to practise hearing, that hearing will take place as soon as practically possible.

"Dr Bracken, thank you for attending today. This concludes your hearing. You will receive a copy of this Determination from the Tribunal Clerk, if you would be kind enough to wait in your conference room."

Julian was stunned. He and the two lawyers returned to their conference room.

"Shall I get some coffee?"

"Please Eugene."

Eugene returned with three coffees and their copies of the Determination. After a few minutes of silence, Jonathan said, "I'm sorry doctor—I'm sure you're very disappointed."

"I'm devastated—is there any way we can overturn this decision? Can I appeal?"

"Technically yes—we can appeal the decision but—it would only be overturned if we could demonstrate that the suspension was an order that no reasonable tribunal could have made and on the allegations, we've heard about, an order of suspension, whilst it may seem harsh to you, was not unreasonable.

"Just to confirm—the order is now effective so you will not be able to return to work, until the outcome of the fitness to practise hearing."

Julian nodded.

"We now need to discuss the next steps. Eugene will write to you to confirm everything. Although 12 months seems a long time it will soon come around.

"I am sure that you're very disappointed, but this is a temporary order and although it will be of little comfort it will not have any influence on the outcome of any fitness to practise hearing. That will be a fresh hearing, where you will be able to give evidence and we will be able to cross-examine witnesses.

"The Case Management Protocol, which consists of telephone conferences with both GMC Legal and the MPTS will now be initiated, aimed at ensuring an early hearing date and addressing matters such as which witnesses are required to attend to be cross-examined and which witnesses' evidence can be agreed. Eugene will participate in the Case Management telephone conferences on your behalf and update both of us.

"Following on from our previous discussions Eugene will contact Professor Hunter and arrange to take a statement from him regarding the operation that was interrupted because of the improperly placed catheter. Did you say his first name is James?"

"Yes—James Maxwell Hunter."

"Perhaps you can review your diaries and CPD lecture hand-outs to try to recall where you first heard the expression "Wonderbra manoeuvre" so that we can obtain a statement from the author of that phrase to rebut any suggestion that you invented it "for your own gratification" which I'm sure will be suggested at the full hearing by the GMC.

"We will also need an expert witness report from a suitably qualified anaesthetist—I'm sure you will know plenty of them, but we need to ensure impartiality, so Eugene and I will look through our data-bases—we did a case together a few years ago and we used a Professor Andrew Whiteman who was excellent—have you heard of him?"

"Yes—but only by reputation—I think he practises in the Nottingham area."

"That's right—so you have no objection to Eugene instructing him to provide an expert report on your behalf?"

"No, none."

"Well, now we need to discuss the letter from Samantha Brown's family and unfortunately there is no easy way to advise you about this other than give you the hard facts. I'm afraid there is more bad news—potentially at least."

"How can it get any worse? Is the letter from the Brown family of no use?"

"I'm afraid only as a source of comfort but not evidentially—the patient was anaesthetised so will not be able to give evidence about what happened, one way or the other—and of course her parents whist supportive, were not present, but the real problem here, which is why I said things could get much worse, is that if those allegations are found proven, then irrespective of what the patient—or her parents think the hospital, or the GMC could refer all three allegations to the police or Nurse Keaveney and Sister Johnson could make complaints of sexual assault and voyeurism to the police. I'm sorry to be so negative but we have an obligation to advise you of your position.

"Currently, these allegations are before the MPTS—your professional regulatory body, whose powers in relation to sanctions extend to imposing conditions, a period of suspension or erasure—in other words professional sanctions against you as a doctor.

"However, if proven and a complaint to the police follows, then the allegations could form the basis of criminal charges under the Sexual Offences Act, if the police become involved. If they do I'm afraid the outcome might be very different."

Julian was listening in disbelief.

"In what way? What's the worst outcome?"

"Well, the Domesday scenario is, if you were convicted and I stress if, on all three charges they would cross what we call the custody threshold so the outcome would be a prison sentence I'm afraid and an immediate one too—given the current Sentencing Guidelines I can't see any judge suspending such a sentence."

"How long?"

"Between three and four years."

"Three and four years! Jesus!"

"However—let's not get carried away—the standard of proof is different—before the MPTS, the standard is the lower one—on the balance of probabilities—but in criminal proceedings the higher standard of beyond reasonable doubt is required.

Much will depend on the outcome of the substantive fitness to practise hearing. If the GMC fail to prove their case to the lower standard, then, logically, unless further evidence comes to light the Crown Prosecution Service, will be unlikely to begin a criminal prosecution. Now, one final piece of advice—you may be photographed when you leave."

"So, is this going to be reported in the papers?"

"Well, not today's hearing, which was in private, but I'm afraid this is just the sort of case that will attract publicity—but they will wait until the fitness to practise hearing, which will be in public, but they might have sent a photographer today to get some pictures for future use."

Julian's stomach turned.

"On the photographing issue—if they want a photo—they'll get one, so give them one—and make it your best one—look as dignified as you can—you've nothing to hide—don't try to pull a coat over your head, run down the nearest alley or hide behind a lamp-post—you'll just look silly—and worse—guilty."

"That's good advice from Eugene—I know they may ambush you but try to give them your "best side"."

Chapter Twenty-Seven

Julian left St James's Buildings in silent despair and began his walk back to the hotel. He found it difficult to believe he was not only now suspended from work but if the hearing went badly, could face criminal prosecutions for sexual assaults, voyeurism and if convicted immediate imprisonment—and Saoirse—the one person who could provide him with any comfort was thousands of miles away in New York.

When he had set out this morning, he had hoped, apparently naively, that by now it would all have been over.

As he stopped at traffic lights, waiting for the walking green, he heard a shout, "Dr Bracken!"

He turned and a photographer with a telephoto lens began snapping away at him from the pavement opposite—his camera shutter click-click-clicking—tut-tut-tutting at Julian.

He dreaded telling Saoirse—she too had hoped it would all be over and had put all her trust in him once and now he would have to tell her the outcome of today's hearing and what might happen if the police became involved—just two weeks ago everything seemed perfect, but now!

He made his way back to the Hilton Hotel and began to pack—he would speak to Saoirse before he checked out when he had had time to collect his thoughts. He sat down. Nervously, he Googled "Bristol Evening News—Dr Julian Bracken"—thankfully nothing came up.

He saw an incoming call, from Saoirse.

"Hi—how did it go?"

"Badly—I've been suspended for 12 months, so I can't go back to work and my lawyers raised other problems that I'd not even dreamt about. I was just about to call you before checking out and driving back to Bristol."

"I'm so sorry to hear that but, don't check out—I've just spoken to my brother Patrick—he's the doctor in Leicester—my mother appears to have taken a turn for the worst so Aoife's trying to get me on a flight back this evening—there's one at around 7.00pm—if she can get me on that flight then I'll be in Manchester by about 6.30 tomorrow morning and I'll come straight to the Hilton. Patrick told me my brother James has managed to get an afternoon flight out of Philadelphia. Can you wait for me? Unless you have to get back to Bristol?"

"No, no—it would be so nice to see you after the day I've had. If you text me your flight number I'll track it—I can pick you up from Manchester airport."

"And then, perhaps you could come along with me to see Mum? If you don't mind? I'd like you to meet her, despite her illness."

"No, not at all—I'd love to meet her. How serious is it?"

"I think it's bad, Patrick told me to get there as soon as possible, which I think can only mean one thing—I just hope I make it—she's only 85 but has been somewhat frail for some time now so we'll just need to see what the Matron at the home tells us. She's been seen by the doctor, so we'll find out more tomorrow. She had a bad fall one evening about a year ago, when she was getting some washing in from the back yard. She spent the night out there, on the floor before she was discovered by Esther who lives next door.

"She was in MRI three weeks, until we managed to get her a place at the Primrose Bank Care Home. The Infirmary told us she'd had several minor strokes in the last few years. It was fortunate that it was a very mild night when she had her fall otherwise, she might not have survived.

"Oh—I've just seen Aoife's email—she's got me on the flight—I'll text you the flight number—can we talk about the GMC tomorrow? I'm sorry about your news—there must be something your lawyers can do—can't wait to see you."

"Me too."

"See you tomorrow morning."

As Julian put his phone down, he noticed an incoming email—from Eugene Kennedy:

Dear Dr Bracken,

Re GMC v Yourself

I have just spoken to Professor Hunter's secretary at St Bart's. I thought I'd better let you know, unfortunately, Professor Hunter died from a heart attack on Christmas Day—in fact his obituary was in The Times on January 6th—copy attached.

(You were indeed right about him—I quote "he demanded the highest standards for both himself and his students, yet at the same time was a man of great compassion and conviviality—at his regular house parties, he was a most congenial host, dispensing copious amounts of vintage champagne"

Eugene.

Julian sat down on the bed, closed his eyes and let out a long sigh."For fuck`s sake!"

Chapter Twenty-Eight

THE PRIMROSE BANK CARE HOME
SOUTH MANCHESTER

7.30 am
2 February

Saoirse stepped back down the steps after ringing the doorbell and waited. After a few minutes, a friendly looking woman in a suit came into the porch and opened the front door.

"How are you Saoirse?"

"I'm fine thanks Maria—this is my partner Julian—how's Mum?"

"Hello Julian. Just the same love—very weak I'm afraid—you've just missed your brothers—they've gone home for a few hours' sleep. I said I'd call them if there was any change—she's in her room—do you want to go through? She was asleep a few minutes ago—you know the way. Will you just sign the visitors' book for me, Julian dear?"

They passed through the TV lounge where the volume was deafening, negotiating their way around several Zimmer frames and down the corridor to Saoirse's mother's room—identified by her name and a photograph of a younger Mary Fitzgerald on the door—on her wedding day with Dermot and various family photographs. A nurse was just leaving her room.

"Hello Saoirse—she's very tired."

Mary Fitzgerald was sat up in bed, supported by several pillows, her pale, white skin was stretched thinly across her forehead and cheekbones so that Julian could see the skull and jaw beneath.

"Hi Mum—it's me—Saoirse."

She opened her eyes, looked at Saoirse and smiled weakly. Mrs Fitzgerald spoke in a barely audible whisper, "Oh you've grown so much—wait until your father sees you—he'll be home in a minute. Who's this?"

Saoirse sat down and took her mother's hand. "This is Julian—my partner."

"Hello."

"Hello Mrs Fitzgerald."

"And what do you do?"

"I'm a doctor."

"Oh, I see." She looked at Saoirse. "You should have married that Kevin Finney—he was very keen on you."

"Well, I know, but he never asked me Mum—and we were only fourteen."

"Oh, I see."

Mrs Fitzgerald closed her eyes and eased back onto her pillow. She swallowed slowly and with a wince.

"Would you like some water Mum?"

"Yes please."

Saoirse held a cup up to her mother's lips and Mary Fitzgerald took a tiny sip without opening her eyes.

After a few minutes, she opened her eyes.

"Have you finished the welding yet?"

"No Mum, I don't do any welding—I work in fashion—do you remember now?"

"Fashion? I never knew that."

"Yes Mum—all my life."

"Oh, I see. Well, you should have said." After a few minutes pause, she continued, "You've just missed Richard Branson and Ted Heath—such nice men—they said they would come back tomorrow and bring some cakes. Do you know who was with them?"

"No Mum, who was it?"

"Pope John XXIII, of course." After a few minutes silence, Mrs Fitzgerald looked back up to the ceiling. "Look at the tiny birds? Look! Up there—one, two, three—aren't they pretty?"

"Yes Mum."

"Your father is going for an interview tomorrow—for promotion at work—Danny's going with him—but if he doesn't pass the interview do you know what we've got to do?"

"No Mum."

"We've all got to join the Communist Party and vote for Mr Khrushchev."

"I don't think it will come to that Mum."

"How are your children?"

Saoirse looked at Julian and shook her head slightly. Julian smiled gently.

"All fine thanks Mum."

"It's five now isn't it."

"Yes, Mum."

"Good! There's a family of five just moved in upstairs—a family of dwarves—and the mother and father can't have taught the children how to cross the road—you remember the Green Cross Code—one of them will get run over and that will be the end of that! Have you come to take me home?"

"No Mum—this is your home now."

"Is it?"

"I didn't ask to be here. Well, it's just the same as where I used to live and it's half-past five already—your father should be home soon then—as soon as he gets the nod from John. He'll be so glad to see you. Are you staying? I've made some cakes."

"Yes—of course Mum—we'd love to stay."

"Your father and brothers will be so pleased to see you. They'll be home soon—home from work and school. That'll be nice. It'll be lovely. Just like a family again!"

Mrs Fitzgerald smiled then closed her eyes and leant back onto her pillow. After a few minutes her breathing slowed. She moved her head to one side and didn't move again.

Julian waited a while and then took Saoirse's hands in his and whispered, "I think she's passed away. Shall I get the Matron?"

Saoirse shook her head, her eyes full of tears. She waited and then leant in, towards Julian and whispered, "When Mum was discharged from hospital after her fall and came here she was so weak—there's a DNR in place."

"Oh, I'm so sorry Saoirse." He put his arms around her.

"Can we just sit with her for a while?"

"Of course."

Chapter Twenty-Nine

**HILTON HOTEL
DEANSGATE
MANCHESTER**

**12:30pm
Tuesday 2nd of February**

"James's family are on their way from Philadelphia—we'll need to go and see Father Paddy tomorrow with Kevin and Patrick. I'm so sorry—I've been pre-occupied with Mum. So, is there is any prospect of overturning the decision to suspend you?"

"No, I asked and the answer was technically yes, but practically no and to make matters worse I got an email from my solicitor Eugene Kennedy yesterday afternoon, after the hearing saying that Prof Hunter died from a heart attack on Christmas Day. So—Professor Hunter is dead, I can't remember the detail of the incident with Nurse Keaveney, and I can't remember when I first heard of the Wonderbra manoeuvre."

"But, I've got some even worse news—my lawyers are concerned that if any of the allegations are proven at the main hearing then that may open up the possibility of criminal charges and—a prison sentence, measured in years—between three and four—and on release the Sex Offender's Register, a Sexual Harm Prevention Order and other orders—including a restriction on travel abroad."

"Saoirse, do you really want to be coming up to a prison to visit me with our two-year-old and then have travel restrictions on our holidays together? And on top of all that I was photographed, just after I left the MPTS building, so at some stage it will be all over the papers—and maybe the TV. So, I need to ask you again if you're prepared to stand by me? I'll understand if you aren't."

"Julian—of course I am—I believed you in Dublin when you told me what happened and as far as I'm concerned nothing has changed—it won't come to that—honestly—believe me—and more importantly—believe in yourself!"

After a few moments thought, Julian got up and embraced Saoirse. "I don't know how I would have managed without you—it was a miracle we met."

"Well sort of!" Saoirse smiled—and then widened her eyes at him.

"Oh God Saoirse! I love you so much. You can make me laugh even now."

"Right! I know you were unsuccessful yesterday morning and you're disappointed but let's think positively—I presume there's nothing to stop you from travelling whilst this order is in force?"

"No, but my lawyers said it would be wise to inform the Trust if I was going to be abroad."

"So, come and live with me—in Dublin—it will take your mind off things—it sounds like you'll have nothing to do and besides we can be together—like we said we both wanted to be—remember? And I can look after you."

Julian couldn't think of a reason to say no.

"Yes—you're right."

"Let's get some fresh air and maybe some lunch—before the jet-lag kicks in."

2.30 pm Tuesday, 2 February
Hilton Hotel
Manchester

There was a gentle knock on the bedroom door and when Saoirse answered a smartly dressed young woman asked for Miss Saoirse Fitzgerald.

"That's me."

"I'm from Jones, Hughes and O'Flynn solicitors—I'm Mr O'Flynn's trainee—Mr O'Flynn told me to ask to see your passport, if you don't mind, please."

"Of course—here it is."

"Thank you—I've been asked to give you this." She handed Saoirse an envelope marked.

BY HAND—PRIVATE & CONFIDENTIAL—ADDRESSEE ONLY
FAO MISS SAOIRSE FITZGERALD
C/O THE HILTON HOTEL DEANSGATE MANCHESTER
FROM—JONES, HUGHES AND ASHA SOLICITORS LLP

"Thank you."

"And also asked to ask you to sign this receipt please, if you don't mind?"

"Yes, of course."

The girl stepped back.

"I'm Kevin Finney's daughter—my Dad said to say he was sorry to hear about your Mother. Sorry for your troubles."

"That's very kind of him—please say hello and thank him—from me."

Saoirse paused.

"Do you have any sisters or brothers?"

"Yes—two of each."

"And would I know your Mum?"

"You might—she was at St Cuthbert's but a few years below you and my Dad—she was called Sarah Finnigan then."

"Yes—I remember her—she was good at hockey. Will you remember me to her also? And give them my best wishes?"

"I will. Thank you, Miss Fitzgerald."

Saoirse closed the door and leant against it for a few moments with tears in her eyes. She opened the envelope and took out various documents—a letter, a copy Will, several handwritten pages, which looked like notes and an old, faded sealed envelope.

BY HAND

3 February 2016

Dear Miss Fitzgerald,

I was sorry to hear of your mother's passing away—Maria telephoned me this morning and told me you were staying at the Hilton—please accept my sincere condolences.

We are the executors of your late mother's estate and are currently engaged in obtaining probate of her will—a copy of which is attached—copies have also been forwarded to your three brothers, Patrick, Kevin and James as all four of you will share equally in your late mother's estate, apart from a specific bequest to you of her wedding and engagement rings and your father's wedding ring, which we will forward to you when we have received the Grant of Probate.

We have been holding the enclosed sealed envelope addressed to you on your mother's express instructions to forward it to you immediately on her death.

Please do not hesitate to contact me if there is anything you wish to discuss or have any questions.

Yours sincerely,
JONES, HUGHES AND O'FLYNN SOLICITORS LLP
BEECH ROAD
CHORLTON-CUM-HARDY
MANCHESTER 21

Saoirse recognised her mother's handwriting on the envelope *Saoirse* and opened the envelope and began to read.

344 Claremont Road
Moss Side
Manchester
15 April 2008

Dear Saoirse,

I have just returned from seeing Dr Cassidy, who told me that that I have early signs of Alzheimer's—he cannot say when and how quickly the condition will progress, but it seems likely that at some stage my mind and memory will fail me, so before they do I wanted to say how much your father and I loved you all and that I am sorry that I couldn't bring myself to talk about your father's death and answer your questions—the ones you were always asking me after your father died. So, I will answer them now.

I didn't want to talk about your father's death because it wasn't a silly bet or dare after a few drinks, like your brothers told you and I let you all carry on believing—it was me—I persuaded him to go to Tenerife for the golf with his friends—I didn't just persuade him—I bought his ticket and insisted he went—he always had a real fear of flying—and how right he was.

I got his friend, Danny Kilmartin to take me down to the travel agents on Wilmslow Rd and I booked the flight for your father as a surprise—I took Danny because he had all the flight and hotel details—if I hadn't booked him on that flight he would still be alive today and you would have had a father to spoil you with his love all these years—he loved you so much. You all lost a wonderful father and I lost a wonderful husband. I have regretted what I did every day of my life since.

He didn't want to leave you—not even for a day but he had been working such long hours—even over Easter that year and I could see he needed a break.

He even wanted to work on Good Friday, but I put my foot down at that—he was dead on his feet—I told him you would still be here when he came back—but of course he didn't come back and it was all my fault. I could never forgive myself for buying that ticket—I sent him to his death—and I didn't want anyone to know because I was afraid everyone would blame me.

Saoirse, you must have known that you were the apple of his eye—he had almost given up hope of a daughter when I became pregnant with you—I was 45 and I knew straightaway I was carrying a girl—just knew—it was so different from your brothers—I was so sick! Every morning, for the first few months! You were a determined child—even then!

Your father was overjoyed—he had always wanted a daughter to spoil—in a nice way—even before your first birthday he was planning your wedding and you will remember he took you to buy your St Cuthbert's Prep School uniform months before you'd started there. He loved to see you trying it on—he felt he'd achieved something—giving all of you an education he never had.

He was right to call you special—with those eyes of yours—he thought it was a miracle—never stopped telling people about you and your eyes. He was the happiest I've ever seen him when you were sat on his knee, playing games before bedtime.

He would have been so proud of you and what you have achieved—flying all over the world—just like you said you would.-and the struggles he had with you to put on matching socks—he would come into the kitchen in the mornings, close the door behind him bursting with laughter, saying you didn't want to be posh and live in Cheshire! She'll grow up to be bold he would say.

As to your school fees—I really don't know to this day who paid them, but I would probably guess they were paid by John Kavanagh—your father's boss. He was the only one who knew what I'd done apart from Danny Kilmartin—and he died on the plane alongside your father.

I had to speak to John to arrange for the time off work for your father—it was all meant to be a nice surprise but it went horribly wrong. I overheard your brothers telling you that they couldn't believe your father had got on an airplane and it must have been a silly bet, made in drink, but it wasn't—it was me—I made him do it—may God forgive me!

John tried to persuade me that I wasn't to blame but I was so worried that you and your brothers might not see it that way, I made him promise never to even talk about it and he never did. He kept his promise and he never spoke about it ever again—not even to me. I'm sure you'll want to ask him and I can't have any objection now because if it was him, you and I owe him a great deal.

When the compensation eventually came through, John tried to persuade me to move to Cheshire or somewhere but I had all my friends in the Moss and of course I didn't want you to think I was turning "posh"—I would have missed popping next door to have some of Esther's goat stew, so I put it to one side—to help you through college—it was what your father would have wanted.

Whenever you read this I hope you will be sure that your father and I loved you all—I want you to know that because there will come a time when I will not even know what it means or why or when to say it because I have no idea what awaits me—except Dr Cassidy has told me that my mind and memory will desert me at some stage, so I have already made an appointment with Simon Jones at your father's solicitors on Beech Road to make my will, while I still can. I will take this letter with me.

I will leave you my engagement and wedding rings for when you marry—as I'm sure you will one day—perhaps you can wear them around your neck under your wedding dress as I'm sure you're fiancé will want to give you some of your own—and also you father's wedding ring which was the only item of his recovered from Mount Esperanza—funny that they told me Esperanza means "hope"—and I still hoped that in some way he was alive—hoped he had missed the flight—until they told me that they'd recovered a wedding ring with the date of our wedding inscribed on it—a wedding ring that was meant to bring love and hope, not despair—so I would like that—it would be a comfort for me to know that a little part of him will be close to you—as it has been to me.

I have written down all my recipes for the cakes you and your brothers enjoyed so much—chocolate eclairs, Savoy cake, maids of honour, vanilla cake, coconut macaroons—they're all there—so, please God, you can make them for your children.

The solicitors will send you and your brothers a copy of my will with this letter—what is left of the compensation and the proceeds of sale of the house on Claremont Rd is to be shared equally between you and them.

Finally, can you please forgive me? Or at least, not think too badly of me? I hope you can.

All my love,
Mum.

Chapter Thirty

**THE IRISH CLUB
CHORLTON-CUM-HARDY
MANCHESTER**

**4:00pm
Wednesday 3rd of February**

Chorlton Irish Club was a series of well-maintained extensions added, as the Irish community in south Manchester expanded and assimilated, to what had been a large, detached Victorian villa. The size of the neatly tarmacked car park also suggested that the Club was well supported.

The rear entrance was open and Julian and Saoirse walked through to be confronted by a larger-than-life sized statue of Our Lady of Lourdes—arms held wide in welcome.

Amongst the notices for televised GAA finals, broadcast live from Croke Park, open days at St Cuthbert's, Notre Dame College for Girls and St Boniface's College for Boys and a "For Sale" board of various items ranging from Irish dance costumes to pre-owned JCBs and other heavy plant and machinery was a poster for:

BOP-LOCAL—EVERY LAST FRIDAY FROM 10.00 PM 'TIL LATE

The DJs included local TV and film celebrities and members of the Manchester bands of the '80s. This month Mike Joyce of *The Smiths* was the guest DJ, followed by Maxine Peake in March.

Underneath was pinned a flyer for:

OUR LADY & ST JOHN'S BOXING CLUB
TRAINING EVERY THURSDAY AT THE PARISH CENTRE

CONTACT SISTER FRANCIS AT THE SISTERS OF MERCY, HIGH LANE CONVENT

A mobile telephone number was alongside.

Saoirse and Julian could hear voices from within the bar area and pushing the door open stepped in.

There were pendants, flags, pennants and pictures of Gaelic football and hurling teams and the two Manchester football clubs—City and United, of George Best, Kevin Moran and Sir Alex Ferguson, presenting cups and other trophies to football teams and players of various ages in green and white hooped strip and a giant, framed, black and white photograph of a beaming Sir Matt Busby, clasping the European Cup amongst a cheering crowd of bleary-eyed club members—with the very same statue of Our Lady of Lourdes looking on in the background.

They approached the barman, a giant of a man with red hair and freckles on his hairy forearms, who was methodically polishing already shiny pint glasses. They knew how to serve a pint of Guinness at Chorlton Irsih!

"Father Paddy told us John Kavanagh might be in the club."

Continuing to polish, he nodded and then shouted across the bar, "Big John—there's a fella here askin' after yer."

"Is that so?" Came a reply from a jovial looking, well-built man in his seventies. Well, you've found him—and at the right time—we've just finished our meeting.

Big John was dressed immaculately in a navy-blue suit, pale blue shirt with double cuffs and a red silk tie. He was wearing highly polished black Oxford brogues. He offered his hand which Julian took—the hand was enormous—and the grip, like iron.

"John Kavanagh—pleased to make your acquaintance my lady and gentleman—and to whom do I have the pleasure of speaking?"

"I'm Saoirse Fitzgerald—Dermot Fitzgerald's daughter and this is my partner—Julian Bracken."

The big man's face broke out into a huge smile. "Saoirse Fitzgerald—I haven't seen you since you were a little girl—come here!" Saoirse disappeared in a bear-hug for a few seconds. "I should have recognised you from the eyes—Dermot never stopped talking about you and those eyes—you've grown into such a beautiful woman—let me have another look at you—come here, let's sit down. Now, you're taking me back." Big John fell silent and sat back into his chair. "Dermot—*Irish by birth and Cork by the Grace of God*! Fitzgerald—your father was my right-hand man for twenty years—we went through thick and thin together.

"There he is, up there, in the photograph with Matt and the European Cup that week-end in May '68. Matt brought the cup down here on the Saturday night and we filled it full of Jameson's then drank it dry. The Irish lads Shay, Tony and Georgie played their part in winning it for Matt after what happened at Munich—they wanted to win it for him—and for the people of Manchester—to show we all belonged.

"You were so young when Dermot was killed—they'd gone on a golfing break—he'd been working long, long hours for weeks on end—we'd won big contracts for motorway extensions and then that happened—terrible news—I couldn't believe it—just couldn't believe it."

Big John paused then looked up. "And what have you been doing with yourself? You look as pretty as a picture."

"Well, after Cuthbert's I graduated from college in fashion and design and I've been working in the fashion sector since then—I'm living and working in Dublin now."

"So, you made the trip back to work in Ireland? Your father would have been pleased at that. And who do you work for there?"

"A fashion-house called Cristiano a Fiorentina—we're based in the International Financial Services Centre."

"I know it—just near Connolly St Station, and creating jobs for others there by the sound of it?"

"Yes—quite a few—in fact last year we recruited a new Irish designer through the work we're doing helping the British Embassy in Dublin to promote trade between the Republic and the UK."

"And more importantly keeping the Good Friday Agreement going—something dear to my heart. Your father would have been very, very proud of you." Big John paused. "And your brothers?"

"Patrick is a professor at Leicester Royal Infirmary—he's a paediatrician and specialises in leukaemia, James lives in Pennsylvania and works for a large pharmaceutical company near Princeton in their research and development department—working on cancer drugs and Kevin manages tours for rock bands."

"That's nice to know—your Mum kept me updated until she became ill, so I've lost track of all of you over the last few years, even though Vera and I visited her she didn't know us. Your mother and father would have been proud of all of you—putting something back. And what brings you here? To Manchester? To the Irish Club?"

"I came to thank you—because I now know it was you who paid my school fees—so I could stay at St Cuthbert's."

"I see—and what makes you think that?"

Saoirse took her mother's letter from her handbag and passed it across the table.

John Kavanagh picked it up and began to read—as he read, tears silently filled his eyes. After he handed it back to Saoirse. he slowly placed his head into his huge rough-skinned hands.

After a long pause, he carried on, "Well now, I'm sorry for your trouble. I hadn't heard. When was this?"

"Yesterday morning, Julian and I were with her at the end—it was very peaceful."

"I'll have to tell Vera—she'll be very upset."

"I couldn't have started at St Cuthbert's Prep and gone on to the College without your kindness I wouldn't be here today—you were very, very generous."

"Well, there's no point in keeping the secret anymore now—your mother blamed herself so much—I tried to make her see sense, but she was beside herself with grief and guilt—she was never the same. She convinced herself that everyone, including you and your brothers would blame her. She knew that Dermot was so afraid of flying—but she insisted he go—she couldn't have known what would happen—no one could."

"I told her everyone would understand—especially you and your brothers, but she wouldn't have it and made me promise never to tell anyone and so I didn't—even though I knew she was wrong. I had to respect her wishes."

After a few moments' silence, Saoirse continued, "I want to thank you so much for what you did for me. I couldn't have achieved what I have without my education and I have you to thank for that."

"Well, what else could I do? And from what you tell me it was money well spent. Your father had worked for me for nearly twenty years. He and your mother paid to put your brothers through school—he would have paid for you too—we were both determined that our children wouldn't need to work with their hands—he wanted you to be free to choose what you did in life—that's why he called you Saoirse.

"You were a very late surprise after all the boys—he loved you so much—like your mother said in her letter—didn't like to spend time away from you—would hurry home to you as soon as the work was all organised for the next day—when he'd everything ship-shape I would give him the nod—he was a tower of strength to me. I couldn't have survived without your father—I nearly didn't."

"I could have done with him when the bombs went off in the 90's and the bricks started coming through the office and the Club windows. After the Arndale bomb it was worse—far worse. It could have gone either way.

"There were threatening, abusive phone calls, but as you know the Irish have been around Manchester for a few generations and there aren't many people in Manchester who are far away from Irish blood, so the hotheads and bully-boys didn't get their way.

" Fortunately, we had friends at the City Council and although Manchester was Labour and the Conservatives were in power at Westminster they put aside their differences to rebuild Manchester. Michael Heseltine, Richard Leese, Graham Stringer were big supporters and made a public visit to the Club. My friend, Sir David Trippier was very supportive, helping to recreate Manchester city centre. The Irish Association organised a protest march against the bombing."

"So, it was just a little something to repay his loyalty when the times were rough for us Irish in Manchester and we had to stick together—you know an act of kindness makes its way all around the world.

"We were lucky—this country gave me and your father an opportunity for which I will always be grateful—I arrived here from County Mayo with nothing except my *"one-man operated earth-excavator"* and I couldn't have done it without your father—so, since we sold out, I've spent my time trying to put something back—you have to put aside your differences and put something back, getting Westminster, Stormont and Leinster House talking to each other— like you and your brothers, all a credit to your mother and father—are doing the same—and so it gets passed on—it gets passed on."

"And I have you to thank for that John—I'm ever so grateful."

"You're welcome Saoirse—most welcome—you'll be sure to let me know when the funeral is?"

"Oh, it's on Friday at 11.00am—we're just waiting for James's family to fly in tomorrow afternoon from Philadelphia—we all went to see Father Paddy at St John's this morning—it was Father Paddy who told us we would probably find you here this afternoon."

"Ah, well Father Paddy will give her a good send-off for sure."

Saoirse stood up and disappeared in another bear-hug.

Big John gripped Julian's hand again.

"Goodbye Mr Kavanagh—it's been a real pleasure meeting you."

"And you, Julian."

Chapter Thirty-One

OUR LADY & ST JOHN'S CHURCH
CHORLTON-CUM-HARDY
MANCHESTER

1:00am
Friday 5th of February

Father Paddy Kinsella, in black cope, took up his position at the head of Mary Fitzgerald's bier, flanked by Mary Fitzgerald's two youngest grandsons, Dominic and Clement, a little jet-lagged and in borrowed funeral vestments. The congregation rose in respect—for Father Paddy and for the deceased. Father Paddy began:

"The sorrow of death encompassed me

And the pains of hell came about me

Kyrie eleison

Christe eleison

Kyrie eleison

Enter not into judgement O Lord with thy servant for in thy sight shall no man living be justified except thou grant unto us remission of all our sins. Therefore, we beseech thee, let not the sentence of thy judgment fall upon her whom the faithful prayer of Christian people commendeth unto thee: but by the succour of thy grace, let her, who, while she lived, was sealed with the sign of the Holy Trinity, be found worthy to escape avenging judgment. Through Christ Our Lord.

Amen."

Father Paddy took the aspergillum, offered by Dominic and slowly circled Mary Fitzgerald's bier, sprinkling her coffin with holy water—three times on the right, and three times on the left—then replaced it in the aspersorium. He took the thurible from Clement and slowly circling, incensed her coffin, again, three times on the right and three times on the left. He handed the thurible back to Clement.

He stepped back and bowed solemnly to Mary Fitzgerald's three sons, Patrick, James and Kevin and her three eldest grandsons, Benedict, Francis and Xavier, who all moved forward and taking their places on either side, lifted her coffin from the bier onto their shoulders then linked their arms under the coffin.

They gently turned Mary around so that her feet would lead her down the aisle of her parish church one final time. Julian put his arm around Saoirse's waist and pulled her into him.

The church bell began to toll as they slowly processed down the aisle—an aisle along which, nearly sixty-five years ago, the newly-married Mr and Mrs Dermot Fitzgerald had happily processed, in their youthfulness, smiling, arm in arm, towards the bright sunshine of an August afternoon—their married life ahead of them, to a more joyous bell-ringing, surrounded by their friends and followed by their smiling parents and Dermot's best man, John Kavanagh and Mary's chief bridesmaid Vera Casey.

"Into Paradise may the Angels lead thee
At thy coming may the Martyrs receive thee
And lead thee to the Holy City, Jerusalem.
May the choir of Angels receive thee
And with Lazarus, once a beggar,
Mayest thou have eternal rest."

Book Two

Chapter One

**APARTMENT 26
31 MERRION RD
BALLSBRIDGE
DUBLIN 4**

Tuesday 28th of June 2016

In the morning, after the traffic on Merrion Rd had died down, Julian had run out to Poolbeg Lighthouse and back in under 1 hour 45 minutes—a personal best, taking care as usual, as Saoirse had warned, to watch out for the dip in the Great South Wall, although the weather was fine and the Liffey calm. He had then taken a warm-down run around the ornamental lakes in Herbert Park before calling in to Roly's Delicatessen on the Merrion Road and returning to the apartment with his shopping.

Showered and changed, listening to BBC Radio 4 in the kitchen, he had made chorizo sausage in baked tomatoes—chopping the sausages and tomatoes and adding several tablespoons of extra virgin olive oil, a sprinkling of sea salt and a handful of black peppercorns—and had left it to slow-cook in the oven. He selected a bottle of Rioja from the kitchen wine rack, sliced a ciabatta and wrapped it in foil ready to put in the oven to warm up before serving. He stood a sprig of fresh basil from Roly's in some fresh water. That was the evening meal prepared. Saoirse's flight from Milan was scheduled to land at 8.00pm and Cristy would have her home for 8.30pm prompt.

He then went for a walk along Sandymount beach. On the way, back he jumped onto a DART at Sandymount Station and getting off at Pearse wandered through the grounds of Trinity College and up to the Irish Film Institute in Temple Bar for a matinee showing of *The Clouds of Sils Maria*.

As he retraced his route he paused, sitting in the Summer sunshine on a bench in Trinity and watched a few overs of cricket on the College pitch alongside

Nassau Street. He mingled with the early evening commuters at Pearse and alighted from the DART at Sandymount, stopping, as usual, on Merrion Rd, to exchange pleasantries with the guard outside the British Embassy.

Saoirse breezed in early at 8 pm.

"Hi—the flight was early and so was Cristy." She kissed him.

"How was Milan?"

"Busy—a gin and tonic please, Doctor B. Something smells good—what's for dinner?"

"Chorizo sausage with baked tomatoes, warm buttered ciabatta and ripped basil. I've put in a handful of whole black peppercorns just for you too! There's a bottle of Rioja to go with that."

"Sounds lovely!"

"That's not all—I'm doing King Prawns Pil-Pil a la Marckwicks for starters—with a glass or two of chilled Peroni."

"Even better. Any news from the GMC, or your lawyers?"

"Not yet but there is a Case Management Conference scheduled for 27th July and Eugene promised to update me after that."

"How have you been?"

"Well—I've had a lovely day really, but I could fill Trinity College library with the books I've read just this month alone—and I've as good as got my own seat at the Irish Film Institute!"

"Never mind—it will soon be over. I'm starving—can we eat soon? Do you fancy an early night?"

"Yep, I do—but I really think dinner will taste all the better for another 15 minutes—what do you think?"

She smiled at him and narrowed her eyes. "I think you may well be right!"

"By the way I received my invitation to the British Ambassador's Summer Garden Party today—I'm looking forward to it."

"Yes—it's nearly all finalised. I meant to mention that Gavin Thompson from the Embassy emailed to say that the Ambassador had received a phone call from John Kavanagh who wanted to sponsor our show. Isn't that kind of him!"

"Yes—very—and typically generous!"

Chapter Two

**APARTMENT 26
MERRION RD
BALLSBRIDGE
DUBLIN 4**

Wednesday 27th of July 2016

Dear Julian, Re GMC v Yourself

Please find attached the expert report of Dr Harold Stonefire, dated 10 May 2016 received from the GMC yesterday. No doubt you will wish to read his report yourself. I would welcome any comments you may have at your convenience, I suspect there is little to take issue with in it and it is capable of agreement in due course.

I am pleased to inform you that after a considerable amount of time on the internet my assistant Lisa has managed to trace the author of the phrase "Wonderbra manoeuvre"—he is Professor J P Arthur Shandwyck Jnr, now retired and living in Boothbay Harbour, Maine, United States.

I had a lengthy telephone conversation with him last week—he seems to be quite a character—ex US Navy and confirms that he coined the phrase Wonderbra manoeuvre in the late 80's and incorporated it into his seminars. He delivered one of those seminars annually at the John Hopkins Medical School in Baltimore, Maryland, which tallies with your recollection of hearing the phrase at a lecture in the Eastern United States.

This undermines any suggestion that you created the phrase "for your own gratification" as alleged at the Interim Orders Hearing by GMC Counsel, Connie Cornwall QC. I attach a copy of Professor Shandwyck's statement for your information.

I participated in a Case Management Conference this morning with the GMC Legal Team and I can inform you that a hearing date has been fixed for your fitness to practise hearing—commencing on Monday 9th January 2017, being the first date convenient to all parties—so just within the 12 months ordered by the interim panel—with an estimated length of hearing of two weeks.

Also, during the Case Management Conference the GMC applied for Nurse Keaveney to give evidence by video link as she will then be seven months pregnant.

In view of the hearing taking place so early in January I have arranged a final conference with Jonathan Bliss to take place at our offices at 10.30am on 23rd December 2016.

I look forward to hearing from you with your comments and seeing you again at our offices in Manchester on 23rd December at 10.30am.

Best wishes,

Eugene Kennedy

CAVENDISH & BEAUCHAMP SOLICITORS LLP

THE IRISH TIMES

Friday 28 September 2016
DUBLIN

British and Irish Army Bands Play in Harmony

In previous decades it would have seemed impossible, but last night, members of the Irish Army No 1 Band and a British Army band came together to perform at a garden party in the British ambassador's residence in Sandymount, South Dublin.

said It was a historic occasion and a sign of the strengthening ties between both countries, commented Ambassador, Sir James Ballard. The Band of the King's Division travelled to Ireland on Wednesday to rehearse with the Army No 1 Band at Cathal Brugha Barracks.

King's Div

The King's Div is one of 23 regular British army bands and provided nine musicians, while 17 came from the Army No 1 Band.

Capt. Richard Walsh, Army No 1 Band conductor shared conducting duties with Capt. Richard Marks of the King's Div – both agreed that it was "a real joint effort.".

Not surprisingly, there were no rebel songs or triumphalist anthems that might have caused a diplomatic incident - carefully chosen playlist included everything from classical pieces to arrangements of songs such as Tom Jones' *It's Not Unusual* and Coldplay's *Viva La Vida*.

Capt. Walsh said: "When you are sitting beside a stranger who is playing the same instrument as you, you have to get on immediately because you are doing exactly the same job even though the accents are different."

Capt. Marks said it was a momentous occasion for his band, which had never performed in Ireland before. "They've been playing very well indeed together. The wonderful thing about music is it's an international language and we all speak the same when we sit down and play."

Musical echo

Sir James said yesterday that they had been deliberately brought together as a 'musical echo' of what is actually happening on the ground.

British and Irish soldiers are serving in a combined unit in the West African country of Mali as part of an EU mission to bring stability to the region.

Fashion Harmony Too

The fashion house Cristiano a Fiorentina reprised its debut show from last year when the emphasis was on a modern take of the Irish leine by Irish and British indie designers.

This year, as its theme, the same designers updated the surcoat, a garment popular in the royal courts of Europe from the 13th century, with models from all twenty-eight members states of the EU gracing the catwalk.

Sir James added, "And by all accounts, this has been a terrific success and both sides have got an enormous amount out of it. I am grateful to the two bands who performed splendidly and to the young Irish and British designers at Cristiano a Fiorentina who combined together to produce such a spectacular show as well as supporting women's rights throughout Ireland, the UK and Europe."

Some 1,300 attended the party in Sandyford last night, including business people, politicians, gardai and members of the Irish Defence Forces and figures from the arts, fashion and entertainment world.

Chapter Three

**CHRISTMAS EVE
TERMINAL TWO
DUBLIN AIRPORT**

Friday 24th of December 2016

Julian had attended the final conference with Eugene and Jonathan yesterday in Manchester which had gone well—everything was ready and his long wait was nearly over. Julian knew he could explain his conduct regarding the two patients on the basis of clinical procedure, but he and his lawyers were worried about the allegation of touching Nurse Keaveney inappropriately for which he had no convincing answer.

In the absence of anything other than Saoirse's female intuition, his lawyers were still advising against suggesting that she had in some way been giving him the "come-on", an assertion which was hard to justify on the facts and which would lead to allegations of a lack of insight into his conduct towards a junior colleague. Worse—if the Tribunal disbelieved him on that allegation, they could find his actions to be not only inappropriate, but also sexually motivated and could then use that finding as evidence to support the GMC case that the other two incidents were sexually motivated. He wished he could remember the incident more clearly.

He'd had two other appointments in Manchester—one at Fruhman & Esterkin, jewellers, in St Ann St and the other at the King St Clinic, before he had taken the 16.00 Aer Lingus flight from Manchester and arrived at Dublin shortly before 17.00.

He emerged into the Arrivals Hall, decorated for Christmas, to be greeted, on this occasion not by screaming Jedward fans but by the choir of St Malachy's Primary School, Donnybrook. They were on the third verse of *Away in a Manger* and the brightly lit hall resounded to their young, clear, soprano voices.

Julian stood and took in the scene. Countless Christmas scenes came back to mind—Christmas Carols at end of Short Half at Downfield, at home with his family, at the Bart's Christmas Concerts and those precious few with Eleanor. There were no Garda Siochana in the background this time, but he was struck by the number of families—awaiting the return of the Irish diaspora for the Christmas gatherings and homecomings.

There were homemade banners—WELCOME HOME DADDY—WELCOME HOME UNCLE PADRAIG decorated with giant three-leaved Shamrocks and the like. Children rushed forward in short races to be the first to be embraced and were swept up and hugged close and then closer still—toddlers following on with tiny tottering steps—mothers waiting in the background to give and receive a welcoming embrace which told them that absence had indeed made the heart grow fonder.

He imagined a similar scene would have greeted a young Dermot Fitzgerald at Cork railway station, returning to visit his parents a few generations ago and wondered how far his fellow travellers had come as they emerged into the Arrivals Hall—how long they could stay before the demands of earning a living would take them away again from their family and country.

He checked that the engagement ring he had collected form from Fruhman & Esterkin in St Ann's Square that morning in Manchester was still in his bag.

The choir finished *Away in a Manger* to a sustained round of applause from everyone in the Arrivals Hall—including the staff in the shops. Julian stepped forward and placed a Euro 50 note into the charity box. The choir mistress announced the next carol—*O Little Town of Bethlehem* as Julian turned to leave the hall.

With the opening lines of the carol ringing in his ears he walked across the Arrivals Hall and took the down escalator to the taxi queue—Cristy had taken his wife Kathleen to Boston for Christmas to see their new grand-daughter Aisling.

Outside Terminal 2 Julian climbed into the first waiting taxi and asked to be dropped outside Leinster House on Kildare St—just a few steps away from The Shelbourne Hotel where he was meeting Saoirse—after her office Christmas lunch. As the taxi passed through Drumcondra and swung left into Frederick Street North he took in the view as he passed along O'Connell Street.

A giant Christmas tree stood opposite the GPO. The Army No 1 Band was playing carols opposite The Gresham Hotel and on a covered stage a little further down an Irish dance troupe of girls, dressed alternately as Santa Claus and elves, their backs as straight as rods and their feet and legs, bending. kicking and flying here and there, was dancing to a syncopated version of *God Rest Ye Merry Gentlemen,* accompanied by a Gospel Choir—their flowing robes, flashes of red and white as they swayed from foot to foot and with arms outstretched, clapped out the rhythm of the carol.

A necklace of children's amusement rides, food and drink stalls stretched along the wide central pedestrianised area of O'Connell Street as far as the Liffey—children skipped and families walked between them as snow began to fall.

As the they sped along Nassau Street along the playing fields of Trinity College Julian noticed the cricket square and the rugby pitch starting to whiten with the slowly drifting snow—the driver turned right into Kildare St and pulled up just short of Stephen's Green.

The snow was falling more heavily now as he turned the corner and was greeted by the three over-coated doormen at the entrance to The Shelbourne Hotel who began to turn the door for him

"Merry Christmas, Sir. How 'ya doin'?"

"Grand, thanks, gentlemen. And Merry Christmas to you."

Julian stepped into the hotel lobby and stood for a few minutes by the open fire in front of the Lord Mayor's Lounge enjoying the warm glow from the burning logs. The hotel was full of guests and locals, anticipating the start of the Christmas holidays.

He took off his coat and shook the snow-flakes from it and crossed the lobby into the crowded long bar and immediately saw Aoife and then Saoirse sat on tall stools at the far end, overlooking Kildare St. Saoirse looked different from usual.

He began to push his way through—as he reached them Aoife stood up and gave him a hug and a kiss.

"Here, take my seat, I was just going—the office Christmas party has tired me out—and I've still got some presents to buy! Enjoy yourselves! Merry Christmas Julian and Happy New Year—I hope everything goes well in Manchester." She gave him another hug. "Take care of her now! We've been at the champagne!"

Julian settled into the stool and looked at Saoirse. She was wearing a new fine cable-knit jersey dress of electric blue and red suede ankle boots with silver buckles and heels. On her left hand, just below the sleeve of her dress she wore the diamante cuff and harness she had been wearing on her glove in Turnbull & Asser nearly a year ago.

On her right, where the dress was sleeveless she wore an opera glove of soft red leather and entwined around her right upper arm was a silver amulet of a serpent's snarling head with a flared, feathered tail. Her blonde hair was pulled tightly to the crown of her head in a severe ponytail bound in a column of silver braid, accentuating her high cheek-bones and full red lips.

Her eyes were heavily made up—one black, the other purple, with long red, glittery cat flicks. The high-necked dress clung to her full bosom and hips. The deeply slashed hem of her dress revealed her crossed legs and a few inches of fine black fishnet stocking.

The other stocking was bright red. Her slim waist was encircled by a wide triple-buckle red leather belt from which were suspended several loops of silver chains. Her skin was glowing with health and had just a slight flush of colour.

She leaned forward and exaggeratedly kissed him briefly but fully on the lips, then leant back and smiled at him. She seemed a little tipsy.

"You look great! And did you dress like this for me or for the Christmas lunch?"

"For you of course!" She smiled at Julian and reaching forward took hold of his wrists. She leaned into him and Julian breathed in her perfume. She kissed his ear and whispered, "I just wanted to make it very, very clear—just in case you are in any doubt—that you can be as sexually motivated—and inappropriate as you want with me—because I am going to be as sexually motivated and inappropriate as I want with you! So, sod the GMC and Connie Cornwall QC!"

She stared unblinkingly at him for a few seconds and then widened her eyes teasingly. Julian returned her stare then took her left hand in his. Reaching inside his jacket he picked up the engagement ring he'd collected from Fruhman & Esterkin that morning. He held it up in front of Saoirse who smiled broadly and nodded. He slipped the ring on. Saoirse leaned forward.

"It's about time, Doctor!"

A ripple of applause surrounded the two of them and rippled out as the other occupants of the Bar.realised what had just happened.

"Shall we get a taxi?"

They left, arm in arm and slipped into the back of the last taxi in the queue in front of the hotel.

Chapter Four

**CHRISTMAS DAY
APARTMENT 31
MERRION RD
DUBLIN 4**

Julian woke to the smell of fresh coffee and the sight of their clothing scattered around the bedroom floor. An empty champagne bottle was on the floor. Saoirse appeared, with the coffee and slipped back into bed.

"Here's what we're going to do for Christmas—we're going to celebrate—because the company is finally about to float and I'm going to be rich—so rich I can stop work tomorrow—so let's get your case over and done with and get on with the rest of our lives! How does that sound, Dr Stinker?"

"Merry Christmas!"

"Well, for once, I've got some good news for you—of course I knew with Eleanor being pregnant that I wasn't infertile, but I thought I might as well get checked out and so I had a check-up in Manchester. I'm pleased to say that my sperm count is very high—160 million at the last test—and there's nothing wrong with my motility—45%—or morphology either—5%—so we've got millions to choose from!"

"Millions?"

"Yes—millions." Saoirse threw her arms around him.

"Wow! I only wanted two or three!"

"I love you Saoirse!"

"Now, there is something I want to propose too—now that I have the chance to do it—John Kavanagh set me thinking—I want to help someone else in the way John helped me—so that someone with talent but without money can achieve their ambitions, like I did—I now have the money and like John said—"it gets passed on"."

"What do you think?"

"Well, I was very impressed with John Kavanagh—his resilience in the face of adversity and his commitment to reconciliation—putting the past behind us—his response to the bombings in Manchester and determination that the Good Friday Agreement shouldn't fail so I've been thinking too—whatever money you want to donate I will match it! But for any other Cuthbert's student who wishes to study medicine—what do you think?"

"I think you're wonderful—I can't believe we met—it was so lucky!"

"Was it? I thought you planned every detail of it!"

"You know what I mean!"

"There's something else I wanted to ask your thoughts about—do you think John Kavanagh would give me away?"

"I would be very surprised if he refused! I think he would be honoured."

Chapter Five

MPTS
GMC V DR JULIAN BRACKEN

8:45am
Monday 9th of January 2017

DAY ONE
Hearing Room Three
St James's Buildings
Manchester

Jonathan, Eugene, Julian and Saoirse had been in Defence Conference Room Three since 08.30am—surrounded by ring-binders of hearing bundles, witness statements, expert reports, copies of *Good Medical Practice,* Minutes of the Case Management Conferences, notebooks and correspondence logs—all feathered with a wide variety of coloured post-it stickers. For the lawyers, this was the moment when the outside world and all other demands were set aside and their focus was on one single matter—a successful outcome.

They had been ready for several weeks but for good measure had held a last conference just before Christmas, although both lawyers knew that even when a case has taken the best part of a year to reach, new developments often come to light—when the teams of lawyers had to concentrate on presenting and defending their cases—intellectual athletics were under the starter's orders.

"We'll be starting on time at 09.30—this is the procedure—we will all go into the hearing room together and you will be asked to identify yourself and state your GMC registration number, then you will be introduced by the Tribunal Chair to the other members of the panel, the Legal Assessor and the Tribunal Secretary.

"Provided there are no preliminary issues I will then make the various denials and admissions we agreed on just before Christmas—in particular, the admission that your conduct regarding Nurse Keaveney was inappropriate—let's just go through the allegations to remind ourselves."

Jonathan opened a large green ring-binder and ran his finger down the page and began reading.

That being registered under the Medical Act 1983 (as amended):

1. At all relevant times you were employed as a consultant anaesthetist at Somerford Royal Infirmary. *Admitted*
2. On the 20th January 2016, shortly prior to commencing an operation to correct scoliosis, a spinal deformity on a fifteen-year-old female, Patient A, who was anaesthetised and in a prone position on the operating table,

    a) you announced that you were going to perform the "Wonderbra Manoeuvre" *Admitted*
    b) you subsequently touched Patient A's breasts *Admitted.* that touching was
    c) excessive in duration *Denied* and therefore

        i. not clinically justified *Denied*
        ii. inappropriate *Denied*
        iii. sexually motivated *Denied*

1. On the 11th January 2016, you were being assisted by Sister Johnson to prepare a female patient—Patient B, for surgery. Sister Johnson was placing a urethral catheter when you took up a position alongside Sister Johnson from where you could view Patient B's pubic area and subsequently focussed a theatre spotlight on and continued to view Patient B's pubic area—*Admitted* that conduct was

    a) excessive in duration *Denied* and therefore

        i. not clinically justified *Denied*
        ii. inappropriate *Denied*
        iii. sexually motivated *Denied*

2. On the 19th March 2014 you were alone with Nurse Keaveney in the Recovery Room at Somerford Royal Infirmary, when Nurse Keaveney

asked you a question regarding the surgical incision and resulting scarring arising from spinal corrective surgery. *Admitted*

Without obtaining her consent, you placed your finger just above Nurse Keaveney's natal cleft and moved it, maintaining contact, the full length of her back as far as her neck and in doing so touched Nurse Keaveney's bra strap and bare skin at the nape of her neck. *Admitted*

Your actions on that occasion were

    i.   Inappropriate *Admitted*
    ii.   sexually motivated *Denied*

By reason of the matters set out above your fitness to practise is impaired because of your:

    a)   misconduct in respect of paragraphs 2 i), ii), iii) 3 i), ii) and iii) and 4 i) and ii). *Denied*

"Is that all agreed Julian?"

"Yes."

"So, for the rest of this week you can just follow what is happening—but whatever you do—do not make any comment whether by word or body language—no matter what you feel or how outrageous the statement—I will deal with anything and everything that arises. Please make a note of anything you wish to discuss because we will have a conference every time we break and every morning first thing—OK?"

"Yes."

"We will have a further chat about how best to give your evidence when the time comes—probably on Monday morning of next week, just before you give your evidence—otherwise you may well forget."

"Yes, I think I'll feel better when things get underway."

"I'm sure you will Connie Cornwall QC tapped gently on Defence Conference Room Three's door and stepped politely back a few paces." Jonathan excused himself and left the room—through the glass Julian could see the two barristers in earnest conversation nodding and smiling in their professional way.

Saoirse took a closer look at Connie Cornwall—an ice-maiden she might well be in court but someone clearly loved her—on the fourth finger of her left hand was an engagement ring which clasped a French-cut white diamond of at least 3 carats and a wedding ring encircled with diamonds. Her only other adornment was a ring on the little finger of her right hand which contained a Pendeloque cut ruby the size of her carefully manicured bright red fingernail.

Jonathan returned to the conference room. "Just a revised witness running order—slightly out of chronology because of nursing commitments—Connie will open the GMC case this morning then call Sister Johnson this afternoon then Nurse Griffiths and Nurse Keaveney tomorrow, Tuesday.

"Nurse Keaveney, as we know, is now seven months pregnant and is giving evidence by video-link from the Education Suite at Somerford Royal Infirmary. That has been booked to link in at 2.30pm tomorrow afternoon so that is a fixture—by the way—Nurse Keaveney is now married and is called Parrington-Weaver."

Julian snatched up the witness running order.

"Did you say Parrington-Weaver? How did that happen? He must be nearly twice her age!"

"Do you know her husband, Julian?"

"Yes—he's an orthopaedic surgeon at SRI—he specialises in sports injuries and has an extensive practice in medico-legal reports."

"In other words, he's very rich?" Asked Saoirse.

"Yes—very well off, indeed!"

"So—a good catch for a nurse in her 30s?"

"A very good catch."

The two lawyers exchanged glances.

"Julian—what is Mr Parrington-Weaver's first name?"

"Anthony."

"And we already know it was Mary Keaveney. Eugene, do you think you could phone your office and ask Lisa to do some research and find out the date of their marriage? And if possible, obtain a copy of their marriage certificate?"

Eugene left the conference room, mobile phone in hand.

"That's an intriguing development—it may be that your intuition was right all along, Saoirse. It will be interesting to see the relationship between the date of their marriage and her anticipated confinement—perhaps some moral blackmail was employed. We can return to that when we have a copy of the marriage certificate.

"So back to the witness list—on Wednesday, James Broadley, the lead surgeon will be called and also Professor Somerville, Medical Director whose evidence is now agreed and will be read. Then on Thursday the GMC are going to invite the panel to read the expert report of Dr Harold Stonefire, again angeed and if necessary go over onto Friday morning and close their case after lunch early Friday afternoon, which means we should get an early finish and get you both home to Dublin for the week-end.

"But it does mean that you will be giving evidence first thing next Monday morning so I suggest that you return to Manchester on Sunday, so you are fresh to face Connie."

Another gentle knock on the door but this time it was the Legal Assessor, John MacPherson.

"Just the panel profiles you asked for, Eugene." He passed another sheet of paper to Eugene and closed the door. Jonathan looked over Eugene's shoulder.

"We have Thomas Winterton, Lay Member in the Chair, Professor Williams, cardiologist and Helen Turnberry, lay panel member."

"Julian—here are the profiles—please have a read. Do you know any of these panel members personally or have any reason to believe that any of them may not be impartial?"

Julian took the sheet of paper from Eugene and studied it, then placed it on the desk. "No—I don't believe so."

The Tribunal Secretary, Ann Richardson, now appeared at the conference room door and announced that the Panel were ready. The lawyers, Julian and Saoirse followed her to the Hearing Room door where the prosecutrix eminence, Connie Cornwall QC was already waiting and after a short pause the door was opened and everyone entered, taking their designated places.

"Good morning, Dr Bracken, I am Thomas Winterton, a lay panel-member and I am chairing this hearing—could you please state your name and GMC registration number?"

"Yes Sir—I am Dr Julian Bracken—GMC registration number—6389755."

"Thank you—can I introduce the other two members of the Panel—Professor Williams, cardiologist on my right and Helen Turnberry another lay member on my left. Then there is John Macpherson QC, our Legal Assessor and Miss Ann

Richardson, the Tribunal Clerk. As you may know Ms Cornwall QC appears for the GMC. Ms Cornwall, Mr Bliss—are you ready to commence?"

"Yes sir."

"Are there any preliminary issues?"

"No sir."

"Very good—Ms Cornwall?"

"Thank you, Sir."

"This is a new fitness to practise hearing. The GMC case is that Dr Bracken, in respect of each Head of Charge acted inappropriately and that his actions were sexually motivated. Indeed, we submit that each of those actions alone if proven would call into question Dr Bracken's fitness to practise on the basis of serious professional misconduct but, taken together, if proven, demonstrate a serious, pre-meditated and sustained departure from *Good Medical Practice* and the relevant *Guidelines,* and represent a fundamental breach of trust expected of any doctor and especially one who holds himself out as so experienced.

"In relation to Head of Charge 2, we say on behalf of the GMC that the time taken to undertake the repositioning of breast tissue was excessive in duration and as to the way performed, in light of Nurse Griffith's evidence as set out in her witness statement took Dr Bracken's actions outside the limits of good clinical practice and were therefore not clinically justified, were inappropriate and sexually motivated.

"Dr Bracken we submit was sufficiently—we would say supremely confident to act in this way because he was relying on the trust his colleagues had placed in him over the last 12 years since he took up his post as a consultant anaesthetist at SRI, but unfortunately for him, failed to realise that Nurse Griffith was observing his conduct for the very first time and had no such preconceptions.

"In relation to Head of Charge 3 the GMC case in short is that once again the time spent in observing Sister Johnson placing the catheter was excessive in duration and therefore cannot be clinically justified.

"Sister Johnson, according to her witness statement is an experienced Theatre Sister who has placed many hundreds of catheters in this way and informed Dr Bracken of this but Dr Bracken not only failed to take the opportunity to explain his behaviour, which, in the circumstances, we say was clearly and obviously called for, but, rather, focussed additional lighting on Patient B's pubic area despite no such request being made by Sister Johnson who furthermore, maintains she already had sufficient illumination to perform the procedure successfully which, and this is not disputed—in fact she did—you may therefore ask yourselves the question. What on earth was the purpose of all that staring and the addition of unnecessary and unrequested lighting if not for personal gratification?

"On behalf of the GMC we submit that neither the excessive duration of Dr Bracken's presence, nor the focussing of unnecessary additional illumination can be justified clinically and that his actions on that occasion too were both inappropriate and sexually motivated. Once again, we submit that Dr Bracken was abusing the trust placed in him by his colleagues—in this case Sister Johnson to conduct himself in this way and did not expect her to raise the concerns she in fact did. You will no doubt bear in mind that Sister Johnson, like Nurse Griffith, was working alongside Dr Bracken for the very first time and again, like Nurse Griffith, casting a fresh set of eyes on Dr Bracken's surreptitious behaviour.

"In relation to Head of Charge 4 the GMC case is that Dr Bracken did not obtain the consent of Nurse Keaveney to touch her and that therefore his touching of her was not only inappropriate, which has, unsurprisingly, now been admitted on his behalf, but also sexually motivated. Taking into account the very particular circumstances in which that touching took place it is the GMC's case that either his conduct was sexually motivated to satisfy a private, latent desire or a "come-on" designed to elicit more intimate sexual contact—a come-on, we submit, he quickly abandoned, pretending nothing untoward had happened, when he realised that Nurse Keaveney was not responding to his improper advances.

"We submit that in all three cases his conduct was a serious and obvious departure from the standards expected of a registered medical practitioner of his experience and standing.

"I will now call the first witness on behalf of the General Medical Council. Because of professional commitments, Sister Johnson, whose evidence relates to Head of Charge 3 will be called first in accordance with the revised Witness Running Order we circulated to the Panel, Legal Assessor and my learned friend earlier this morning. Mr Bliss has no objection to that."

***

Panel Chair: "Good morning, Sister—please take a seat. Please proceed, Ms Cornwall."

"Thank you sir. Sister Johnson—could you please take the Oath?"

"Yes—I swear by almighty God that the evidence I shall give will be the truth, the whole truth and nothing but the truth."

"Thank you—could you please look at the Witness Statement Bundle in the red folder before you at page 76—it's behind Tab 7—is that your statement?"

"Yes."

"Could you please turn to page 84? Is that your signature next to the Statement of Truth?"

"Yes."

"Could I just briefly ask you—does that statement relate to an incident in the preparation room at Somerford Royal Infirmary on 11 January 2016?"

"Yes."

"Were you were assisting Dr Bracken to prepare a female Patient—Patient B for surgery?"

"Yes."

"In particular—you were inserting a catheter into Patient B's urethra?"

"Yes."

"And—this perhaps sounds obvious but that would mean that Patient B's pubic and vaginal area would be exposed?"

"Yes."

"Had you undertaken that procedure before?"

"Yes—on many occasions—hundreds."

"Successfully?"

"Yes—always."

"Before you began that procedure did you ensure that you had sufficient illumination to carry out the procedure successfully?"

"Yes."

"And on this occasion too, did you in fact successfully place the catheter?"

"I did indeed."

"Without any assistance from Dr Bracken?"

"Yes—I didn't need any assistance."

"At some stage did Dr Bracken provide extra lighting?"

"Yes."

"Was there anything unusual about Patient B's pubic area?"

"Yes—there were two tattoos—of a serpent and an apple—and she had a carefully trimmed "airstrip"."

"How long did you take, from start to finish, to fit that catheter on Patient B?"

"About five minutes."

"Was Dr Bracken present for all of that time?"

"Yes—he suddenly appeared as soon as I opened the sterile pack—as if from nowhere and began staring over my shoulder. I kept moving around to try to block his view but he kept moving too."

"And, having now taken the oath, do you adopt the whole of that statement as the truth?"

"Yes, I most certainly do."

"Thank you Sister. Would you please remain there? I'm sure there will be some questions from Mr Bliss who represents Dr Bracken"

"Jonathan Bliss. Sister Johnson, I see from your statement that you qualified as SRN in 2000, after graduating in Nursing from Cardiff University."

"Yes."

"Some sixteen years before this incident?"

"Yes."

"So, you would regard yourself as a very experienced nursing Sister?"

"I've placed hundreds of catheters for both male and female patients—without any problems—if that's what you mean Partly—but as an experienced, shall we say very experienced sister you would agree that problems can occur if the catheter is not placed correctly?"

"Yes—but not with me."

"Well I'm happy to accept that—and to be clear I am not questioning your competence. And placing a catheter is a little more difficult when the patient is female?"

"It can be."

"Usually it is isn't it?"

"I've just said—it can be."

"Because the urinary meatus is obscured by the labia, isn't it"

"Yes—as I said it can be, but not for me—I knew what I was doing."

"Thank you. Now, for the moment setting aside your own skills and competence which as I say are not in issue, do you agree that problems can arise with other nurses who might not be quite as skilled as you are?"

"Yes—but only very occasionally."

"Leaking urine?"

"Yes."

"Tears and soreness?

"Yes."

"Leading, potentially to subsequent infections and painfulness?

"Yes."

"Furthermore there can be abnormalities of the female urethra, usually a narrowing—can't there?"

"Yes, but that's more usually found in males."

"Yes, you're correct. But stenosis—a narrowing of the urethra can also be caused by trauma can't it?"

"Yes."

"And this patient had been in quite a nasty car accident where she had sustained a fractured pelvis and a double fracture of her tibia and fibula.

"Yes."

"So perhaps all the more reason to be careful?"

"I was being careful."

"And all the more reason to have the very maximum amount of illumination."

"I didn't need it—I placed the catheter correctly I don't disagree, but ultimately it is the anaesthetist's responsibility to ensure that none of these things happen?"

"Yes. It is."

"Thank you very much. How long had you worked at Somerford Royal Infirmary prior to this incident?"

"Three weeks—before that at St David's Hospital Cardiff."

"So, you and Dr Bracken had never worked together before, had you?"

"No."

"Would you agree that teamwork is a part of good surgery?"

"Yes."

"And you say Dr Bracken was staring at Patient B?"

"Yes—and I told him I could manage And he then focussed a spotlight on Patient B illuminating what you were doing?"

"Yes, but I already had enough light."

"And you say continued to stare?"

"Yes."

"If I used the words "continued to observe" rather than "continued to stare" would that amount to the same description of what Dr Bracken was doing?"

"No, he was staring And would you say that you were staring—or observing?"

"I was busy placing a catheter."

"So, you were looking at what you were doing."

"Yes—of course—observing what you were doing?"

"I wasn't observing—I was doing it."

"Well, you were looking at what you were doing—so that you didn't make a mistake?"

"I didn't make a mistake—and I didn't need his help."

"Well, let me put it another way—Dr Bracken was looking at what you were doing too. He was observing what you were doing—just as you were observing what you were doing—to ensure that you did it correctly, he was doing the same as you. His behaviour amounted to that didn't it?"

"He was ogling—at her and her tattoos—Patient B was a glamour model—everyone in the hospital knew that!"

"So, you say you were looking but Dr Bracken was staring or ogling?"

"I didn't need any help—he was staring."

"And to help you even more, Dr Bracken provided more illumination so you could see more clearly—didn't he?"

"No, I could see clearly—the extra light was so he could ogle the patient—he didn't stop staring until I covered the patient up."

"After he had observed you successfully complete the procedure?"

"Yes."

"When you and he returned to other tasks?"

"Yes—but by then I'd covered the patient up so there was nothing left for him to stare at. So, you felt that he wasn't showing the patient any dignity?"

"No—he certainly wasn't!"

"And you felt that was inappropriate?"

"Yes—of course."

"And from what you say that his conduct was in some way sexually motivated?"

"Yes."

"And if you are right about that it was a serious matter, wasn't it?"

"Yes—very serious."

"You thought that at the time, did you?"

"Yes—it was obvious what he was up to."

"Are you sure you thought that at the time?"

"Yes—I'm very sure."

"His actions failed to afford dignity to the patient, were inappropriate, and sexually motivated—you thought all these things at the time? Right there and then?"

"Yes—it was obvious to me what was happening—you weren't there."

"Raising serious concerns in your mind?"

"Yes."

"Which would have required immediate, urgent action to safeguard other patients?"

"Yes, yes."

"When did you in fact report those concerns?"

"A few days later—when I'd had time to think about them."

"But what was there to think about? You've just given evidence that "it was obvious what was happening", yet, you didn't report your concerns until over ten days later, on the 21st January, did you?"

"If you say so."

"Well I'm only able to say so because that's the date of your initial statement of complaint. You can have a look at that because it's at p…in the bundle. Was the delay in reporting your concerns because at the time you actually thought that Dr Bracken was as a matter of good teamwork observing you and when he focussed the light he was simply trying to make your task easier?"

"But he didn't say anything—"

"No—he didn't because, like you he was concentrating on what you were doing—because he was observing you—not the patient? He wasn't simply looking at the patient—he was observing what you were doing wasn't he? That's right, isn't it, Sister Johnson?"

"He was doing both."

"If you're correct that Dr Bracken was demonstrating a lack of respect for Patient B's dignity and his actions were sexually motivated you must have thought that patient safety was an issue—so why didn't you report this incident immediately?"

"I don't really know—I was thinking it over."

"I suggest that his behaviour at worst amounts to being a fuss-pot—and possibly a failure to communicate properly—you thought he was unnecessarily checking up on you—and you were aggrieved about that, weren't you?"

"No."

"Not even slightly?"

"No."

"Your professional pride was hurt and when you overheard Nurse Griffith talking about the Wonderbra manoeuvre—well over a week later—a week when you had taken no action whatever, you changed your mind about what Dr Bracken had been doing?"

"No, I didn't."

"You changed your mind from thinking that Dr Bracken was being an annoying fuss-pot to being a pervert—because of what you over-heard on the 21st of January—over ten days later—because if you had really thought that at the time there was a serious risk to patient safety you should have reported your concerns immediately—shouldn't you?"

"I would have."

"No, should have—but you didn't, did you?"

"No, I didn't."

"You put two and two together and got six? Didn't you?"

"That's just what you're saying now he's had time to think about it and come up with that excuse—you weren't there—I was!"

"And there's a big difference between being a fusspot and being a pervert, isn't there?"

Sister Johnson didn't answer.

Chapter Six

"CC QC Nurse Griffith—could you please take the oath?"

"I swear by Almighty God that the evidence I shall give will be the truth, the whole truth and nothing but the truth."

"Would you please look at the Bundle in front of you—the red one entitled Witness Bundle—at Tab 6 page 54. Is that your statement?"

"Yes."

'Is it dated 28 August 2016?"

"Yes."

"Why were you in theatre that day?"

"I was there to observe the procedure as part of my professional development plan."

"So, your purpose that day was simply to observe?"

"Yes."

"You had no surgical or clinical tasks which might distract you?"

"No—I was simply there to observe."

"And did your statement include your observations of Dr Bracken just before an operation began on Patient A at the Somerford Royal Infirmary?"

"Yes."

"Was it a spinal corrective procedure?"

"Yes."

"And why do you recollect the incident with Dr Bracken?"

"Because of what Dr Bracken said just before the operation started—he said something about a Wonderbra."

"Have you read your statement before the hearing started?"

"Yes."

"And is there a Statement of Truth at the end of it at p75?"

"Yes."

"Is that your signature at the foot of page 75?"

"Yes."

"Do you adopt that statement as your evidence to this hearing today?"

"Yes."

"Thank you, Nurse Griffith,—would you please remain there? Mr Bliss will have some questions for you."

"Jonathan Bliss. Nurse Griffith—I just want to ask you some questions on behalf of Dr Bracken. I think you've been a nurse for twelve years?"

"Yes."

"And have assisted in theatre on many occasions?"

"Yes."

"So, very experienced?"

"I'd like to think so."

"But, on this occasion, you were observing at an operation of this kind for the first time?"

"Yes."

"As part of your training up?"

"Yes."

"In this particular operation the patient is lying prone—face down on the operating table?"

"Yes—the patient was lying face down and it was the first time I had observed at an operation like that."

"And—have you ever heard of a Wonderbra before?"

"Yes—of course."

"But you had never heard of the "Wonderbra Manoeuvre" before that day?"

"No."

"In fact if I understand your evidence correctly you didn't actually hear Dr Bracken say the words "Wonderbra Manoeuvre" but just "something about a Wonderbra" to use your phrase from just a few minutes ago?"

"Yes—I heard the word "Wonderbra" but not "manoeuvre"."

"So, understandably you were wondering what's he talking about a Wonderbra for?"

"Yes."

"And you must have been wondering what a Wonderbra had to do with spinal corrective surgery?"

"Yes, I was."

"So you looked at Dr Bracken and saw he had both his hands under Patient A's breasts?"

"Yes."

"So you must then have been asking yourself what on earth was going on?"

"Yes, definitely."

"Dr Bracken, and I assume yourself, were both in your operating scrubs?"

"Yes."

"Which includes a mask and a hat?"

"Yes."

"And was Dr Bracken wearing his mask?

"Yes."

"Did the mask cover the lower part of his face?

"Yes."

"Up to say the middle of his nose?

"Yes."

"And his hat was covering his head too, shall we say to just above his eyebrows?"

"Yes—well, just covering his hairline."

"Alright, just covering his hairline—so it follows that the only part of Dr Bracken's face that was visible was from the middle of his nose to just a few inches above his eyebrows?"

"I suppose so."

"Well that must be right, mustn't it?"

"Yes."

"In any event you couldn't see his mouth, could you?"

"No."

"So, you would have been unable to see any gesture—such as a smile he was making with his mouth?"

"No."

"You could only see his eyes?"

"I suppose so."

"Were you aware then of any reason why a doctor would have to touch a female patient's breasts before an operation?"

"No."

"And were you shocked when you saw Dr Bracken with his hands underneath Patient A's breasts?"

"Yes—very."

"You thought—they shouldn't be there, didn't you?"

"Yes."

"And you said in your statement that he had his hands "all over her breasts for a few minutes"?"

"Yes."

"But no one else in the theatre apparently noticed this?"

"No."

"Despite this touching of the patient's breasts lasting according to your evidence for as long as two minutes?"

"No."

"Do you think your estimate of time may have been affected by a combination of your shock and surprise and the fact that you could think of no reason for what Dr Bracken was doing?"

"Well it seemed like a long time—maybe not as long as two minutes now I think about it."

"You have already accepted that you couldn't see whether he was smiling?"

"No—I couldn't but he was up to something—there was a twinkle in his eyes!"

"What kind of twinkle?"

Nurse Griffith bristled slightly and then frowned. "A big one."

"Compared to what?"

"Compared to a small one—he had—yes, a very big twinkle in his eyes—it was obvious to me what was going on—I know you're trying to trick me Nurse Griffith—I am not trying to trick you—I am just trying to get to the truth—it could have been a twinkle about anything, couldn't it?"

"Not when he's got his hands all over a teenage girl's breasts for a long time and that's the truth You say in your statement that he seemed to be "enjoying himself"?"

"Yes."

"On what do you now base that opinion?"

"Well—I'm not sure—it was just my reaction then when I looked up."

"Do you think now, that your reaction—an instant reaction—was an overreaction?"

"I suppose it could have been."

"Because, you were the only one who found Dr Bracken's words and conduct odd?"

"Yes."

"Despite, as you say, Dr Bracken groping, to use your description a teenage girl's breasts for a long time—two minutes in full view of the theatre?"

"Yes."

"And no one else took exception to what he was doing?"

"Well, like I said just before—it may not have been for quite that long."

"Well how long do you now say this went on for?"

"I'm not sure now—long enough!"

"You had not observed in an operation of this kind before—you had not heard of the Wonderbra Manoeuvre before—I suggest that your estimate of the time Dr Bracken had his hands on Patient A's breasts is wrong."

"No—I know what I saw! He was enjoying himself as he fondled Patient A's breasts."

"What you saw was Dr Bracken repositioning the patient's breasts to avoid harm caused by sustained downward pressure."

"Well, it was a funny way of doing it."

"And you were mistaken in the length of time he took?"

"No, I wasn't and when I told all the other nurses the next day they all agreed with me."

"Did they? And was one of those nurses, nurse Keaveney?"

"Yes—and she must have believed me because she said I should report him to HR—she even offered to go with me—to see Julie Lightfoot, Head of HR."

"And did she?"

"Oh—yes—she was very helpful—she insisted I go."

"So, it sounds like Nurse Keaveney a good friend of yours?"

"Not really—she's just a work colleague."

"And was Nurse Keaveney in theatre when the operation on Patient A was in progress?"

"No."

"And were any of the other nurses you spoke to the next day?"

"No."

"So neither Nurse Keaveney, nor any of the other nurses you spoke to the next day witnessed what Dr Bracken was doing, did they?"

"No.

"I have no further questions, thank you, Nurse Griffith."

"Any re-examination Ms Cornwall?"

"Just a few questions please. Were you the only member of staff in theatre that day to observe?"

"Yes."

"Other staff were there to either perform or assist in the operation?"

"Yes."

"So you were the only one with the time to carefully observe Dr Bracken and what he was doing?"

"Yes."

"Nurse Griffith, it's been suggested to you that you're mistaken about what you saw—did you have a clear view?"

"Yes."

"It's been suggested to you that Dr Bracken was undertaking a necessary medical procedure by redistributing pressure on Patient A's breasts—what do you say about that suggestion?"

"He was taking far too long for that."

"Were you mistaken about that?"

"No, I was not."

Chapter Seven

GMC v DR JULIAN BRACKEN
MPTS

"I swear by almighty God that the evidence I shall give will be the truth, the whole truth and nothing but the truth CC QC."

"Would you please identify yourself?"

"Yes—I am Charles St John Gascoigne."

"And, your occupation?"

"I am the Manager of Turnbull & Asser, shirt-makers of Jermyn St, London."

"And how long have you held that position?"

"33 years."

"Is Dr Julian Bracken known to you?"

"Yes—Dr Bracken has held an account with us for the last 15 years."

"When was the last time you saw Dr Bracken?"

"Just over a year ago—the 8th January 2016—to be precise."

"How can you be so sure?"

"I have looked at his account and there is a note in my own handwriting that he collected half a dozen new shirts that day—I remember leaving a message for him at his hotel—Brown's on Albemarle St the day before, asking if I should arrange to have his shirts dropped off at the hotel and Henry the concierge called me back the next morning to say that Dr Bracken was going to collect the shirts himself as he was going to purchase a new tie or two and to expect him at about 4.30."

"And did you see Dr Bracken later that day?"

"Yes—at about 4.30 pm, he came into the shop."

"Was he alone?"

"Yes—I was serving another customer at the time and I excused myself to greet Dr Bracken and went to collect his shirts from my office."

"Was the other customer male or female?"

"Female."

"And do you remember her name?"

"Yes—Miss Saoirse Fitzgerald."

"How old would Miss Fitzgerald be?"

"I would be very surprised if she was more than 35."

"How would you describe her?"

"Yes—she is a very elegant, very attractive lady—always well dressed and very charming. I remember she was wearing a red trench coat—a Burberry—and her choice of perfume was exquisite."

"And is she tall?"

"I would say about 5'7", slim, with shoulder length blonde hair and well—to me she is the very epitome of modern womanhood."

"Do you know Miss Fitzgerald well?"

"Yes, very well."

"And is that Miss Fitzgerald—sat at the back of this hearing room?"

"Yes—indeed."

"Did Dr Bracken collect his shirts and leave?"

"Well he collected his shirts but he didn't leave straight away—I had expected him to be with us for only a short while—he's very decisive—he normally picks his ties very quickly—usually yellow—he started to look at some of our new ties. He seemed to be taking his time I must say which was very odd because he usually makes up his mind very quickly."

"Was Miss Fitzgerald still in the shop?"

"Oh yes—Dr Bracken left before her after paying for his new tie."

"When did you next see Dr Bracken?"

"He came into the shop about 30 minutes later—I asked him if he'd forgotten something but he said he hadn't—he seemed a little embarrassed."

"Was Miss Fitzgerald still there?"

"No, she had gone back to her hotel—she always stays at Brown's—in fact the same hotel where Dr Bracken was staying. I imagine that's where he'd first spotted her—it's not a very large hotel."

"Did Dr Bracken tell you why he had returned to the shop?"

"Yes—but not straight away—I must say his behaviour seemed rather odd—after some hesitation he asked me if I would give him the contact details for Miss Fitzgerald."

"And did you?"

"Indeed not—that would have been a serious breach of customer confidentiality—I told him that I couldn't do what he was asking."

"How did Dr Bracken react to your comments?"

"He asked me to pass on a message."

"Did he tell you what message he wanted you to pass on?"

"No, because I told him I couldn't."

"How did Dr Bracken react when you refused to do what he wanted?"

"He seemed very disappointed and a little annoyed but he could see I wasn't going to be persuaded and so he apologised and left the shop. To be honest I think that he was—what's the expression—"stalking" Miss Fitzgerald—looking back I distinctly recall he came into to the shop about five minutes after Miss Fitzgerald—as if he'd been waiting for her outside or following her—yes—stalking would be the right word."

"So, your distinct impression was that Dr Bracken was stalking Miss Fitzgerald?"

"Oh yes—most definitely—you could tell by the look in his eyes! It was definitely the look of what's the phrase? A sex predator!"

"A sex predator?"

"Yes."

"Is that your firm opinion?"

"Yes—most certainly."

"Thank you, Mr Gascoigne—would you please remain there—I am sure that Dr Bracken's barrister will have many, many questions for you."

Connie Cornwall QC looked across the hearing room directly at Julian—her face broke into a broad smirk—then she winked at him as if to say, "Get out of that!"

Julian sat up with a start—he felt a sense of foreboding and doom—something hanging over him. He looked at the bedside clock—03.35 am. He looked around the hotel room and held his head in his hands—a bad dream! A nightmare! Saoirse was still asleep—her chest slowly rising and falling with her steady breathing.

He padded over to the window and looked out on a frosty and becalmed Manchester city centre—small plumes of steam spiralled upwards from office blocks and the occasional car meandered silently through the streets far below. A small group was making its way homewards—one young woman in a red sequinned mini-dress, linking arms with her boyfriend—the other couple were larking about swinging each other around and racing from lamp post to lamp post, their breath pluming in the cold night.

God!

He heard Saoirse stir behind him.

Julian sat down on the bed beside her and stroked her hair. "I've just had the most terrible nightmare—I'm so glad you told me you were "stalking" me when we first met."

Chapter Eight

MPTS DAY 2
GMC V DR JULIAN BRACKEN
EVIDENCE OF AND CROSS EXAMINATION OF NURSE
PARRINGTON-WEAVER (NEE KEAVENEY)

CC QC "This witness is going to give evidence by video-link from Somerford Royal Infirmary's Education Suite as agreed with Dr Bracken's solicitor at a Case Management Conference on the 27th July 2016. Could I also mention that the witness has asked that she have her husband present in the room with her to provide support—I have mentioned this to Mr Bliss and he has no objection."

Jonathan Bliss said, "Yes sir, I understand from the GMC that the witness is now seven months pregnant and 36 years of age and was therefore advised by her GP to avoid any unnecessary travel as this is her first pregnancy. The defence have no objection to this course of action, nor to the witness having the support she has asked for."

Nurse Parrington-Weaver took the oath.

"Nurse Parrington-Weaver—did you make a statement to the GMC dated 28 June 2016?"

"Yes."

"And do you have that statement in front of you now? It's at Tab 5 page 63—is there a Statement of Truth at page 74?"

"Yes."

"Is that your signature next to it?"

"Yes."

"And have you read the statement recently?"

"Yes—last night and this morning."

"The statement relates to an incident in the recovery room at SRI on the 19th March 2014 when you say that Dr Bracken touched you on your back."

"Yes."

"Did you at any time agree to Dr Bracken touching you on the back as described in your statement?"

"No."

"And is everything in the statement true and correct?"

"Yes."

"And do you adopt that statement in its entirety as your evidence?"

"Yes."

"Thank you—would you please wait there? Mr Bliss who represents Dr Bracken may have some questions for you Jonathan Bliss. I have just a few questions for you—I hope you won't find them too taxing—in your present state as I understand you are—what seven months pregnant now?"

"Yes—that's right—I'm due at the start of March."

She smiled. "I'm having twins."

"I see. Just to be clear for my note and the record—if you can just look at your statement dated 28th June 2016 the name on the front of the statement is Keaveney, not Parrington-Weaver—is that right?"

"Yes."

"And the signature at the very end of the statement is also Keaveney—is that right?"

"Yes."

"So, before you were married your surname was Keaveney—is that right?"

"Yes—that's right."

"So, when did you change your name?"

"Well, when I was married, on Saturday 17th September 2016."

"So that was just, let's see—some four months ago?"

"Yes."

"And do you prefer to be called Nurse Keaveney or Nurse Parrington-Weaver?"

"Nurse Parrington-Weaver, please."

"Thank you for clearing that up—just for the record you see.

"I don't know what you mean, when you say that.

"Well I suppose "just for the record" in this context means when I look back at my notes, it's clear to me and anyone else that for example Nurse Keaveney became Nurse Parrington-Weaver on the 17th September 2016 and that they are the same person—not two different but perhaps related nurses and also that for example there is a sequence for the events you're giving evidence about. Does that help?"

"I'm not sure but think so."

Nurse Parrington-Weaver looked suspiciously at Jonathan—as did Connie.

"Again to be clear—you were not assisting on the procedure with Patient A on the 20th January?"

"No."

Nurse Parrington-Weaver looked a little more puzzled.

"But you had a discussion with Nurse Griffith on the morning after—on the 21 January 2016?"

"Yes."

"And because of that conversation did you go with Nurse Griffith to Julie Lightfoot, Head of HR?"

"Yes—I think I did—I think we went together."

"In fact, did you offer to take Nurse Griffith to see Julie Lightfoot?"

"No—she said she was going to go and I just offered to go with her."

"You didn't persuade her to go?"

"No—well, not that I can remember."

"You didn't insist that she go?"

"No—I just offered to go with her—we're good friends actually."

"Good friend—I see. So the reason for you making that offer was because you are long-standing friends?"

"Yeh—just being helpful really—for moral support—like I say—being a good friend."

"So you thought Nurse Griffith might not report the matter if it was left to her?"

"I don't know—I just thought it would be helpful if I went along with her."

"Thank you. Now, nearly three years ago in March 2014, you say you were on duty in the recovery room at the SRI?"

"Yes."

"And you were alone with Dr Bracken."

"Yes."

"Wearing just your underwear as would be normal under your scrubs?"

"Yes."

"And Dr Bracken was in scrubs too?"

"Yes."

"And, as you've said—it would be normal for all the surgical team, including

Dr Bracken, to be wearing just their underwear under their scrubs?"

"Yes."

"You would be well aware of that?"

"Well yes—everyone knows that, don't they?"

"Well you say so and "everyone" includes you, doesn't it?"

"Well, yes."

"And, to be fair to Dr Bracken—it was you who asked the question about the surgical scar that would be left after spinal corrective surgery?"

"Yes."

"I mean, Dr Bracken didn't just suddenly start a conversation about scars, did he?"

"No."

"And he didn't suddenly offer to show you where the scarring would be, did he?"

"Well, no."

"Well, no, he didn't because it was you who initiated the discussion, wasn't it?"

"I suppose so."

"Well, there's no suppose so about it is there? Just look at your statement at Tab p65: "I asked Dr Bracken about the scarring left by spinal corrective surgery" so you initiated the discussion by asking that question, didn't you?"

"Yes—I've already said so, haven't I?"

Nurse Parrington-Weaver looked to her left and then back at Jonathan Bliss.

"And why was that?"

"Well, because I was interested."

"And this would be a long-standing interest?"

"Well I suppose so."

"Going back a few months or even years?"

"Well I've been a Nurse for ten years."

"And after 10 years, for the first time you ask a question about scarring?"

"Yes."

"There are books you could have looked at? Over the years?"

"I suppose so."

"You could have gone online."

"I suppose so."

"You could have asked Mr Broadley, the surgeon?"

"I could have."

"And, in fact, as the lead surgeon he might have been better informed?"

"I suppose so, but he wasn't there."

"No, he wasn't. You were alone with Dr Bracken, weren't you?"

"Yes—I've already said that too." Nurse Parrington-Weaver glanced again to her left.

"Was Dr Bracken the only doctor you worked with at SRI?"

"No."

"Did you work with many of the surgeons there?"

"Yes—nearly all of them."

"And your evidence is that this was the first time you ever asked a surgeon about scars?"

"I think so. Yes."

"Including your husband?"

Nurse Parrington-Weaver looked again to her left and then back at Jonathan.

"Well it would be surprising if you hadn't as I understand he has a very extensive orthopaedic practice, hasn't he?"

"Yes."

"Did you ever ask any of the other surgeons about surgical scars?"

Nurse Parrington-Weaver quickly glanced again to her left. "I can't really remember now. I may have done."

"Did you ever ask your husband about the location and extent of surgical scars?"

Nurse Parrington-Weaver looked again to her left and shook her head vigorously. She then twisted around in her seat, looking over her shoulder.

There came the sudden sound of a door slamming out of sight and with tears beginning to well up, Nurse Parrington-Weaver glared at Jonathan. She took a deep breath through flared nostrils before she suddenly pointed at Jonathan and began shouting, "I know what you're going to suggest—you're all the same, you lawyers—that's not the reason I married him—so you needn't start asking me questions like that—just like everyone says I'm a gold-digger—just because I had a boob-job and wear expensive bras and knickers under my scrubs – so I could bag a doctor for a husband, but there`s nothing wrong in looking nice!—

—everyone is always saying that and they're all wrong! I'm fed up of people saying things like that about me so no, no, no—it's not true—that's the answer to all your questions, so you needn't bother asking them! No, no, no, no! I married him because …I love him." Her voice trailed off into a whimper.

Nurse Parrington-Weaver started sobbing and then snatched up her handbag and swiftly turned away. "I'm going now, I've said all I'm prepared to say. I hope you're pleased with yourself!"

There came the sound of a slamming door again.

Connie, fuming, looked across at Jonathan. She put her finger on her microphone but thought better of it and took it away and sank back into her seat, then her finger went forward to her microphone again—then away again.

"In the circumstances, I have no further questions for Nurse Parrington Weaver—nee Keaveney," said Jonathan.

Panel Chair: "Miss Cornwall—do you wish to have the witness recalled for any re-examination?"

Connie, still fuming, spat out, "No thank you Sir."

DAY3
GMC V DR JULIAN BRACKEN

CC QC: "I now propose to call Mr James Broadley—senior surgeon."

"I swear by Almighty God that I shall tell the truth, the whole truth and nothing but the truth."

"Mr Broadley—can you please turn to Tab 8 at page 85 of the Witness Bundle? Is that your statement?"

"Yes."

"And is there a Statement of Truth at page 93?"

"Yes."

"The statement relates to an operation which took place on 20th January 2016 on Patient A when you were the senior surgeon?"

"Yes."

"Are you familiar with the phrase The Wonderbra Manoeuvre?"

"Yes—I know what it means."

"Is it a phrase you use yourself?"

"Not really."

"Is that because it is really a teaching aid?"

"Yes."

"So, not a phrase in common in use in theatre?"

"Not especially."

"Thank you—I believe Mr Bliss who represents Dr Bracken may have some questions for you."

"Mr Broadley—when Dr Bracken used the phrase Wonderbra Manoeuvre on 20th January—what did you understand him to be saying?"

"That he had checked that Patient A's breasts were positioned to minimise downward pressure—to avoid post-operative pain and possibly worse—tissue necrosis."

"So, his comment was significant?"

"Yes."

"Helpful to you?"

"Yes."

"And to everyone else who was familiar with spinal corrective surgery?"

"Yes, indeed."

"If Dr Bracken hadn't said what he did, what would you have done?"

"I would have checked and if necessary repositioned Patient A's breasts myself."

"So, quite important, as far as you were concerned?"

"Yes."

"Yes—thank you, Mr Broadley."

Connie by way of re-examination:

"Mr Broadley—if you'd had to reposition Patient A's breasts, how long would it have taken you?"

"I suppose several seconds."

"Not two minutes?"

"No, not as long as that."

"And you wouldn't have used the expression Wonderbra Manoeuvre?"

"Probably not."

"Thank you. Sir, the defence have agreed the evidence of Professor Somerville, Medical Director at Somerford Royal Infirmary, Julie Lightfoot, Head of HR at the hospital and the GMC expert, Dr Andrew, Stonefire, consultant anaesthetist, in their entirety and so both statements and the expert's report can be read—do you wish to retire to do so?"

"Thank you, Ms Cornwall,—Mr Bliss—we will retire to do that and since there are nearly 100 pages in total can I suggest we reconvene at 04.00 this afternoon?"

"Thank you, Sir,—and can I tell you—that is the case for the GMC."

Chapter Nine

GMC V DR JULIAN BRACKEN

4:00pm

"Ms Cornwall, I can confirm that the panel have read the witness statement of the, Professor Somerville, Julie Lightfoot and Dr Harold Stonefire's report during the afternoon."

"Thank you, Sir—do you have any questions?"

"No thank you—you indicated that Dr Firestone was the last witness for the GMC—is that still the case?"

"Yes sir."

"Thank you—Mr Bliss—do you have any submissions of no case to answer on any of the charges?"

"No Sir."

"Thank you. In that case, shall we begin Dr Bracken's case at 09.30 on Monday morning?"

"Thank you, sir."

Chapter Ten

In their conference room, the two lawyers went through their advice to Julian about giving evidence. "Whilst we've made inroads into the GMC case with the cross-examination of their witnesses, Connie will come at you well prepared—so—it is important to remember—do not lose your temper—no matter how provocative the questions—all you have to do is to persuade the panel that your version of events is to be preferred—or at least undermine—make them doubt the GMC case—we have heard from James Broadley that the repositioning of breasts is clinically justified and we have Professor Shandwyck giving evidence tomorrow afternoon about his coining of the phrase "Wonderbra manoeuvre"—you know the experts' evidence is essentially that your conduct in relation to Patient A and Patient B could be regarded as clinically justified—it is the length of time and what was going through your mind when you were doing those things which is important—even Connie concedes that.

"When it comes to Nurse Parrington-Weaver, you have admitted that your actions were inappropriate and will have to accept that in retrospect your actions could have been misinterpreted but that you were simply answering her question by demonstrating the line of incision and you were not sexually motivated—but—in the circumstances you accept that your conduct was inappropriate—this may sound like a generous concession—given her outburst in her evidence but it demonstrates insight and therefore adds credibility to your other evidence which we need the panel to accept on the very much more serious allegations.

"A couple of other things—don't go "off proof"—sorry, a lawyer's term—keep to what is in your statement which Eugene carefully prepared—it covers everything we need to put in as evidence.

"Secondly, Connie has a habit when cross-examining a witness of asking a question and staring silently at you after you have given your answer, which gives you the impression you have not fully answered her question but it's a ploy to tempt you to keep talking and go "off proof"—keep to what's in your statement—just give your answer and then wait for the next question.

"Finally—don't try to anticipate the line of questioning—you won't see it coming and if you're telling the truth you won't be caught out! OK?"

"Yes, thanks."

It was 09.25—the Tribunal Secretary appeared at the conference room door.

"Will you come with me please Dr Bracken—the panel is ready."

***

"I swear by almighty God that the evidence I shall give shall be the truth the whole truth and nothing but the truth.

Jonathan Bliss: "Dr Bracken—there is a statement in the Hearing Bundle in front of you at Defence Bundle—Tab 9—it's page 94—do you have it?"

"Yes."

"It is dated 5th October 2016?"

"Yes."

"And if you turn to page 118 of the same bundle, do you see your signature next to the Statement of Truth?"

"Yes."

"Is that statement your statement?"

"Yes."

"And having now taken the oath, do you confirm that your statement is true and correct?"

"Yes—indeed."

"At the outset of this hearing, you heard me admit on your behalf that your conduct in relation to Head of Charge 4—regarding Nurse Parrington-Weaver was inappropriate?"

"Yes."

"You deny that you acted inappropriately or in a sexually motivated manner in relation to all the other charges?"

"Yes."

"Very well, Doctor Bracken—would you please remain there keeping the Bundles to hand as I am sure there will be some questions for you from Ms Cornwall on behalf of the GMC and perhaps later from the Panel."

"Thank you."

Connie Cornwall QC briefly rearranged her papers in front of her and looked directly at Julian. She smiled gently as if contemplating a forthcoming pleasant event—an event Julian imagined she had been looking forward to for some time. She leant purposely forward and firmly pressed the button at the base of her microphone—a red light came on to indicate the start of her cross-examination of Dr Julian Bracken.

"Doctor Bracken—would you accept that patients should be able to trust their doctors?"

"Yes."

"And that would especially include an anaesthetised patient?"

"Yes."

"And particularly a patient you yourself had anaesthetised?"

"In fact, it's hard to think of a more vulnerable patient than Patient A, isn't it?"

"I agree."

"Because you have rendered her unconscious and you have complete control over when she regains consciousness?"

"Again I agree."

"And that trust not just Patient A, but all patients places in you in you would include trusting you not to touch them inappropriately?"

"Yes."

"Nor gain sexual pleasure or gratification from staring at a naked patient's genital area?"

"Yes."

"And it would also be the case that nurses working alongside you would be entitled to trust that you respected their dignity?"

"Yes."

"And that your behaviour towards them was always appropriate and not sexually motivated?"

"Yes."

"Thank you, it follows does it not that any such conduct would be a serious breach of that trust and would fall far below the standards required by *Good Medical Practice*?"

"Yes."

"And also far below the standards expected of an anaesthetist of your experience and standing?"

"Yes."

"So, we agree on everything, so far?"

"Yes."

"Good. We have heard that you are well respected and indeed eminent in your specialty."

"That would be for others to comment upon."

"That's very modest of you, doctor, but please bear with me. Is it true that you are an elected consultant member of the Council of the Royal College of Anaesthetists?"

"Yes."

"And one doesn't get elected to such a position, shall we say, "by accident"?"

"No."

"Very well. Let me ask you about the incident regarding Nurse Parrington-Weaver. This incident occurred at SRI where you have held the post of consultant for 12 years—is that right?"

"Yes."

"The incident occurred in the recovery room?"

"Yes."

"You had just finished an operation and were both still in your scrubs?"

"Yes."

"The patient had been handed over to the ward nurses following the post op check?"

"Yes."

"And you and Nurse Parrington-Weaver were therefore alone?"

"I believe so."

"Well the witness wasn't challenged on that point."

"No."

"And in your statement there is no reference to anyone else is there?"

"No."

"So you were alone, weren't you?"

"Yes."

"You saw Nurse Parrington-Weaver on the video link? She is approximately 5'6"."

"Yes."

"She is slim?"

"Yes."

"And has long blonde hair?

"Yes."

"And we know because she told us she is 36 and explained that she runs marathons for charity?"

"Yes."

"And Nurse Parrington-Weaver asked you a general question about the surgical scar that would be left on a patient's back following an operation to correct scoliosis?"

"Yes."

"Did she at any time indicate to you by her conduct or ask you to demonstrate this by touching her back?"

"No, not that I recall—I don't remember."

"Underneath her scrubs Nurse X was wearing only her underwear—wasn't she?"

"That would be normal. Yes."

"And in response to her question, you took up a position behind Nurse Parrington-Weaver and put your finger on her back at the base of her spine?"

"Yes."

"Just above her buttocks?"

"Yes."

"Patient records are increasingly electronic these days but do they still have pens, biros and markers at the SRI?"

"Yes."

"Presumably many of them—doctors still need to write things down from time to time?"

"Yes."

"And according to Nurse Parrington-Weaver, there was a white-board in the recovery room—presumably to keep a note of progress—time of operations, patients, procedures, surgeons and the like—is that right?"

"Yes."

"So, can we assume that if you had wished you could have easily found a pen, biro or marker?"

"Yes."

"And you could have illustrated the scar by drawing a diagram on the white-board?"

"Yes."

"Which would have meant that Nurse Parrington-Weaver would have been able to see the line of incision rather than just feel it?"

"Yes."

"I suggest that would have been more educational than using your finger to trace a line along her back?"

"I suppose so. Yes."

"Or you could have used a pen to trace the line along her back? Two simple, practical alternatives to touching her back with your finger? But you didn't, did you?"

"No."

"You used your finger, didn't you?"

"Yes."

"And you used your finger because you wanted to touch her, didn't you?"

"No."

"You touched her to begin with just above her bottom?"

"Yes."

"And then, according to her evidence you slowly moved your finger up her back and towards her neck and in doing so, across her bra strap?"

"Yes—if she says so but I don't really remember—but not for the reasons you say."

"You wanted to touch her in an intimate way?"

"No."

"You have a fascination with bras—don't you? I suggest a mild but real fetish—with Wonderbras and bra straps?"

"No, I don't."

"You wanted to do exactly what you did do—for your own private reason, disregarding her dignity—you touched her near her buttocks and along her back and felt her bra strap as you slowly dragged your finger to the bare skin at the nape of her neck?"

"I accept I must have done that—but not in a sexual way."

"Well you say so but let's just look at that, again, can we? You are a consultant, alone with a young nurse—you, a senior member of the surgical staff and as you've just acknowledged a member of the council of your Royal College and a younger and if I may suggest—it's a matter of course for the panel—attractive junior member of staff, who was wearing only her underwear underneath her very light surgical gowns—in response to an indirect question you approached her from behind, and without her consent, placed your finger just above her natal cleft between her buttocks and traced a line from the top of her buttocks up her back across her bra strap ending on the exposed bare skin at the nape of her neck. What I'm suggesting to you Dr Bracken is that the more senior you get the more circumspect your behaviour should become. Do you see how in the circumstances I've just outlined, this Tribunal might easily find that your conduct was sexually motivated?"

"Yes, but it wasn't—although in the circumstances I accept that it was inappropriate."

"But not sexually motivated?"

"No, not sexually motivated."

"But, inappropriate?" Connie stared at Julian.

"Well in retrospect—inappropriate but it simply never crossed my mind at the time."

"Never crossed your mind at the time? Really? Are you really saying that this was an innocent mistake?"

"Yes."

"Are you really saying that despite your many years of experience, in the circumstances described above you honestly didn't think at the time that your actions were inappropriate?"

"It just never crossed my mind."

"It never crossed your mind?"

"No."

"Doctor Bracken—are you familiar with the GMC's Guidelines for Intimate Examinations and Chaperoning?"

"Yes."

"Those guidelines include any examination of the genitals, rectum and breasts, don't they?"

"Yes."

"And the guidelines also go on to state—and I quote—"Any examination which the patient may perceive as intimate." It's in the Hearing Bundle at Tab 17 p 433."

"Yes—I am aware of the Chaperone Guidelines."

"So, you don't need to read them again—to refresh your memory?"

"No."

"And many doctors, as well as patients, might regard an examination of the area of a young female which would involve touching of her lower back close to her buttocks, her bra-strap and neck as an examination requiring a chaperone, or at least offer a patient the opportunity of having a chaperone—wouldn't they?"

"That's possible."

"If that's possible and you accept you are familiar with the guidelines—so familiar that you don't need to consult them why did you touch her in that way—with your finger? In circumstances in which you've just admitted you might have offered a patient a chaperone?"

"I simply didn't think—I was trying to explain to her."

"You were alone with her?"

"Yes."

"Why didn't you use the Whiteboard?"

"I can't explain."

"Or just use a pencil or a pen or a marker?"

"Again—I can't explain."

"You see, doctor with a patient, you have no choice—you have to touch her in order to examine her but here you did have a choice, didn't you? You didn't need to touch Nurse Parrington-Weaver at all—there were many alternatives to touching—so why did you?"

"As I've said—I can't explain."

"Well—there is one obvious explanation and I put it to you in the clearest of terms so there can be no misunderstanding—it was a "come-on", wasn't it? A come-on that you hoped would lead to greater intimacy?"

"No."

"Well the only other person present thought there was something odd about your behaviour because she says in her witness statement: "I froze—it didn't feel right—it seemed to go on for ages"."

"It didn't go on for ages—it took a matter of only a few seconds—I can't speak for her, only me."

"And when she didn't respond to your come-on, you just simply ignored her?"

"I didn't ignore her—I was responding to her question."

"You realised from her reaction that you'd overstepped the mark and so you pretended it had never happened—didn't you?"

"No—that's not the way it happened."

Connie stared at him silently. "Well let's move on. That incident was reported to your Medical Director and he and the Deputy Head of HR undertook an investigation which resulted in you being informally advised about your conduct—is that right?"

"Yes."

"So, you must have thought you had gotten away with it?"

Legal Assessor: "Ms Cornwall?"

"I'm very sorry—I will withdraw that question and rephrase it. You weren't referred to the GMC on that occasion?"

"No."

"I suggest that when one looks at all the facts of that incident there are only two sensible explanations as to why you didn't use the Whiteboard or a pen or some other inanimate object such as a biro or marker which all appear to have been readily available and that is you needed and wanted to touch Nurse Parrington-Weaver as either a come-on or for you to achieve some form of private sexual gratification—that's right, isn't it, doctor?"

"No, it most certainly isn't."

"Well, let's move on—you weren't referred to the GMC but advised to consider your conduct in the future. Did you?"

"Yes."

"What steps did you put in place because of that advice?"

"Well I have never touched a nurse since."

"Yes, we can also agree that's right—because the next complaint we have—less than two years later is that you were paying unwanted, inappropriate attention, not to a nurse but to a young female patient—and not to her back this time but to her genital area. Now your evidence—at page 226 of your statement is that the reason you were doing that was because of an incident about 12 years ago."

"Yes.

"And your evidence was that a Professor Hunter was the surgeon on that day?"

"Yes."

"And Professor Hunter is, unfortunately no longer with us. Tell me Doctor—assuming this happened—which the GMC do not accept—how did Professor Hunter communicate his disapproval to you?"

"He glared at me across the theatre."

"Glared at you across the theatre?"

"Yes."

"With his scrubs on?"

"Yes."

"His gown and hat?"

"Yes."

"So, you were able to interpret Professor Hunter's state of mind despite being able to see only the small—tiny part of his face between his mask and his hat?"

"Yes."

"Just like Nurse Griffith?"

"Yes."

"And what about the other theatre staff on that day? Assistant surgeon?"

"I simply cannot remember?"

"Your anaesthetics assistant?"

"Again—can't recall."

"Nurses? Can you remember anyone else at all from that incident? You've forgotten about the other three or four."

"No—I've tried but I've have not been able to remember anyone else who was there—apart from Professor Hunter."

"Yes—we know about him—he can't assist us, can he? What about the name of the patient?"

"No—I'm sorry—I can't remember—I've tried."

"So, this is another example of you not being able to remember. Is that because this incident never happened?"

"It did happen."

"Except, we only have your evidence for that?"

"Yes—but I'm telling you the truth—it was a long time ago."

"And you say this incident stuck in your mind because of the look on Professor Hunter's face—despite your observations being restricted in the same way that Nurse Griffith's observations were restricted?"

"Yes."

"And yet you ask the Panel to believe you and not believe Nurse Griffith?"

"Yes."

"Have you read Dr Smith's report?"

"Yes."

"Can you please turn to Tab 13—GMC Hearing Bundle—Expert Report—on the table in front of you—have you found it?"

"Yes."

"Dr Stonefiresays at Page 73 Para 23: *It is in my experience unusual for anaesthetists to place catheters and many, in my experience, will leave this procedure to an experienced theatre sister or nurse.*

"So, putting aside the alleged incident with Professor Hunter—which we suggest simply never happened, there was no need for you to get involved was there?"

"Yes, because once the patient has anaesthetised, her or indeed his care is my responsibility."

"You disagree with Dr Smith's expert report."

"Yes—with that part of it anyway—I will frequently—always check that catheters are placed correctly especially if I do not know the nurse in question very well—and on this occasion, I hadn't worked with Sister Johnson before."

"Frequently or always?"

"Always."

"You just said frequently a moment ago—which is it?"

"Always."

"And your justification for that is the leaking catheter from 12 years ago where you are the only witness of fact that it actually happened?"

"Yes."

"But—it's not the end of the world is it—urine on the table?"

"It shouldn't happen—it's preventable."

"But lots of things shouldn't happen in theatre—but they do?"

"Yes."

"Arteries rupture, patients stop breathing hearts stop beating—that's what happens and what you as a team are supposed to do is deal with them—aren't you?"

"Yes—but you can't predict or prevent those events—this was predictable and so preventable—I hadn't worked with Sister Johnson before and I was simply checking."

"The patient was a model—a glamour model, wasn't she?"

"I believe so."

"Is that a Yes or a No?"

"It's a Yes.""

"And you were aware of that at the time?"

"Yes—but it didn't make any difference to me."

"You had seen her prior to the operation for assessments, consent?"

"Yes—briefly—she was admitted as an emergency following a road traffic accident."

"Sister Johnson told you she could manage—didn't she?"

"Yes."

"Yet you continued to look—didn't you?"

"Yes—I was checking."

"Checking on a sister who has 16 years' experience?"

"Yes."

"Well, why didn't you say so?"

"I didn't think I needed to—none of the other nurses ever complained."

"Well, perhaps they should have!"

Legal Assessor: "Ms Cornwall?"

"I'm sorry—I'll withdraw that remark. Well let's look at the Wonderbra manoeuvre next. Just like the catheter incident—where there was no need to observe an experienced nurse performing a task she had performed many times before—there was no need to say anything like that at all, was there?"

"I suppose not—I didn't have to use that phrase—no."

"You didn't need to make any reference at all to a piece of underwear that sexualises and stereo-types a woman's breasts, did you?"

"No."

"Then why use it?"

"Because it describes the way the breasts should be placed to minimise pressure."

"Why not say something along the lines of—I am now going to reposition the patient's breasts to avoid any post-operative complications from sustained downward pressure?"

"Well, with respect, I think you may have at least partly answered your own question—because that's quite a long description and in my view even then a little incomplete—Wonderbra Manoeuvre is basically short-hand and most people are familiar with the symmetry achieved by a Wonderbra."

Connie glared at Julian for a few seconds. "You used that expression because you like females to look like that, don't you?"

"No."

"No?"

"Well we all have certain images of attractive women."

"You had seen Patient A on several occasions, hadn't you?"

"Yes."

"Spinal curvature doesn't affect normal adolescent development, does it, doctor?"

"No."

"In fact, Patient A was well developed for her age?"

"She was a nice, pleasant girl—and yes—a pretty girl—and yes—she was well into puberty."

"And that was your weakness, wasn't it, Doctor? Because you find that stereotypical image attractive?"

"No—well… I'm a heterosexual male—as a man of course I find women attractive but most certainly not anaesthetised patients."

"Nurse Griffith's evidence was that you spent a few minutes doing this and she believed you were achieving sexual gratification—a sexual gratification that was more intense because you were being outrageous in doing it in front of the whole operating theatre—because you didn't think for one minute that anyone would suspect you—and you got a big private thrill from that didn't you? It was excitement added, wasn't it?"

"I did not. I was in a good mood—I was working alongside friends—colleagues who knew me well."

"Yes—you make my point for me—colleagues who knew you so well they wouldn't dream of suspecting you—except for Nurse Griffith and Sister Johnson—both coincidentally having never worked alongside you before who saw things with fresh eyes, didn't they?"

"No—that's not true."

Connie stared at Julian in silence.

"It was supposed to be a perfect day."

"And what exactly was going to make your day so perfect?"

"Because I was meeting someone very special that night—a woman I'm quite happy to admit I do find attractive—for the first time in the ten years since my wife died—the woman sitting there behind my lawyers."

Connie looked at Saoirse and smiled—she turned back to Julian. "The lady there?"

"Yes."

"Well, I'm sure we can all understand that to varying degrees—so yes—and your feelings ran away with you didn't they Dr Bracken—you were looking forward to the evening—quite properly—no one can complain about what two consenting adults do. I am happy to concede that but you lost control—only for a while—I'm also prepared to accept that—and whilst you may have performed the Wonderbra manoeuvre on many previous occasions—perfectly properly and professionally—because as you've just admitted—you were anticipating the evening ahead—you didn't on this occasion—Nurse Griffith was right—wasn't she? Observing this procedure for the first time, she saw something that your colleagues didn't see—didn't she?"

"No—absolutely not."

"Because you couldn't resist an opportunity to carry on feeling a young girl's breasts for longer that was clinically necessary—didn't you?"

"No."

"Nurse Griffith's evidence was that you spent a few minutes doing this and you were achieving sexual gratification—by arranging a young female's breasts into a shape you find erotic?"

"I did not."

"And but for the fact that you carried on longer than necessary you would have got away with it—wouldn't you?"

"That's not right—Professor Shandwyck uses the phrase also."

"But usually only when he's teaching, like Mr Broadley—as an educational device to retain the attention of medical students. It's the case isn't it Doctor Bracken that in these three incidents you were motivated by sexual gratification—tracing a line along a young nurse's back from her buttocks, over her bra strap up as far as her neck, whether it was a come-on or not, viewing a young glamour model's vagina, decorated with tattoos and fondling an anaesthetised patient's breasts whilst hiding behind the trust that nurses and patients place in both you in particular and in the medical profession in general?"

"That is not true—I did not act in a sexually motivated way on any of those occasions or indeed ever whilst in theatre or any consultation with any patient—I most certainly did not."

"And you were exposed by two witnesses—Nurse Griffith and Sister Johnson who were prepared to speak up tell the truth about what they saw because they were not taken in by your bravura?"

"No."

"And Nurse Parrington-Weaver who wasn't prepared to put up with your inappropriate conduct towards her?"

"No."

The room was silent for a while as Connie held Julian's stare. "I have no further questions." Connie sat back in her chair and interlinked her fingers—contemplating another erasure.

Panel Chair: "Do any of my colleagues have any questions. No? In that case, can I ask you some questions please, Dr Bracken?"

"Yes—of course."

"What percentage of these operations involve female patients?"

"Research suggests that about 90% of adolescents affected by idiopathic—that is unexplained curvature of the spine are females."

"And what ages?"

"From about 10 years of age to early teens."

"So much of your surgery involved female teenage patients?"

"Yes—mostly female teenagers."

"And can you tell me Doctor—how you came to specialise in this area?"

"I don't recall any decision to do so—the procedure is like general surgery—except that the patient is in the prone position it's just that the procedures are much longer—I simply drifted into it and then the requests came from the surgeons."

"So, can you tell me how many such procedures you've been involved in?"

"I would say about 80."

"So, you would have repositioned the breasts of approximately—how many female patients?"

"Well as Mr Broadley says, he and the other surgeons would from time to time perform the same task so I would say about 60 times altogether."

"Thank you, doctor."

Chapter Eleven

The Residence of Emeritus Professor JP Arthur Shandwyck Jnr
Boothbay Harbour
Maine
USA

At 09.20 am East Coast Time in Boothbay Harbour, Maine, Professor Shandwyck Jnr—JP—as agreed had taken his place behind the desk in his office overlooking Linekin Bay from where he loved to watch the ospreys swooping into the water and emerging with wild Atlantic salmon, wriggling and twisting—literally for life in their talons—numbers of these magnificent birds had increased since his retirement here so he always kept his old naval binoculars to hand on the desk beside him. Although he had logged on to the number given to him by the attorney from Manchester, England as soon as he had taken his place behind his desk nothing had happened—apart from a red light which had started to flash at the top left-hand corner of his screen.

His attention strayed and he noticed the familiar shape of a fully-grown osprey hovering, perfectly still over the bay a little to the right of his field of vision. The screen on his laptop was still inactive so he picked up his binoculars and focussed on the bird as it remained some 100 feet or so above the surface of the bay—a more graceful bird in flight or efficient hunter he could not imagine.

The huge wingspan enabled the bird to hover above the water, picking out fish far below with its powerful vision and then swoop on its unsuspecting prey—indeed so awesome are its powers that medieval thinking was that it could mesmerise fish into turning belly-up in surrender. On a few occasions, the professor had even seen an osprey rise from the surface with a fish in each set of talons. He had also noticed that in flight the bird presented the head of the fish forward—he presumed to minimise drag and so conserve energy.

One of the bird's three naturally forward-facing talons is reversible so that when hunting, in the moment before striking, as the osprey's body jack-knifes into an elegant V shape the outer talon swivels round to provide a more balanced grip with two talons on either side. The spicules on the underside of the toes and reversed scales on the talons, in combination, mean no fish ever escapes. As someone who had first-hand experience of warfare he couldn't help but conclude that no designer of modern naval weaponry could have improved on the osprey's natural evolution.

As he watched, the osprey pulled in its wings and began to drop swiftly down. In a few seconds, it was just above the surface of the bay and extending its wings pulled out of the dive, plunging its talons into the water, sending silvery arcs and spumes upwards, momentarily disappearing below the surface and then with a powerful flap of its wings pulled skywards with a large salmon wriggling back and forth between its talons. The bird soared upwards and disappeared beyond the trees. JP sat back and recalled his schooldays and one of the poems the Jesuits had taught him by rote:

> I caught this morning morning's minion, king-
> dom of daylight's dauphin, dapple-dawn-drawn Falcon, in his riding
>   Of the rolling level underneath him steady air, and striding
>   High there, how he hung upon the rein of a wimpling wing
>   In his ecstasy! Then off, off forth on swing,
> As a skate's heel sweeps smooth on a bow-bend: the hurl and gliding
>   Rebuffed the big wind. My heart in hiding
> Stirred for a bird—the achieve of, the mastery of the thing!
>
> Brute beauty and valour and act, oh, air, pride, plume, here
>   Buckle! AND the fire that breaks from thee then, a billion
>   Times told lovelier, more dangerous, O, my chevalier!
>
> No wonder of it: sheer plod makes plough down sillion
>   Shine, and blue bleak embers, ah my dear,
>   Fall, gall themselves, and gash gold vermillion

What was it Einstein had said?

"There are only two ways to live your life—the first is that nothing is a miracle and the second is that everything is a miracle."

His reverie was interrupted by his wife, Gayle, who slowly backed into the study carrying a tray of coffee, mineral water and cookies. She was wearing her running gear—mirrored sunglasses, black leggings with purple flashes and her old Crimsons cheerleader top, her long black hair held back in a tight ponytail.

"Here you are JP, I'm just going down to the lakeshore for a run—back in about an hour." She squeezed around the desk and placed the tray on the desk in front of him. Not for the first time did JP admire her triumvirate of perfectly formed glutei and reaching out gave the maximus a gentle pinch. As he expected, Gayle looked playfully back over her shoulder at him. "And I do believe it's time to take your medication," she said with a broad smile and placed a blister pack on his desk. JP could still detect her educated, Louisiana drawl.

"I'll be back in an hour." At the door, she put on her mirrored sunglasses and blew him a kiss from the doorway. "Adieu ma cher!"

The door of the study closed behind her and JP picked up the blister pack, popped a 100mg tablet of Viagra, split in two and swallowed one with a gulp of mineral water. He still really didn't know why a woman of thirty-five had committed to living with him in the middle of nowhere, but was perfectly prepared to subscribe to Professor JP Shandwyck's "General Theory of Miracles".

After a few minutes thought he picked up his binoculars again and looked out of the window. The osprey had long since disappeared—but no matter—he wasn't looking for ospreys any longer. At the five-bar gate by the mailbox at the end of the drive, amongst the snow-drifts, Gayle was doing her stretches against a backdrop of sunshine-dappled red maples, balsam poplars and Atlantic white cedars.

As JP slowly took in her agile figure, he reflected on the fact that she was still in the same, if not better shape than when he'd first noticed her as lead cheerleader of the Crimsons at the Harvard v Princeton annual football fixture 10 years ago.

As he watched Gayle stood up and turning to the house, blew him a kiss, then gave him a smile and a vigorous wave before opening and closing the gate and taking the track down to the lake, disappearing amongst the leafless woodland in flashes of black and purple, her ponytail bouncing left and right. He reached for a cookie and settled back into the soft leather of his captain's chair and looked forward to her return—as he did so he felt an incipient vasodilation.

***

In Manchester, the Panel Secretary was unable to perform any miracles with the IT—it was now 3.50 pm in Manchester and 09.50 am in New England—at least there was plenty of time to fix things. The Legal Assessor hovered nearby, leaning left and right to get a better view of what the Tribunal secretary was doing. Jonathan Bliss was awaiting the connection, ready with Professor Shandwyck's statement—post-it stickers neatly highlighting the important parts of the Professor's evidence on the various paragraphs of his statement.

Suddenly the screen flashed with disjointed, pixelated images but no recognisable picture, then a clear image of a bearded man in his sixties wearing a blue checked lumberjack shirt seated at a desk, with a pair of binoculars around his neck, magically filled the screen. Behind this man were numerous framed photographs—of United States fighter jets taking off from or landing on the deck of an aircraft carrier and to the left a large Stars and Stripes fringed with gold—close by was another flag of mainly blue with a multi-coloured badge in its centre—the flag of the State of Maine. A display case contained a large-scale model, seemingly of the aircraft carrier in the framed pictures.

"Hello! Hello! Professor Shandwyck?"

"We seem to have a picture, but no sound," observed the Chair. The Tribunal Secretary and Legal Assessor began to press the buttons at the base of the microphone but were hampered by a combination of impatience and the brief time lag between Manchester and New England. The light at the base kept switching in a delayed fashion from green to red and back again but neither knew which colour indicated the sound was active.

Professor Shandwyck looked at his laptop screen to see a suited man with a sign on the desk in front of him saying "Panel Chair Thomas Winterton".

"Professor—thank you for joining us today—I am the Panel Chair, Thomas Winterton—this is my colleague, Professor…and…we are hearing a case brought by the GMC against a consultant anaesthetist—Dr Julian Bracken—I am going to hand you over to Mr Jonathan Bliss who is counsel for the doctor."

"Good morning, or should i say good afternoon, Professor?"

"Good afternoon to you all."

"Professor, my name is Jonathan Bliss and I represent Dr Bracken—I believe you made a statement to Dr Bracken's solicitor Mr Eugene Kennedy who in fact is seated to my right here. Could you please confirm that you have a copy of your statement in front of you? Is it dated 20 July 2016?"

"Yessir."

"I am going to ask you now to take the oath—I understand you will swear on the New Testament—is that right?"

"Yessir."

"And do you have a copy of the New Testament to hand?"

"Yessir. I swear by almighty God that the evidence I shall give will be the truth, the whole truth and nothing but the truth—so help me God!"

"Starting at page 1, could you briefly confirm your qualifications?"

"Yessir—at the age of eighteen, I was commissioned to the rank of ensign in the United States Navy Reserve under the Health Professions Scholarship Program, I undertook my medical degree at Harvard Medical School, Mission Hill, Boston. On graduation, I was promoted to lieutenant and began my internship at the Chelsea Naval Hospital, Mystic River, Boston. I completed my full training in anaesthesia there in 1974, the year the hospital was decommissioned, when I became a fully qualified Naval Physician.

"I was then deployed to the aircraft carrier **John F Kennedy** and served mainly in the Mediterranean because of the deteriorating situation in the Middle East, I last saw active service on Big John off Beirut following the Beirut barracks bombing in 1982."

"When Big John was dry-docked at Norfolk Naval Shipyard, Virginia for an extensive overhaul and refit I applied for a post as consultant anaesthetist at the Massachusetts General Hospital Boston from where I retired two years ago. For the last 10 years of my career, I specialised in spinal corrective surgery. I no longer practise medicine but three times a year I give a course on leadership together with a colleague of mine from Santa Fe in New Mexico. My wife is the administrator and accompanies me on those trips."

"Thank you, professor. Would it be correct to say that most of those surgical procedures are lengthy?"

"Yes."

"And would the patient be prone, i.e., face down on the table?"

"Yes."

"Does that present a risk of harm to the patient?"

"Surely—well apart from pressure on the airways, sustained pressure on any soft tissue can cause post-operative discomfort at least and tissue necrosis if the blood supply is impeded or cut off."

"And how would you minimise the risk of harm or discomfort?"

"With soft padding—for example—there is a "Montreal Mattress" which is specifically designed to minimise pressure on soft tissues."

"Which areas of the body are susceptible to harm?"

"All soft tissue."

"Would that include the breasts in a female patient?"

"Yes—particularly so and depending on body mass index, also in a male patient."

"Professor—have you ever heard of a Wonderbra?"

"Yessir. Who hasn't? The Wonderbra was invented just across the border from here in Canada."

"And have you ever used the expression "The Wonderbra manoeuvre"?"

"Yessir. I started to use that expression in the late 1980s, just after I'd seen one being worn, when I was teaching medical students how to avoid soft tissue injuries to breasts in prolonged surgery."

"And this may seem a somewhat obvious question but, why was that?"

"Well because the symmetry achieved by the Wonderbra was the symmetry I thought best to avoid or minimise any harm."

"Did you also lecture more widely?"

"Yes—I would lecture across the whole of the United States and occasionally in Europe."

"Do you recall delivering one such lecture at The John Hopkins University Hospital in Baltimore, Maryland?"

"Yessir—I recall that lecture was pretty much an annual event."

"And you would use the expression "The Wonderbra manoeuvre" during most of those lectures?"

"As far as I can remember—in all of them."

"Professor—did anyone ever complain about your use of that expression to you?"

"No."

"Or were you ever criticised by your regulatory body?"

"No—not at all—I thought it was an unusual but novel and effective way to teach and to keep the students' attention. Everyone got the point, especially the male medical students."

"Thank you, professor,—will you please stay with us as there may be some questions for you from Ms Cornwall—the lawyer representing the GMC."

"Professor, good morning, I represent the GMC and would now like to ask you some questions if I may."

"Of course, Ma'am."

"Can I ask—have you seen the allegations Dr Bracken faces?"

"Yes Ma'am."

"Was your use of the phrase "Wonderbra manoeuvre" mainly confined to your teaching duties?"

"Well mostly."

"So, you wouldn't frequently use it when in theatre?"

"Perhaps, from time to time."

"But not always?"

"Not always."

"A patient who is anaesthetised is, because they are unconscious, especially vulnerable—would you agree?"

"Yes."

"And therefore, relies on her anaesthetist to treat her with respect and dignity?"

"Yes."

"So, any departure—"

"Mr Chair—can I remind my learned friend that this witness is a witness of fact and not an expert witness?"

"Agreed and I am asking him questions not as an expert witness but as a witness with many years of experience as an anaesthetist dealing with many patients who are unconscious—I am simply establishing that the duties of a doctor to a patient whom that doctor has rendered someone unconscious are the same in the United States as here in the United Kingdom."

Jonathan Bliss: "If Ms Cornwall's point is that it is an aggravating factor to inappropriately touch a patient in those circumstances then that is dealt with in the GMC's expert report and repetition doesn't make it any more or indeed less serious—indeed if it helps I can concede the point—it is not in issue—what is in issue is the state of my client's mind—in simple words his intentions when he:

a) announced his intention to and in fact performed the Wonderbra manoeuvre—the physical act being admitted
b) observed Nurse Y inserting the catheter, again—the physical act being admitted

c) demonstrated the surgical incision on Nurse Parrington-Weaver's back—again the physical act being admitted."

CC QC: "Noted."

"Well I'm glad we're agreed on those very important points—I am very grateful to my learned friend and in that case I only have a few further questions for the Professor. Professor—bear with me—do you agree that we are dealing here with Dr Bracken's state of mind?"

"Yes."

"And of course, you can't help us with that because you were not present?"

"No, I can't because I wasn't."

"And it is perfectly possible for a doctor to perform the Wonderbra manoeuvre either professionally or inappropriately, depending on his state of mind?"

"Yes—and as I understand it that is what you must prove—but could you prove what I am thinking right now?"

JP's mischievous question was prompted by Gayle's silent return—she was now standing by the door to his study. Professor JP Shandwyck fixed Connie with a knowing smile, bordering on a very smug smirk and looked across his sun-filled study as Gayle first removed her crimson running vest and then her sports bra and leggings, leaving her wearing just her sunglasses and ankle socks.

JP's smirk was returned with a bemused smile by Connie, across the cold and watery Atlantic.

"I have no further questions—thank you, Professor."

"Mr Bliss—do you have any re-examination?"

"No thank you sir."

Panel Chair: "Professor Shandwyck—we are very grateful to you for your time in assisting us today."

"You're welcome. Good afternoon."

Professor Shandwyck watched Connie Cornwall QC disappear and logged off.

JP would have been very surprised indeed if Connie Cornwall had been able to imagine and then prove what was in his mind.

Back in Manchester, neither the weather, nor the view was so uplifting—a slight drizzle was falling onto the windows of Hearing Room 3 as Jonathan informed the Panel that he intended to call no more evidence and that the case for Dr Bracken was now closed. The chair announced that as it was 3.45pm the panel requested Skeleton Arguments on the Facts to be filed by 09.30am tomorrow and would hear Submissions on the Facts at 10.30am and then retire to consider their determinations.

In their conference room Eugene, Jonathan, Julian and Saoirse reviewed the evidence of the last few days and Jonathan outlined his draft Skeleton Argument on the Facts. Eugene and Jonathan let Saoirse and Julian depart at 4.30 but worked on together until 6.00pm—Jonathan promised to email the perfected submissions by 9.00pm and Eugene to review and email any comments by return.

Chapter Twelve

MPTS

3.55pm

At 3.55 pm the usher brought the parties and their lawyers to the door of Hearing Room 3 once again. After a short pause, they entered and took their seats.

Panel Chair: "Dr Bracken, Ms Cornwall and Mr Bliss—we have reached our decision and I will now read our determination in full—as follows:

Determination

We are very grateful for the submissions made this morning by counsel but do not propose to recite in full those submissions which are a matter of record but will refer to the relevant points made by Ms Cornwall for the GMC and Mr Bliss on Dr Bracken's behalf.

Standard of Proof

We have accepted the advice of the Legal Assessor that we must be satisfied, after considering all the evidence in the case, called on behalf of both the GMC and Dr Bracken, that what is alleged by the GMC is more likely to have happened than not. We also accept that the more serious the allegations the more persuasive, compelling and consistent the evidence should be.

Definitions

We accepted the advice of the Legal Assessor that there is no legal definition of "sexually motivated" and therefore, it should have its ordinary meaning of "motivated by sex".

Evidence

The Tribunal heard evidence from Nurse Griffith, Sister Johnson and Nurse Parrington-Weaver and the lead surgeon—Mr James Broadley. The evidence of Professor Somerville and Julie Lightfoot was agreed and read together with the report of Dr Stonefire, the GMC expert whose evidence was also agreed. We therefore accepted that report, where relevant in its entirety.

We also received evidence from yourself and Professor JP Shandwyck by video-link from the United States.

The Case Against You

The GMC case is that at the time of these events you were employed as a consultant anaesthetist at Somerford Royal Infirmary, (SRI).

On the afternoon of 19th March 2014, you were in the recovery room at SRI with nurse Parrington-Weaver who asked you an open question regarding the extent of a surgical incision to correct scoliosis—a form of spinal deformity. In answer to her question you took up a position behind her and without obtaining her consent put your finger on her back, just above her buttocks and moved it upwards, along her back to the nape of her neck. In doing so your finger crossed her bra strap. At some stage, you made contact with Nurse Parrington-Weaver's bare skin—either through the opening in the back of her scrubs top or above it. Nurse Parrington-Weaver stated that she was surprised and felt uncomfortable at your behaviour and later complained to HR and the result of that complaint was that you were informally warned about your conduct but not, at that time referred to the GMC.

Ms Cornwall for the GMC submitted that there was only one realistic explanation for your conduct and that it was not only inappropriate, which was admitted on your behalf, but sexually motivated since there was a Whiteboard in the Recovery Room and there were also markers and pens which could have been used, either to illustrate, by diagram the answer to her question, or to use in place of your finger to trace the line on Nurse Parrington-Weaver's back. Ms Cornwall submitted that as a member of the Council of the Royal College of Anaesthetists, you were perfectly aware of the GMC Guidelines on chaperoning—indeed so well aware that you stated in cross-examination that you did not need to consult the Guidelines when invited to do so by Ms Cornwall.

She invited us to accept that touching a female in the way you did was tantamount to an intimate examination and that most, if not all doctors would have readily appreciated that and this was a matter that should have been self-evident to you with your considerable experience. She submitted that you momentarily gave way to a desire to touch Nurse Parrington-Weaver's buttocks, back, bra strap and bare neck with your finger and further suggested that this was a "come-on" to initiate more explicit sexual activity. She reminded us that Nurse Parrington-Weaver was, as normal, wearing only her underwear beneath her scrubs whilst in theatre.

On 11 January 2016, nearly two years later you were preparing a young female patient—Patient B for surgery. The patient was anaesthetised and you were being assisted by an experienced theatre sister—Sister Johnson who was placing a urethral catheter. You took up a position behind Sister Johnson and observed her as she was performing this procedure. Despite Sister Johnson's protests that she was capable and competent to perform this procedure you continued to observe her until the catheter was in place.

At some stage, you focussed a spot-light on Patient B's lower body, further illuminating her pubic area. Ms Cornwall submitted that at the time you were aware that Patient B was a young glamour model and that there was no alternative explanation, in the light of Sister Johnson's experience, her protests and the duration of your observation of the procedure, which she alleged to be excessive, together with your continued viewing, particularly after the repositioning of the spotlight, other than your private sexual gratification. She relied on the opinion of the GMC expert witness Dr Stonefireat p35 Para 6 of his report *that in my experience it is unusual for a consultant anaesthetist to always place a urethral catheter and that it was his own practice to commonly rely upon an experienced Sister or Nurse.*

Ms Cornwall reminded us that your explanation for observing this procedure so closely was an experience you had when first in post at St Bart's when you were implicitly criticised by the surgeon, Professor Hunter, when urine leaked from an improperly placed catheter during an operation, was not corroborated by anyone else present. Ms Cornwall further pointed out to us that even according to your version of that event the criticism was implicit as nothing was actually said. She submitted that you had succumbed to a temptation to look at Patient B's naked lower body attracted by the fact she was a glamour model and had intimate tattoos.

On 20 January 2016, you were the senior anaesthetist in theatre when a spinal corrective procedure was being performed on a young female patient—Patient

A who was lying face-down on the operating table. You had held several pre-operation consultations and assessments with Patient A and accepted that Patient A was well into her puberty and had developed fulsome breasts. Shortly before the operation began you used the words '*I am now going to perform the Wonderbra Manoeuvre* 'and placed your hands underneath her breasts, touching and moving both of Patient A's breasts.

Ms Cornwall's submission regarding this final incident was that, whilst she accepts that this procedure is clinically justified, we can rely on the evidence of Nurse Griffith's observations regarding the manner in which you announced your intention to "perform the Wonderbra manoeuvre"—that is your "body-language", your facial expression and the length of time you took to complete the procedure, and that taken together this amounts to compelling, cogent and consistent evidence bearing in mind once again the excessive duration of your touching that your acts were sexually motivated and proven to the required standard. She reminded us of the evidence of both Mr Broadley and Professor Shandwyck, who has gave evidence on your behalf that both regarded the use of the phrase "Wonderbra manoeuvre" primarily as a teaching aid and did not usually use the phrase in surgery. Miss Cornwall invited us to infer that you had momentarily lost your self-control whilst subconsciously contemplating the evening ahead of you which may have involved consensual activity of a sexual nature.

It is the GMC's case that your actions on all three of these occasions, whilst only lasting a brief period of time were inappropriate and sexually motivated and represented a serious breach of trust and therefore a serious departure from Good *Medical Practice*. It is the GMC's case that you were attracted to these two female patients and Nurse Parrington-Weaver and that you used the trust that patients, your colleagues and nursing staff placed in you to perpetrate these acts for your own sexual gratification, although, she conceded, for relatively short periods of time.

Whilst Ms Cornwall accepted that our starting point should be that each allegation should be considered individually she also submitted that if we found any allegation proven to the standard required then we could rely on that finding as evidence of a propensity on your behalf to act in a sexually motivated way and we might therefore be assisted in our deliberations regarding the other allegations she brings against you on behalf of the GMC. She invited us to find that all the charges were proven to the required standard and supported by consistent, compelling evidence from truthful witnesses.

The Tribunal's Decision

We have considered each allegation separately and considered very carefully both the oral and documentary evidence put before us by both parties and the helpful submissions of both Ms Cornwall on behalf of the GMC summarised above and the equally helpful submissions of Mr Bliss referred to below and made to us succinctly and forcefully on your behalf yesterday morning. We have exercised our own independent judgment.

Findings

We found that the witnesses were all honest and that the matters in issue were, in the end, all quite narrow. Indeed, we accepted Mr Bliss's submission that what was critical and axiomatic to this case—and was indirectly referred to by Professor JP Shandwyck in his resolute exchange with Ms Cornwall, was that the GMC had to establish to the required standard what was the state of mind of Dr Bracken when he was doing the three acts the GMC complain about and if proven amount to, what in Ms Cornwall's lengthy and detailed submissions, sustained sexual misconduct.

We found that Dr Bracken was an honest and straightforward witness of fact, who did his best to remember the events in question although one of them—the operation with the late Professor Hunter took place several years ago and another now more than three years ago. Considering all the witness evidence we found as proven and indeed admitted, the GMC's assertion in relation to the charge that Dr Bracken did, without seeking consent, touch with his finger Nurse Parrington-Weaver's 's back and that this was without asking for her explicit consent to do so. We bore in mind the Legal Assessor's advice that the more serious the allegation the more compelling and clear the evidence would need to be.

We felt compelled to consider the spontaneous and unsolicited outburst by Nurse Parrington-Weaver during her brief cross-examination by Mr Bliss, regarding her husband and the cosmetic surgery she referred to was admissible—this was not evidence of the witness's previous sexual history but of fact. We particularly noted that it was Nurse Parrington-Weaver who spontaneously provided this evidence.

We felt obliged to consider, in the light of that evidence, whether or not the question she herself posed to Dr Bracken in the Recovery Room was itself sexually motivated and whether it amounted to an act of "agente provocatrice"—we cannot be sure that it wasn't—indeed we went further and took the view that Nurse Parrington-Weaver whilst not explicitly giving consent—because we accept that Dr Bracken did not seek such consent was not objecting and indeed was implicitly agreeable—for reasons of her own to such contact having invited it and so have properly taken this it into account when considering whether the GMC has satisfied us that Dr Bracken's conduct was sexually motivated.

We accept his evidence that it simply did not cross his mind that his actions could be regarded as anything other than an attempt to answer Nurse Parrington-Weaver's question. We noted the admission made by counsel on his behalf—against his interest, at the outset of this hearing that he acknowledged that his conduct on that occasion, in retrospect had been inappropriate and accepted that admission and acknowledgement as evidence of Dr Bracken's insight into his conduct.

We find that considering all the evidence, his actions were in fact motivated by his desire to provide a detailed answer to Nurse Parrington-Weaver's question and were not sexually motivated but were in the circumstances inappropriate, but not seriously inappropriate, bearing in mind our finding that Nurse Parrington-Weaver had implicitly consented.

Consequently, we find that in relation to charge 4 the GMC have failed to satisfy us that Dr Bracken's conduct to the required standard of proof was sexually motivated.

In relation to Charge 3, whilst we noted Ms Cornwall's submission that there was no evidence to corroborate Dr Bracken's assertion regarding the previous incident involving the improperly placed urethral catheter, we accepted Mr Bliss's submission on this point that firstly it was not an issue where legally, corroboration was required and secondly that as the incident referred to by Dr Bracken in his evidence took place many years ago we should properly and fairly take into account the difficulty Dr Bracken faced in remembering and tracing other witnesses. Our Legal Assessor agreed with both of those submissions. We also accepted Mr Bliss's submission that it is the responsibility of an anaesthetist to care for a patient he or she has anaesthetised and noted the GMC's own expert agreed with him on that discrete point.

Whilst we accept that Sister Johnson was very experienced in placing urethral catheters, it was common ground that she had not worked with Dr Bracken previously, so that whilst we accept that many anaesthetists will allow an experienced nurse to place a catheter, we do not see how we can criticise Dr Bracken for adopting a higher standard of care in discharging his responsibility to his patient on this occasion. We also noted that Sister Johnson accepted that she did not report her concerns about Dr Bracken's conduct regarding the incident until more than 10 days later and therefore attached considerable weight to Mr Bliss's submission that if she had held those concerns at the time, she would and should have acted sooner in expressing those concerns and that her recollection may well have been adversely influenced subsequently by comments made by the witnesses to the other incidents.

We found that she was to some extent aggrieved that Dr Bracken appeared to be scrutinising her competency of which she appeared to be especially sensitive. In arriving at this conclusion, we also placed reliance on Mr Bliss's cogent submission that Dr Bracken was aware that Sister Johnson was a new member of the staff at SRI and therefore Ms Cornwall's argument that Dr Bracken was relying on her trust lost much of its force.

We also noted that as soon as the catheter was correctly inserted Dr Bracken turned away to attend to his other tasks and whilst this was potentially equivocal we accepted that it was more likely to be consistent with him supervising Sister Johnson placing the catheter than sexually motivated conduct as alleged. We accepted Mr Bliss's submission that on this isolated occasion there was an innocent failure to properly communicate, especially as they had not worked together before.

Our finding in relation to charge 3 is that the GMC have failed to persuade us, to the required standard, of their case that Dr Bracken's actions were inappropriate or sexually motivated.

Finally, in relation to Charge 2, we accept the evidence of Dr Bracken and Professor Shandwyck regarding the provenance of the phrase "The Wonderbra Manoeuvre" and furthermore that it is a convenient shorthand to describe the correct position of female breasts to best avoid post-operative complications. We noted Ms Cornwall's forceful comments that Professor Shandwyck and Mr Broadley the lead surgeon accepted that the expression was more properly useful in the teaching arena but also noted the evidence of Mr Broadley that the announcement communicated to the other members of the surgical team, that the soft tissue checks on the breasts had been undertaken.

Whilst we had considerable difficulty in assessing the weight we should attach to the interpretation of partially obscured facial gestures, we accept that a frown or glare is, on balance, more easily recognisable than a smirk or smile. We note that it would have been very difficult to observe any expression on Dr Bracken's face and that this was the first procedure attended by Nurse Griffith—where there was a discrepancy as to the length of time Dr Bracken took to reposition the breasts we have accepted and preferred his evidence on that point.

We considered the observations of Mr Bliss that as Nurse Griffith was not expecting to see anyone re-positioning Patient A's breasts, she would have been extremely shocked and this in our view would have significantly affected the accuracy of her recollection of the incident in terms of its duration. We also noted the evidence of Mr Broadley that he had on occasions undertaken the same manoeuvre when Dr Bracken was occupied in other pre-operative procedures. We were not satisfied from the evidence of Nurse Griffith, although honest, that the behaviour of Dr Bracken when conducting this manoeuvre can support an allegation of sexually motivated or indeed inappropriate conduct.

We also considered the evidence of Professor Shandwyck on this point that it was he who had had coined the phrase "Wonderbra Manoeuvre" and rejected the GMC submission that Dr Bracken had invented the phrase as part of a subterfuge to disguise his sexually motivated conduct. We accept, as referred to above, Dr Bracken's evidence that the phrase was a convenient shorthand to alert Mr Broadley to the fact that he had carried out the necessary checks on re-positioning soft tissue likely to be affected by sustained downward pressure. We find that the GMC has failed to demonstrate to our satisfaction that Dr Bracken's actions were either inappropriate or sexually motivated and so we find Charge 3 not proven.

To conclude therefore we find all the allegations not proven, apart from the one admitted - Ms Cornwall—we would like to hear from you as to whether we should issue a Warning to Dr Bracken regarding the incident with Nurse Parrington-Weaver.

CC QC: "Given your findings and indeed Dr Bracken's insight as demonstrated by his admission at the very outset of this hearing that he accepted that his behaviour towards Nurse Parrington-Weaver was inappropriate, coupled with your finding that it was an innocent course of conduct and was not seriously below the required standard, I do not ask you to consider issuing a Warning to Dr Bracken."

"Thank you, Ms Cornwall—the Panel Secretary will now print off and hand out copies of the Determination. Dr Bracken—the case against is concluded and you are free to go."

Julian stepped out of the hearing room into the corridor and the arms of Saoirse. Eugene and Jonathan stood close by with their notebooks into which they slipped their copies of the Determination exonerating Julian. They looked at each other and then the embracing couple and silently turned away in the direction of conference Room Three. Gathering their various folders together they turned to see Connie Cornwall in the doorway.

"Well done, you two! That was the right result, although you were sailing a bit close to the wind with your cross-examination of Nurse Parrington-Weaver—nee Keaveney! I think things will be a bit frosty in the Parrington-Weaver household for a few days to come!"

She smiled and turned away before either Jonathan or Eugene could react. As she passed Julian, she smiled again and offered her hand. "I think that was the right result doctor—good luck! I hope you're back to work soon!"

Julian was too surprised to do anything except take her hand, whilst Saoirse's reaction was somewhat cooler. Jonathan and Eugene both shrugged at Julian who shrugged in return as Connie walked away down the corridor—her papers under her arm.

Saoirse glared at Connie's receding back.

"Come on you—I don't want the love of my life charged with causing grievous bodily harm to a QC! One trial a year is enough for me!"

Saoirse smiled back and took hold of Julian by the arm. They joined Eugene and Jonathan in the conference room for the last time. "Does this mean that it's all over?"

"Yes."

"Oh, thank God. Thank God!"

"Yes, that's it, doctor, you are free to go and more importantly, I think you can almost certainly forget about any criminal proceedings, in view of the fact that none of the allegations were proven—not even to the balance of probabilities and so there is very little prospect of proving them to the criminal standard which is much, much higher."

Julian looked at the desk littered with sets of hearing bundles, witness statements, exhibits and expert reports—documents which he had lived with for the last year, but which had now lost their significance. It was as if he had just passed from another world into a new one. He took Saoirse's hand.

"Do I need those?"

"Not unless you want them?"

"No, he doesn't! I'm taking him away for a few days. He has an important task to do now, which both of us have had to put off for far too long!"

"We are truly, truly grateful to you both." Julian stepped forward and shook Eugene and then Jonathan by the hand—Saoirse stepped forward and embraced Eugene then Jonathan.

"Just one last thing," asked Eugene, "what is that perfume you wear?"

"Oh, you have reminded me." Saoirse took out of her tote two small packages wrapped in Cristiano a Fiorentina gift paper. "These are for you—I hope that you will both get a lot of pleasure from them." She stared at Eugene and widened her eyes.

"I am just exhausted—will you forgive me if we simply get back to our hotel—all I want to do is sleep for a week."

"Of course—we feel a little the same."

They left—arms around each other.

"He's a lucky man," said Jonathan.

"No—not really, he had us defending him."

"I wasn't talking about the case!"

"Yes—I know you weren't!"

Eugene and Jonathan packed their bags and Eugene dropped the bundles of documents into the six document boxes already bearing his office address, together with Jonathan's brief—endorsed with the outcome:

Charges not proven No impairment—no Order, no Warning. GMC v Bracken—Jonathan Bliss.

"I'm just going to call the office and arrange for all these boxes to be collected." He walked off down the corridor—phone to his ear.

Two minutes later, he stepped back into the conference room.

The two lawyers were free now and felt the pleasure of a job well done—as Connie had said.

"Fancy a beer?"

"That's your advocate's training for you—only ask a question when you already know the answer."

"Yes—of course!"

"And then I've got something to show you."

***

Julian and Saoirse found themselves unexpectedly alone in the lift—they embraced and shared a passionate kiss. Julian pushed Saoirse up against the lift wall and they kissed again—even more deeply.

"That was sexually motivated conduct—if ever I saw it—or felt it, Dr Stinker!"

"Admitted and proven!"

"Anyway—what's this important task I must do?"

"Can't you guess? You're supposed to be a doctor! The 6th of March is fast approaching! You'll be needing these to do it!"

Saoirse handed Julian two single first-class tickets from Manchester to London Euston.

"I've made an appointment for you at UKFC tomorrow—you're booked into the "Donation Room" at 3.00pm—but don't worry—I'll be there too—in case you need a hand—and just to let you know—I managed to get to Selfridge's last week-end and bought some very fine items from La Perla! I can guarantee you'll like them! Black mesh with silver lacing! Oh, and some new pairs of stockings!"

Julian looked at the tickets—they were dated a week ago. "You never doubted me, did you?"

"No."

Saoirse and Julian stepped out of St James's Buildings and turned in the direction of the Hilton Hotel.

"Dr Bracken!"

Julian turned.

'I hear you've been cleared?"

"Yes, I have…"

"Could I have a picture—of both of you?"

"Of course." They posed on the steps of St James's Buildings.

"Thank you, Dr Bracken, I'm sure you're relieved?"

"Yes, I am—thank you. It's been a nightmare and I'm just glad it's all over."

"Thanks for the picture, Doctor—it will be in the Bristol Evening News tonight."

"Thank you—we'll look out for it."

The photographer walked off.

As they walked along, Oxford Rd Julian saw a Ferrari, pulling up at red traffic lights to his left, with its hood down, driven by Connie Cornwall. In the passenger seat, Julian could just see another female -and noticed that her hand was stroking Connie's inner thigh. On her fingers were exact copies of Connie's rings. The traffic lights turned to green and Connie roared off.

Chapter Thirteen

**THE LASS O' GOWRIE
CHARLES ST
MANCHESTER**

The Lass o'Gowrie was no more than two minutes' walk away. The two lawyers contemplated their untouched drinks—there was nothing wrong with the beer—Eugene looked at Jonathan. "I know what you're thinking."

Jonathan looked up,

"It's always an anti-climax—a year of nervous energy—even with sixty years' experience between us the trial process leaves you emotionally drained—especially when you've got Connie in the other corner!"

"Anyway, now that we've discharged our professional responsibility to our client, what did you want to show me?"

Eugene took his iPad from his case. "I'm sure this is pure coincidence but, do you remember the letter the Brown family wrote to Dr Bracken?"

"The PS said that Samantha was going to do a 10K sponsored walk to raise funds for Somerford Royal Infirmary."

"Look at this—it's a photograph from the Bristol Evening News of Samantha Brown completing her sponsored walk."

Eugene pushed his iPad across to Jonathan—there was a headline:

FORMER PATIENT RAISES NEARLY £5,000 FOR SRI SPINAL INJURIES UNIT

…under which there was a photograph with a caption:

Former patient Samantha Brown finishes her sponsored walk, supported by her parents George and Helen.

"Pretty girl, isn't she?"

"Yes—she is—very pretty!"

"Notice the shoulder-length blonde hair?"

"Yes."

Eugene took the iPad back for a few moments and then returned it to Jonathan.

"The girl in the photograph. Do you know who she is?"

Jonathan looked at the screen, again, a newspaper article from The Bristol Evening News headlined:

BRISTOL MODEL'S TRIUMPHANT RETURN TO THE CATWALK AFTER HORRIFIC CAR ACCIDENT

…above a full-length colour picture.

"No—but I'm guessing it's Patient B—is it?"

"My learned friend is right first time."

"Notice any resemblance to Samantha Brown?"

"Yes—shoulder-length blonde hair!"

"Now—the video-link when Nurse Parrington-Weaver was giving her evidence wasn't the very best, but one thing was clear—"

"She had shoulder-length blonde hair."

"And Saoirse Fitzgerald?"

"Shoulder-length blonde hair."

Jonathan exhaled a slow breath.

"And I'm willing to bet the former Mrs Bracken had?"

"Shoulder-length blonde hair!"

"Well, it's a good job Connie didn't latch on to this—she would have let him have both barrels—she'd still be cross-examining him now!"

"Well, knowing Connie, I thought she would—but it just goes to show that even Connie is human!"

"So, when did you realise this?"

"Well, quite early on, but the question id – is it just a coincidence? I thought the Tribunal Chair had spotted it when he asked how many of the patients were female and then when Julian went off proof and referred to Saoirse sat at the back of the hearing room, alarm bells were ringing like crazy. You remember—Connie took quite a long look at Saoirse.

"Anyway, Connie didn't pick it up and the Tribunal didn't mention it in their determination—although only one in seven of the female UK population is blonde—so work out the odds of that—and Connie seemed more concerned to imply in her cross-examination that he had succumbed to his anticipation of the evening's activities a little earlier than scheduled—but of course, if she'd seen these two pictures and made the connection that I did!"

"However—as Connie said—the right result!"

They both looked at their glasses again. Eugene raised his glass. "To Connie!"

"To Connie!"

"What time is your train?"

"Leaves Manchester Piccadilly at 18.20—into Euston at 20.28—home by 21:30. Thank God for Richard Branson!"

"All that travelling! It must drive you mad! When are you going to join us and move up to live in the future capital of England? Manctown!"

"I don't think Jilly would ever let me—she'd miss the tennis at The Hurlingham Club too much!"

"What are you up to this evening?"

"Nothing!"

Chapter Fourteen

**DEANS COURT CHAMBERS
BYROM ST
MANCHESTER
5:30pm**

Connie burst into the Senior Clerks' room at her chambers.

"Oh, good evening, Ms Cornwall—have you finished at the GMC?"

"Yes—just an hour ago, Chris—flying visit—Alice is outside in the Ferrari on double yellows—is there anything in?"

Chris smiled knowingly. "Well, Miss Cornwall, Sir John Fortune from the Judicial Appointments Commission called and asked if you could call him back before 6.00pm—I've left a note with his number, on your desk."

Connie turned quickly and disappeared down the corridor to her room and for few minutes Chris could hear the sound of muffled telephone conversation.

Very soon afterwards, Connie appeared again in the Clerks' room.

Chris looked up—with a broad smile, he asked, "Well, is it M'ladyship now?"

With a broader smile, Connie answered, "Indeed it is—I start sitting next Term—Mrs Justice Cornwall!"

"Suits you, M'Lady—I shall look forward to accompanying you to your swearing-in ceremony."

"And I shall look forward to that too, Chris—and can I say how grateful I am for all your wonderful support over the last twenty years—it's fair to say that it might not have happened without you! I am very grateful—now—I'm going to tell Alice!"

Book Three

Chapter One

1:00pm
15th of March 2017

RISTORANTE SERGIO A LE GRAND HOTEL VILLA DI CORLIANO
SAN GIULIANO TERME
TUSCANY
ITALY

Eugene stepped out of their hire-car and he and Margaret walked across the white gravel of the hotel car park to the restaurant entrance—on the door was a large graceful handwritten notice:

"Chiuso oggi

Riservato per la festa di nozze di Dr Julian Bracken e Signorina Saoirse Fitzgerald"

In the shady spread of an ancient chestnut tree, a wedding table was set for the bride and groom and their thirty guests. Waiters and waitresses in black and white stood ready and the three chefs were looking on from the kitchen doorway.

The Etruscan sky was azure blue with just a wisp of white cloud here and there. A waiter approached and offered a glass of chilled Prosecco to Margaret and Eugene, who could now hear, in the distance the cacophony of car horns announcing the approach of the fleet of cars carrying the other guests from the Church of the Blessed Virgin in nearby San Giuliano.

They were joined by Jonathan Bliss and Jilly and took in the view as the taxis, festooned with garlands of flowers and ribbons of white entered the grounds of the Palazzo Villa di Corliano through the ornate gates and began to process up the long drive, arriving with deafening sound into the car park in front of the restaurant, followed by Julian's Aston Martin—carrying the bride and groom.

As the wedding car pulled to a graceful halt a band began to play and a beaming John Kavanagh stepped forward and in a deep baritone voice, with his Irish brogue began to sing version of his own version of `That's Amore!'

Rounds of applause broke out as a smiling Saoirse and Julian stepped out of the wedding car and were enthusiastically showered for a second time with confetti by their guests.

More chilled Prosecco was distributed by the waiters and against a the background of muted Vivaldi and Scarlatti fugues and canons the guests introduced themselves to each other and enjoyed the early Spring sunshine as the canapes were served.

Eventually, the guests took their seat at the wedding table.

"Signore e signori per favore bienvenuto a Signora Saoirse Bracken e Dottore Julian."

The guests rose to applaud Julian and Saoirse as they were fan-fared to the middle of the table.

Eugene picked up the menu:

Un pasto di anti-pasto e poi arrosti di maialino con Tiramisu

Prosecco

Barolo

"Glad you could both make it and it's nice to meet your wives—I owe you a lot—my reputation and my profession—there was a time when I thought the whole world and everybody in it—was sexually motivated!"

"You mean you were on planet Connie?"

Eugene raised his glass. "Wouldn't have missed it for the world—in fact, Margaret and I used to holiday a lot around here when the boys were young—we're going on a little trip down memory lane tomorrow—first stop Lucca, where, if I remember rightly, your colleague *Theodoric of Lucca* established the anaesthesia profession with his sponges of morphine and mandragora."

Julian grinned. "He did!"

"Just as well there was no GMC or Connie Cornwall in the 13th century!" Added Jonathan.

"Then on to Sienna for a few days where Margaret and I have a game of tennis to conclude which we started eight years ago and never got around to finishing—it's one set each—I would have fancied my chances more when I was eight years younger—we're then up the coast to Torre del Lago if the weather favours us."

"We were sat next to your brother Gerry and his wife over lunch—a lovely couple."

"Yes—Gerry helped me a lot just after Eleanor died and dealt with the claim arising from the accident—he works for a PR agency representing sports personalities, so he took all that away from me."

The photographer was standing to one side, snapping away and quietly following Julian and Saoirse as they said their 'Hellos' to their guests.

"I wish you both long life and happiness."

"Saoirse and I are celebrating something else—Saoirse is pregnant—with twins!"

"That's wonderful news—when are you due?"

"Late September."

"Where's the honeymoon?"

"Well, a few days here to really relax and then we're driving back to London for the first eight-week scan at the clinic next Wednesday and if all's well catching a flight on Friday from Heathrow to Boston. Saoirse is taking me on a visit to *The Ether Dome* at Boston General Hospital.

When we first met at my favourite restaurant in Bristol I began to tell Saoirse about why I decided to become an anaesthetist and got as far as mentioning *Theodoric of Lucca*—it appears Saoirse has been doing some research of her own and discovered the *Ether Dome* in Boston and the part it played in the history of modern anaesthesia so it seemed a nice thing to organise our honeymoon around—"*Theodoric and The Ether Dome*"—it sounds like a Roald Dahl story!"

"Yes—and we received a lovely email from Professor Shandwyck inviting us to stay with them in Boothbay Harbor, so we accepted. It looks a lovely place and he's going to show us the ospreys he was so engrossed in watching whilst he was waiting for the Tribunal secretary to finally manage to get the video-link working at the hearing. Gayle has promised us some nice walks through the woods surrounding their home—it sounds lovely."

"Give him my regards," said Eugene.

"Well, that should make for one very tired anaesthetist. Back to work after the honeymoon?"

"No, I—we decided—when we found out that Saoirse's expecting—they offered me a phased return to work after the GMC hearing, but I thought—you only need another malicious comment and the whole thing starts all over again—so I thought about it and I came to a very firm conclusion—I thought no! Sod 'em! Besides—God willing, I'm going to be doing the school run in a few years' time."

"And the nappies before then!" Added Saoirse, smiling.

"Thanks for the perfume by the way."

"Does Margaret like it?"

"Not as much as I do!"

"I'll drink to that!"

"Oh mother—have you met Jonathan and Eugene, my lawyers. Jonathan, Eugene—my mother and father."

Mrs Bracken was a tall, elegant lady who, despite her years, had a full head of shoulder-length blonde hair. "Delighted to meet you both—we were so lucky Julian had such a good legal team."

"This is my father - Julian senior."

"Pleased to meet you both - we were so lucky that Julian had such a talented and committed legal team - well done to both of you."

"We were both delighted to assist." said Jonathan.

"Could I possibly drag my father away for a few moments?" asked Julian junior.

Eugene's gaze followed the trio as they passed through the other guests. He noticed that as they were passing an attractive blonde waitress, Julian senior's hand reached out towards her buttocks but was rapidly pulled back by his wife.

Chapter Two

9.30 am
Wednesday 22nd of March 2017

BROWN'S HOTEL
ALBEMARLE STREET

"Good morning, Dr and Mrs Bracken—how lovely to see you both—together. Can I just say how delighted I and the staff are to have played even a small part in bringing you together? A real romance with a happy ending—that apparently started in this very room!"

"Thank you, George—and did you know we are expecting twins?"

"No! That's wonderful news, Doctor—congratulations, Mrs Bracken—and may I ask—when are you due?"

"The end of September, George."

"That's really wonderful news—I hope everything goes well for you—you certainly look very well if I may say so? Can I bring you your usual? Orkney Kippers for you, Mrs Bracken, and Eggs Albemarle for you, Doctor? And decaffeinated coffee and Orange Pekoe tea?"

"Yes please—thank you George."

"Right away doctor."

Julian beamed at Saoirse. "Are you looking forward to the scan? You do look lovely—pregnancy suits you."

"Looking forward—I can't wait!"

"We need to call in briefly at Morley and Casson at 1:00pm to sign the Trust Deed and our Wills—we'll have plenty of time."

"Excuse me—it's here again." Saoirse pulled a face, clutched her mouth and hurried out of the restaurant—George sent one of the waitresses after her.

Julian picked up his copy of The Times and began to skim through. He stopped at –

The Register
Births

Parrington-Weaver

On 15 March 2017 to Mary Bernadette (nee Keaveney) and Anthony Richard Colin—twins, a son, James Aloysius Patrick Bartholomew and a daughter, Andrea Eloise Maria Elaine.

Some minutes later, Saoirse returned.
"Are you Ok?"
"Yes—fine now—it's just that it's as regular as clockwork—I can't do anything about it—I hope it ends soon!"
Julian pushed The Times across the breakfast table. "Looks like we were beaten to it!"
Saoirse picked up The Times, and after a few seconds placed it back down.
"Looks like they made up and she got what she wanted then!"
"And have you?"
"Of course!"
She widened her eyes at Julian and then broke into a beautiful, beaming smile.

Chapter Three

Thursday 23rd of March 2017
THE OFFICES OF MORLEY & CASSON
STAFFORD ST
MAYFAIR

1:00pm

"Richard—thank you for seeing us now."

"Not at all—anything to accommodate the happy couple."

"Could I introduce my wife of just seven days? Saoirse."

"Delighted to meet you—and may I offer you my congratulations—on both fronts—may you have a long, happy and successful marriage—and of course a happy and successful pregnancy."

"Thank you, Richard."

"Now—this shouldn't take long—both of your Wills and the *"Dermot and Mary Fitzgerald Educational Trust Deed"* you have already approved are ready for your final signatures and the funds have been in our client account since yesterday. It's a discretionary trust—you'll see that the purpose is to assist one pupil at St Cuthbert's College Manchester who wishes to pursue a degree course in medicine and one in fashion and merchandising, the Trustees being myself, the Chair of Governors and the current Headmaster—we've all already signed—I'm sure the College and governing body will be delighted.

"Now—if you'd both like to sign where your names are – here, I can deal with the formalities with the Charity Commissioners while you're away on your honeymoon.

"And finally, your new Wills—I'll need to get Jennifer, my PA and her colleague Patricia in to witness you both executing your Wills. I hope you have a wonderful honeymoon—New England, isn't it?"

"Yes—should be lovely now—Spring is finally here."

"I've ordered you a taxi—the UKFC on York Street in Westminster, isn't it?"

Chapter Four

**2:00pm
Wednesday 22nd of March 2017**

**UKFC
WESTMINSTER
LONDON**

"So, here is the ultrasound image—the double embryo transfer has been a success—as you can see—there are the two perfectly healthy babies—here and here." Dr Hayton handed over the printout and leaning over pointed out the two large, grainy embryonic heads and sharply curved spines.

"There are two strong, normal heartbeats and everything is as expected at this stage. Next time, if you like, we should be able to tell you the sex of your babies, depending on their positions." Dr Hayton leant back into his chair and smiled broadly. "Congratulations—I know how much this means to both of you."

Saoirse felt herself welling up and Dr Hayton, noticing this, carried on gently, "So, I look forward to seeing you both again in about six weeks' time for a further check-up and scan. Just follow the advice in this leaflet and if you need to discuss anything at all please call me. You can also access the clinic website to view the FAQs and further advice for expectant mothers.

"I've included our leaflet on *Flying Whilst Pregnant*—it will be fine up to 32 weeks but try to avoid alcohol on board and take a walk around the aircraft every hour or so. Try some leg-stretching and if you can, wear flight socks which will improve your circulation and lessen the possibility of DVTs. I've included a pair for you. I hope you have a wonderful honeymoon."

"Thank you very much, Dr Hayton. Saoirse and I would like you to have this from us—with our sincere thanks." Julian handed over a bottle of champagne.

"Well, completely unnecessary." He looked at the label and beamed. "This is very generous indeed—Perrier Jouet 2002! I'm most grateful. Someone has good taste!"

"Well, it was bought with a celebration like this in mind."

Julian smiled sadly – Saoirse gently squeezed his hand.

Julian and Saoirse left the clinic hand in hand, walking happily along York Street in the direction of Westminster Bridge. They felt a silent sense of achievement. Saoirse had been right after all—the allegation made by Mary Keaveney had been exposed as false and malicious. Julian had been fully vindicated. The panel had exonerated him in relation to his conduct, accepting his evidence that he had acted professionally and in the best interests of his patients.

The results of the scan meant their dreams were now within their grasp—just several months away. Julian reflected on their wedding last week in Tuscany and the forthcoming honeymoon in New England. They could now relax and enjoy the time ahead, following the delight of seeing their healthy babies huddled safely together, side by side in Saoirse's womb. Their lives were now irrevocably interwoven.

It was a beautiful Spring Day and as they reached the junction of York St and Westminster Bridge Road Julian looked at his watch—it was just coming up to 2.30pm. Big Ben was imperiously chiming the half hour. The rest of the day was theirs.

"Why don't we walk up to Parliament Square and take a cab to *Hamleys* on Regent St, to look at toys? It's on our way back to the hotel."

"That would be nice—we'll need two of everything though! Just window-shopping, though—best not to tempt fate! We don't even know what sex they are yet."

"Then back to Brown's for you for a lie down and to get your feet up."

"And do you know what I have a real craving for? A curry!"

"Well there's always that nice Indian—Chor Bizarre just across Albemarle St from Brown's. The chicken chettinad there is superb. So that's agreed then—window-shopping for toys, a siesta for you and we'll take a walk across the road later tonight for curry for both of us to satisfy your cravings."

Once on Westminster Bridge, they crossed over and began to walk slowly, arm in arm towards the Palace of Westminster as they had first done after dinner at Marckwick's. The bridge was teeming with many tourists happily taking selfies. Julian noticed a party of schoolchildren with their teachers, laughing and chattering excitedly away in French.

There were many other accents, including a group of teenagers, talking in the flat Northern vowels of Lancashire. Couples of all ages, happy couples, all with their own private reasons to be happy, just like Julian and Saoirse—walking arm in arm along Westminster Bridge.

Julian paused. "Any other cravings by the way?"

Saoirse looked deeply into Julian's eyes. Julian recalled the unexpected thrill of seeing her extraordinary eyes for the very first time in the mirror is Turnbull and Asser and the same, irresistible look she had given him in Browne's Brasserie on Sandymount Green so many months ago—the day they had first made love.

"Well, there might be!"

She pulled him towards her and they embraced.

Chapter Five

BBC
Breaking News - Breaking News - Breaking News - Breaking News

Thursday, 24 March 2017 3:10pm

Forty injured - five killed in Westminster terror attack

Assailant shot dead after fatal stabbing of police officer beside Parliament

A large part of the City of Westminster remained cordoned off last night after five people died and more than 40 were injured near the Houses of Parliament in the worst single terrorist attack in Britain for more than a decade.

A thick-set man in black clothing mowed down pedestrians as he drove a car across Westminster Bridge. He then left the vehicle, carrying two knives before fatally stabbing an unarmed police officer inside the grounds of Parliament, where armed police shot the attacker dead.

The Palace of Westminster was locked down within minutes, with Membera in the House of Commons and the Lords Chambers told to lie on the floor immediately after the attack.

The incident began around 2.40 pm when a dark-coloured Hyundai drove on to a pavement on Westminster Bridge, running over pedestrians and leaving two dead and others seriously injured.

Three French secondary school students who were visiting London on a class trip were among the injured.

In one act of selfless bravery, eye witnesses say that a couple were embracing and as the vehicle approached them, the male tried to push his partner to safety but were both struck by the vehicle. They were taken to St Thomas's Hospital nearby.

Chapter Six

**THE BRITISH EMBASSY
MERRION RD
BALLSBRIDGE
DUBLIN 4**

Friday 24th of March 2017

The Irish Times

Taoiseach Enda Kenny and the President Michael D Higgins have both signed the Book of Condolence at the British Embassy, for the victims of Wednesday's Westminster terror attack.

President Higgins wrote in the book: *"President of Ireland offering sympathy to the families of those killed and the injured."*

Taoiseach Enda Kenny wrote in the book: *"Mo comhbhrón dom priomh aire agus do mhuintir na Breataine as ucht an tragóid seo."*

He added in English: *"My sympathy is to the families of those who lost loved ones and my support from the Irish Government to the prime minister and her government arising from the tragic events in London."*

Afterwards, he spoke to the French ambassador, Jean-Pierre Thibault, who also signed the book – three French students were involved in the fatal attack. President Higgins said: *"It is very important to see it as the criminal act that it is, affecting citizens going about their orderly business of working in the public space."*

He also expressed a desire that any reaction to the attack *"doesn't fit into the agenda of those who take such criminal action"*.

The table on which the Book of Condolence has been placed also contains a framed message from British Prime Minister, Theresa May.

The message states: *"An act of terrorism tried to silence our democracy, but today we meet as normal, as generations have done before us."*

'Deeply honoured'

The British ambassador to Ireland, Sir James Ballard said he was "deeply honoured" that the President had come to express his condolences following the attack, in which five people were killed and 20 others were injured.

"Since the incident first broke, we have been inundated with people expressing support and sympathy," he said.

"We are deeply grateful to the President for joining us here in the Embassy in a formal way, especially as one of the victims of Wednesday's attack was a personal friend of myself and my Deputy Head of Mission, Gavin Thompson, having worked with us over the last few years to promote closer business links between Ireland and the UK.

We can only hope and pray that she and her husband, who was also injured in the attack will both make a swift and full recovery.

"We are very aware that the people of Ireland have joined with the people of the UK, reflecting the very special and unique bonds that exist between our two countries."

The Book of Condolence for the victims of the Westminster attack is open between 10am and 4pm until March 27th at the British Embassy, Merrion Road, Dublin.

Chapter Seven

MERRION HOUSE
HILL TOP
HALE BARNS
CHESHIRE

11:30am
26th of September 2017

Saoirse descended the stairs of the silent house slowly, one step by one step. She limped across the hall and with difficulty picked up her newspaper and her post from the carpet in the hall. She took them into the conservatory overlooking the garden and settling down in one of the wicker armchairs raised her left leg onto a stool and waited for the pain to subside. She turned the pages until she found what she was looking for.

THE TIMES
REGISTER

26th of September 2017

BIRTHS

To Saoirse Bracken, nee Fitzgerald, formerly of Moss Side and Dublin, now of Merrion House, Hill Top, Hale Barns, Cheshire, and the late Dr Julian Bracken, of The Backs, Bristol—twins, on the 22nd of September—a boy, Patrick Julian Dermot John and a girl, Mary Saoirse Aoife Eleanor.

With sincere gratitude to all the doctors and staff of St Thomas's Hospital Maternity Department and Major Trauma Unit, Westminster Bridge, London.

She fingered the four rings around her neck and took them out from her blouse. Turning her father's wedding ring, she could just make out in the bright sunshine the now familiar tiny engraving on the inside:

To my husband Dermot—Irish by birth and Cork by the grace of God! All my love—18th August 1951

And, on Julian's:

To my darling husband on our wedding day, 15th March 2017, Church of the Blessed Virgin, San Giuliano Tuscany. Yours forever, Posh

Exhausted, she fell asleep and was woken by Sarah gently shaking her elbow. "Mrs Bracken, sorry to disturb you but I think Patrick is needing a feed—Mary is still asleep."

Sarah handed Patrick over and Saoirse unbuttoned her blouse and unfastening her nursing bra, offered her full breast to her baby boy and smiled as his head jabbed quickly left and right before he found her and began to feed. She closed her eyes and thought of Julian and wished he were there to share these moments.

She felt Patrick stop suckling and opening her eyes, looked down on his reddening face.

A few moments later, a high-pitched squeak erupted from Patrick's nappy.

Saoirse burst out laughing and between her giggles whispered, "Patrick Bracken—you little stinker!"

Then her laughter gave way to sobs and her tears dropped onto her naked breasts and Patrick's soft, downy lanugo. She pulled him closely to her and still sobbing, closed her eyes again.